SHADOW OF THE CROWN

JERI GILCHRIST

Covenant Communications, Inc.

Cover images courtesy of istock photo.

Published by Covenant Communications, Inc.
American Fork, Utah

Printed in Canada
First Printing: September 2008

13 12 11 10 09 08 10 9 8 7 6 5 4 3 2 1

ISBN-13 978-1-59811-576-5
ISBN-10 1-59811-576-6

SHADOW
OF THE
CROWN

OTHER BOOKS AND AUDIO BOOKS
BY JERI GILCHRIST:

The Perfect Plan

Out of Nowhere

ACKNOWLEDGMENTS

When I first began to write *Shadow of the Crown,* I had no idea how many people would contribute their time, expertise, and talents to see to its realization. I am grateful to all of you for offering your help, support, and friendship.

To Mom, who told me stories about her childhood in Denmark during the Nazi occupation. This book would never have come to pass without her. This book, though mostly fictional, was inspired by some of her stories. My heart aches to hear her tell me more.

To Dad, who took us on the trip of a lifetime. Going back to Denmark thrilled me. I will always hold those memories close. I love you more than words can say.

To Brad, for the countless hours you spent helping me research. This will always be our book. I hope you know how much I love and appreciate you. I am so grateful to my Father in Heaven for the blessing of having you to share my life with. I'm the luckiest girl in the world.

To my three children, Tyler, Felicia, and Bryan. Thank you for your patience and understanding while I plucked away at the computer. You are my pride and joy. I love you all! Bryan, you are my biggest cheerleader. Your excitement does my heart good.

To my Danish family who showed me a whole new world. I'll be back to Denmark one day. I appreciate your help and technical advice. I thought of you with every page I wrote.

To my friend, Kerry Blair, who has been there for me through thick and thin, sink or swim. I couldn't do it without you. You amaze me with your thoughtfulness and talents. Thank you for everything, especially for being my friend.

To Kim Wright and Monica Taylor for your terrific ideas; to Cori Giardiello for your editing and sense of humor; and to Christina Morrison and Becky Smith for your critiques.

To my temple family and friends who let me run ideas by you and who are kind enough to encourage me to keep writing. I can't begin to tell you how much that means to me.

Thank you to the Pedersen family for your enthusiasm and willingness to help.

I owe a great deal to Kirk Shaw, my editor at Covenant. Kirk, you're the best. It would have been impossible to accomplish this task without a top-notch editor like you.

And to everyone at Covenant, especially Kathy Jenkins. It's my honor to work with such a wonderful group of people. Thank you for everything you do.

1

Teira Palmer stared in dismay at the run-down dwelling that was her ancestral home. Then she looked at the notes that lay on the passenger seat, hoping she had come to the wrong address. It was possible. For all she knew she had read the Danish map upside down and backward. She certainly wasn't familiar with the area. She hadn't been to Denmark since she was twelve, and that was almost fifteen years ago. The only thing she knew for sure was that the house in front of her looked nothing like the one she remembered.

Unfortunately, the notes confirmed that she was in the correct place. Teira shivered. Someone by the name of Magnus Spelman had been hired to care for her grandmother's home. Grethe Pedersen paid him a monthly wage for its upkeep. But judging by the eyesore in front of her, someone hadn't kept his end of the bargain.

Teira leaned back against the headrest. With jet lag catching up to her, it was hard to gather her thoughts. She'd left Salt Lake City International Airport more than twenty hours before. Never one to enjoy flying, she couldn't have been more grateful once the Scandinavian airliner touched down with perfect precision at Copenhagen Airport in Kastrup.

But then she had come here. Her eyes cut back toward the house and she grimaced. Staying in such a derelict place certainly wasn't what she'd envisioned when invited to stay at her grandmother's country home while working abroad for ComTech. The telecommunications firm for which Teira worked had recently acquired the local Danish telephone company, a move that looked to be highly profitable for both parties, assuming Teira did her job well and brought them up to speed quickly. She knew she could do that. She wasn't so sure she could stay here.

Teira looked at the house once more and rolled her eyes. Then she closed them and leaned back against the seat. It shouldn't be a surprise to find things like this. As far back as she could remember, almost nothing turned out to be as it first appeared. As a child, Teira was tucked into bed with magical stories of Hans Christian Andersen as well as tales from her Danish family history. She was told stories of kings and queens, beautiful castles, and golden crowns in a kingdom far away across the sea. There, loyal and courageous subjects laid down their lives for their country. The bravest and best of all the warriors was her own grandfather. Teira had grown up idolizing him until the day reality stepped in and she realized that the hero of her dreams was actually a traitor.

Teira's grandfather, Soren Pedersen, had been a saboteur in the Resistance movement and had worked with the Freedom Council during the occupation of Denmark in World War II. Soren died weeks before the war ended during an act of treason. He had betrayed kingdom, crown, and country. Worse, Teira thought resentfully, he had betrayed his family.

Teira remembered well the day her mother had sadly told her the truth about her grandfather—how he had turned his back on all he once stood and fought for, all he had believed in. Although he died because of the choices he made, his family continued to pay for his mistakes after his death.

Teira yawned as exhaustion overcame her. She looked again at the house, her heart sinking lower. Who knew what she would find inside? Unable to face whatever it was just yet, Teira let jet lag overcome her and drifted off to sleep.

* * *

A man pulled up across the roadway and turned off the engine of his car. From this angle he could see Teira perfectly. She was alone.

He looked at the house. The gathering dusk caused eerie shadows to play across the face of it, but the windows were dark. Deserted.

The yard was badly overgrown. It looked as if no one had been there in some time.

Where was the grandmother?

The man's eyes returned to the woman in the car. He glanced at his watch and tapped his fingers restlessly on the steering wheel, wondering why she didn't get out. When he could wait no longer, he opened the door and made his way toward her.

* * *

Teira dreamed she was running through the hallways of her grandmother's house. Cobwebs brushed her face and rats scurried between her feet. Try as she might, she could not outrun the terror that pursued her. It was mere steps behind in the darkness. She could *feel* it. The fear was so real it crippled her. The harder she tried to run, the slower she moved. As she sank to her knees she heard a tapping nearby. It grew louder, more insistent, until she could feel it pounding in her head. Was it within the wall? Under the floorboards?

Coldness crept up her spine and settled in her shoulders and neck.

Her grandfather had died. Her grandmother was gone. Her mother had left the country. She was here alone—the only one left to pay the price for what *he* had done.

The knocking was relentless. Teira felt as if everyone who had died in the massive explosion was there at her door. Her grandfather had taken their lives and destroyed their loved ones. They wanted retribution. They had come for her.

* * *

Teira let out a terrified scream that woke her from her sleep. Dazed and groggy, she tried to focus. The knocking didn't stop. Her heart raced as she turned toward the left and saw a man's face peering in the window. Her second scream was louder and more terrified than the first.

The man smiled.

Teira's heart hammered in her chest. Her ragged breathing made her lungs feel as though they would burst. Although her hands gripped the steering wheel in terror, Teira's eyes darted around the car in search of a weapon. She had Binaca breath spray in her purse but doubted it would render an attacker immobile. Nor did she have much hope that a thump on the head from a rolled-up magazine would do him any lasting damage.

She glanced at the man again from the corner of her eye. He was still smiling, but it wasn't a crazed lunatic kind of smile like she'd seen in the movies. Under other circumstances she might have found it attractive. Despite herself, Teira turned toward him for a closer look.

The man stood calmly with his hands in his pockets and let her gape. He didn't try to open the door and he'd stopped pounding on it as well. He just stood there.

Teira frowned. He was an incredibly mild-mannered, good-looking attacker, she would grant him that. As if with a mind of its own, her heartbeat changed. Although it still raced, it was a different feeling altogether. It was that smile that did it, she realized. He had a great smile.

Not that she was fool enough to trust a strange man with a great smile.

Cautiously, Teira double-checked the automatic lock. Reassured that at least he couldn't open the door, she spoke to him in rusty Danish, asking through the closed window if he needed help.

The man waited patiently for Teira's tongue to work its way carefully around each unfamiliar word. Then in plain American English he said, "I was about to ask you the same question."

"Ni, tak," Teira said, meaning *no, thanks*. Then she decided that if he could speak her native tongue, so could she. "I'm fine."

"You sure?" he asked. "Because it looked like you were having a bad dream there."

Teira's irritation overcame her fear. "What are you doing on our property? You scared me half to death!"

"When I heard you'd arrived I thought I'd come by to see if—"

"So *you're* the one!" Teira cried.

The man's eyes widened. "Excuse me?"

"You're the one responsible for all this!"

"I guess you could say that," he said with a shrug.

"You admit you're the man in charge?" Teira pressed, glad to know who she had to blame for the ruin of her grandmother's home.

"Well, yes. I guess. But—"

"Why, you dishonest, despicable man!" All her fears and frustration poured out at once, now that she had the culprit in hand. "Taking advantage of a poor, innocent woman like that! And what's with the fancy suit and car? Now you get home and get some work clothes on. I want this place cleaned up tonight, Magnus Spelman, or I will personally drag you before Margrethe, Queen of Denmark, and ask her to guillotine you for taking advantage of the elderly." When he didn't move, she banged a fist against the window for emphasis. "Get going!"

He didn't move. "Who is Magnus Spelman?"

"Don't you play with me," Teira said. "By the look of this eyesore, you've been stealing from my grandmother for years."

The man looked from Teira to the dilapidated house and back again. It was as if she could see the realization dawn on his handsome face. "Allow me to introduce myself. I'm Christian Tanner. If the name is unfamiliar, let me clue you in: I'm your boss. I came by to make sure you made it here okay and to give you this." He reached into his jacket pocket and retrieved a cell phone. "They said you forgot to pick it up when you were in the office earlier. I thought you might need it, what with working in the telecommunication industry and all."

Teira tried to reach for the button that would lower the window, but instead her hands slipped from the steering wheel and fell limply into her lap. Unable to meet Christian Tanner's eyes, she gazed instead at the ruins.

2

So this, Teira thought, *is Christian Tanner.* She had closed her eyes to avoid meeting his, but she could see him just fine in her mind's eye. He was handsome—if you liked tall, black-haired, dark-eyed, athletically built men with smiles that could melt the North Pole. Who didn't? According to office gossip, practically nobody who worked for him. Teira could only wonder what was wrong with the women who *weren't* attracted to him. Were they blind?

Screwing up her courage, Teira opened her eyes and looked out the car window. Tanner was still there. He stood straight and tall, peering in her window with one eyebrow higher than the other. His lips twitched as if he were holding back a laugh.

Teira swallowed twice, hoping to dislodge the big fat foot she had stuck in her mouth. She began to apologize profusely. He didn't seem to be listening. Then she realized that while he might be listening, he probably couldn't hear what she mumbled through the closed window. Still apologizing, Teira pulled the door handle. Was it stuck or what? She rammed her shoulder against the darn thing. At last it dawned on her that a rat had a higher IQ. The door was still locked. Teira took a deep breath, released the lock, and opened the door.

Christian stepped back, smiling at her discomfort.

Trying to ignore the smile, Teira straightened her spine, swiped at the wrinkles in her khaki slacks, and held out her hand. "Mr. Tanner, it's a pleasure to meet you. I'm Teira Palmer." She was prim and proper enough now to make her mother proud.

Or maybe not.

Tanner laughed. Then he said, "You can call me Christian. We're all on a first-name basis at work. I like an informal atmosphere." He took her hand. "It's a pleasure to meet you, too. That is, it will be if I can stop the beheading."

Teira smiled. "Since you're not Magnus Spelman, you're safe. He was supposed to be taking care of this place."

Christian looked around. "Right offhand I'd say a beheading is in order."

"But forgive me for not recognizing you," Teira continued. "At the beginning of each training class I teach I play the DVD with your introduction. I've seen it so many times I could recite it in my sleep. I should know you anywhere. Have you done something different with your hair?"

Christian laughed. It was possibly more attractive than his smile. "I must have changed shampoos."

Teira felt her cheeks turn from pink to red and wondered if it would be too much to ask for a lightning bolt to zap her. "Yeah. That, uh, must be it."

Christian looked at his newest employee. She may not have recognized him, which strangely pleased him, but he'd recognized her from her files. His upper-management position with ComTech almost always guaranteed Christian instant recognition. It was rare to get a reaction from someone within the company who wasn't somehow related to his title. He liked the novelty of this particular situation.

In personally picking each member of his new team, Christian had done his homework. Teira Palmer had come highly recommended, and he liked what he'd heard. For instance, she could be defiant of authority. In his book, that was a plus. On the other hand, she had a reputation for being well liked and easygoing, something much needed in training and management. Finally, her intelligence and knowledge of the system were unparalleled.

While he'd liked what he'd heard from the start, seeing her standing in front of him now, Christian also liked what he saw. Teira was a natural beauty who was totally unaffected, and she smiled easily. Her curly, shoulder-length dark hair glistened in what was left of the sun. Her brown eyes sparkled with expression beneath long lashes, and cute little dimples appeared in her cheeks as she nervously chewed her bottom lip.

Pulling himself back to the conversation, Christian said, "Have you been inside yet?"

"I didn't have the nerve," she confessed. "I stopped off at the store and bought cleaning supplies and a few groceries. After I got here, I sat in the car trying to get up enough drive to go in and start cleaning. I must have dozed off." When he grinned she corrected herself. "Okay, I crashed."

"That must have been some nightmare."

"Well, there were rats in it," she said. "They're my greatest fear. But don't tell anybody. If word gets out, the next thing I know there will be rubber rats on my desk and in my purse. It's happened before."

Christian smiled. "Your secret's safe with me. To clinch the deal I'll even confess that I don't love rats either." He leaned closer conspiratorially. "Mice are okay, but rats are disgusting."

"That's it?" Teira said. "That's the best you can give me?" She tucked her hair behind an ear to get it out of the way.

Cute ear, Christian noted. Then he pretended to be affronted. "Why is my fear of rats less impressive than yours?"

"Well, it's not fitting for our fearless leader to be afraid of a mouse."

"A rat," he corrected. "The difference between the two is about twelve inches where I come from!"

"Where do you come from, the Amazon?"

"No, California. They have man-eating rats there." He looked toward the house. "Maybe they do here, too. You can't stay in this place. The company will rent an apartment for you like we originally planned. In the meantime, we can put you up in a hotel."

"No, really," Teira said. "The inside can't be all that bad. My mother was here two years ago."

He looked doubtful. "Let me at least check it out before I go."

"Would you?" Teira asked, gratefully leaning back against the car. "I'll wait right here."

"Some faithful sidekick you're turning out to be." Christian looked at the house but didn't move toward it.

"Here you go." Teira handed him a ring of two keys. As he walked toward the door, she looked around the yard until she found a large rock. "Wait!" she called, nudging the stone from the ground with her toe. "You might want this."

He walked to where she stood. "Want it for what?"

"Protection," she said, "in case you see any man-eating rodents. But don't put any holes in the walls."

"Right." He frowned. "Tell you what, why don't you join this little expedition? You can carry the rock to make sure I don't damage that valuable property of yours."

Teira fell into step behind Christian as he headed back toward the porch. "Okay, but if I see a rat, he's going down!" she exclaimed. "Did you know that in eighteen months the wretched things can have over a million descendants? They can swim for three days, so building a moat around your house won't even save you. And they can fit through a hole the size of a nickel." She tapped Christian on the shoulder. "You want to know why?"

"Not particularly."

"Because they don't have bones," Teira said distastefully. "They only have cartilage—that's what makes them so flexible. The beastly things can get anywhere to wreak havoc on innocent people. That's just wrong, don't you think?"

"Absolutely," Christian said, testing the first step up to the door to make sure the wood hadn't rotted. "Were you an exterminator before you joined ComTech?"

"No. Somebody gave me a gummy rat once. All this helpful information was on the package. I have a memory like an elephant."

"I'll have to remember that," he said, fitting the key in the door. He opened it and then looked back at Teira. "On further consideration, let's leave the rock outside. I don't trust your aim and I have my head to consider. Besides, from what *I've* read, rats are more afraid of us than we are of them."

"Even the man-eating variety?"

"I'm banking on it."

* * *

A thorough investigation of the house turned up no signs of rodents of any variety—Amazon, man-eating, or run-of-the-mill. Teira felt like dropping to her knees in thanksgiving.

Christian stayed and helped remove dust covers from the furniture. Cobwebs had anchored themselves in the corners, and the musty, dusty place definitely needed to be aired. *But,* thought Teira, *it will be charming after a good scrubbing.* When Christian and Teira tested the electricity and gas and found both in good working condition, Teira felt even more optimistic about the house.

While Christian carried in her luggage, Teira unpacked the groceries and scouted out the cupboards for dishes and utensils. The kitchen was well stocked. There was even a beautiful glass pitcher in the hutch, perfect for lemonade. If there was one thing she loved, it was homemade lemonade. Teira smiled as she sliced her newly purchased lemons.

Soon the kitchen smelled citrus fresh. At least it did until she opened the faucet. With the water came an odor that was horribly rank. Hastily, she stuck a slice of peel down the disposal and turned it on, hoping that would take care of the sour smell.

Next Teira washed the pitcher and filled it. Then she added the lemon slices and sugar and stirred. Meanwhile, she allowed the disposal to run, pushing in the rest of the peel. Just when she noticed the smell was getting worse instead of better, Christian found her in the kitchen. She knew from the look on his face that the rotten egg smell was not her imagination.

"I've never had lemonade that smelled like that," he said, walking over to the counter to look into the pitcher.

Teira followed his gaze and blanched at the brownish green floaters in the water.

"I've never had lemonade that looks like that, either," he added. "What did you put in it?" In the next second he pinched his nose with his thumb and forefinger and held the rest of his hand over his mouth.

Teira did likewise and ran for the door. Christian followed. Moments later she was on the front porch, gasping for air. "Sorry," she managed at last. "I have overactive gag reflexes. I had to get out of there. What *was* that smell?"

"Your lemonade, I presume." When Christian saw that she was about to slap him, he laughed. "Kidding. There's stagnant water in the pipe. Whoever turned it off didn't drain the pipes. The good news is there doesn't seem to be any rust, just gunk that has collected and dried in there. When you turned the water on, all of it flushed out. You just need to run all the faucets until the water's clear." When she nodded, he said, "Is there anything else I can do for you before I take off?"

"No. But I really appreciate everything you've already done. Thank you."

"No problem. I'm glad I could help."

As Christian turned to leave, Teira had an attack of conscience and added, "I know I started off on the wrong foot—like by putting it in my mouth. I'd hoped to make an impression when we first met."

"I don't know," he said. "Threatening me with a guillotine was pretty impressive."

Teira tried to smile but couldn't quite get her face to cooperate.

"And trying to poison me with slimy lemonade—that left a good impression, too. Not to worry."

"If it helps at all," she said, "I assure you I'm very good at my job."

"Better than you are at making lemonade, I hope." With that Christian Tanner waded through the waist-high weeds back to his car.

Teira waved as her boss drove away, then turned back slowly toward the screen door.

Things *had* gotten off to a bad start, she thought as she walked into the house to clean up the kitchen. First she hadn't recognized her boss, then she'd mistaken him for someone else, and finally she'd threatened to have him beheaded—all within the first five minutes of their meeting.

The lemonade hadn't been a brilliant idea, either, she thought ruefully. She had to hand it to Mr. Tanner—Christian—though. He took everything in stride. In fact, he laughed it all off.

Teira felt her conscience suddenly pricked again. Would he have such a sense of humor if he knew the biggest reason for her being there in Denmark had nothing to do with her job?

* * *

The driver cruised down the quiet country lane and slowed to a stop outside the house before moving on. Up ahead he pulled off to the side, half hidden by the shrubbery, and extinguished the headlights.

He pulled out a cell phone and punched a single number. After months of being paid to drive by this house twice a week, he finally had something newsworthy to report to his employer.

"It's me," he said. "I'm outside the house. It's occupied."

At the other end of the line, the phone was slowly lowered back to its cradle. The darkness of the room seemed to close in on the man as he stared ahead.

The tension building inside him at the unwelcome news made his face pale, contorted his expression, and caused him to sweat heavily.

Recklessly his mind raced back to the past as if it was only yesterday. A myriad of images and memories that even the passage of time had not let him forget came crashing down on him.

3

Teira was still fighting jet lag the next day when she showed up for a half-day of work. Christian gave her a tour of the building and introduced her to the people she'd work with. He was friendly, charming, and professional—professional enough to make her blush in remembrance of their first meeting, but friendly and charming enough to make her wish the tour would never end.

Unfortunately, there was one person at ComTech she already knew and was not anxious to see again. Adam Carson. She had met Adam in Salt Lake City. They'd signed up for the same Danish class prior to leaving for Denmark. For Teira it was a refresher course. She'd learned Danish as a child, but rarely spoke it as an adult. Since it was all new to Adam, Teira had volunteered to help him along. She had thought they were friends, oftentimes holding practice sessions after class at a nearby café. But apparently friendship wasn't enough for Adam, and the sessions soon became a trial as Teira spent most of the time fending off his unwelcome advances. She cringed at the thought of working with him here in Denmark after their last meeting in the States.

"I can make your wildest dreams come true," Adam said the last night she'd seen him. It was then he told her that she was "the stuff dreams are made of."

"Oh, yeah?" she replied. "And what would you know of my dreams?" By this time Teira was disgusted by the thought of being in this man's dreams at all.

"I have it all," he said confidently.

"You certainly don't lack self-esteem."

"What I mean is, I have a successful career that's going nowhere but up. The gig in Denmark guarantees me a fat bonus that will add very nicely to my nest egg. All that's left to consider is you and me." He reached for her hand. Teira pulled it away. "Think of the fun we'll have in Europe, just the two of us."

It had made the hair on the back of her neck rise. "Actually, there are eight of us going," she joked.

If she thought the subject had ended at dinner, she was disappointed once it was time to say good night.

"How about a kiss until we meet again?" Adam said, stepping forward eagerly. She stepped back. He tugged at her arm to pull her closer. "Come on, one kiss," he coaxed. "You're playing hard to get."

That was the last thing she was doing. "Look, Adam," she said, "I think we should be straight with one another. I considered you a friend, but the way you're acting tonight, I'm questioning even that. I don't want to be romantically involved with you. We have to work together, so I think it would be best if we forget tonight."

Adam had then glared as Teira pulled her arm from his grasp. She missed the specifics of the curse he muttered, but she didn't miss the way he kicked her trash can into the street on his way back to his car.

It was now a month later. Teira followed Christian into Adam's office, hoping the latter had grown up and gotten over her rebuff. It would be impossible to avoid him, after all. Adam's field of expertise was information technology. In other words, he was a computer genius. If there was anything he couldn't do with a laptop, she hadn't heard of it. Her job was to train management on the systems that Adam constantly updated and perfected. There was no way to avoid interacting with him.

The instant she saw Adam's smug face, Teira knew he wasn't going to make it easy. He hadn't forgotten their last encounter. Nor had he forgiven her for it.

"Oh, believe me, boss, we've met," he said following Christian's introduction. "Teira and I go way back."

Christian raised an eyebrow at the tone of voice.

"We took language classes together," Teira explained quickly.

"Yeah, language lessons." Adam chuckled and turned back to his computer.

There was little Teira could do but follow Christian through the rest of the tour, seething.

* * *

Teira waited anxiously in the lobby of the senior center for her grandmother. Would Grethe recognize her after all these years? As her mind drifted back to her mother's stories about her life in Denmark, her eyes filled with tears. Hanne and Grethe may have had very few material things, but love was in abundance in their home. The day Grethe walked her daughter to the shipyard to set sail for America aboard the *SS Stockholm,* she'd placed into her hand a doily that she had crocheted. Tucked inside were a few coins. It didn't amount to much monetarily, but Hanne knew how hard her mother had worked and sacrificed in order to give it to her. It was most precious because of the love that shone in her mother's tear-glistening eyes as she told her daughter good-bye. Hanne vowed that one day she would find a way to make her mother smile once again.

When Teira had boarded the plane for Denmark, she recalled the vow her mother had made so many years ago. She promised herself that if there was anything she could do to help keep that promise, she'd do it.

Teira held back her laughter as the petite, eighty-seven-year-old woman scurried toward her. Grethe Pedersen was still independent of walkers and canes in spite of a recent hip replacement. In her hands was a box of chocolates and a couple of neatly folded napkins. On her face was a smile that lit up the room.

Giddy with excitement, Teira jumped from her seat and ran to wrap the elderly woman in her arms. *"Mor mor!"* she said. It meant mother's mother—grandma.

Grethe hugged Teira tightly and kissed both her cheeks as she spoke rapidly in Danish. Overcome by emotion, Grethe stood with tears rolling down her soft, wrinkled cheeks. She pulled a lace handkerchief from the cuff of her sleeve and used it to dab at her eyes. Then she tucked it back in place, grabbed her granddaughter once again, and rocked her back and forth, all the while whispering soft words in Danish.

"Jeg elske dig," she said. *"Du komme finde hjem."*

Teira understood the words her grandmother repeated: *I love you* and *You came home.* Tears welled in her eyes. In halting Danish she told her grandmother how she had longed for the chance to visit.

"You have grown into such a beautiful young woman," Grethe told her in her native tongue. "You look so much like your grandfather. I would know you anywhere! You have my Soren's eyes."

"I've always been told I look like my mother," Teira said. "I thought she looked like you."

Her grandmother nodded her head. "Ah, yes. You surely do look like your mother, for Hanne has her father's eyes as well. My Soren had the kindest eyes, but very revealing. He could hide nothing from me." Grethe smiled sadly until Teira squeezed her hand. Then she shook off the reverie. Offering her granddaughter a chocolate, she led the way to a small sofa in the senior center's front parlor.

Soon they were chatting about Teira's work and her parents who were serving a mission in Canada. Teira wasn't surprised to find how much Grethe already knew about their experiences as missionaries. While Grethe had never joined the Church herself, she had been happy for Hanne and respected her desire to be baptized. Grethe admired the way she raised her granddaughter to have such strong faith and morals.

Curiously, Teira thought, Grethe didn't ask about the condition of her house or property. Teira counted it a blessing. She didn't want to upset her.

Teira's first visit with her grandmother was too brief. The time flew by and she could only promise to return the next day. As they said good-bye, Grethe held her tightly and said softly, "How my Soren would love to know his granddaughter is so much like him."

Teira's heart plummeted, but she didn't reply. Instead she forced a smile and told her grandmother again how much she loved her. Finally she turned and left.

Teira drove the streets of Copenhagen, caught up in her thoughts. How was she like her grandfather? Her looks, she hoped, rather than her character. Certainly she believed she had the courage and integrity that history indicated he had lacked.

By the time Teira thought to focus on a street address, she was hopelessly lost. She stopped in downtown Copenhagen to ask directions and was relieved to learn that the outlying cemetery would be less difficult to find than she had feared.

Several minutes later she arrived at the cemetery. Teira climbed from the car and hesitated in front of the wrought iron gate, the intricate pattern atop it holding her attention momentarily. Then she looked around to take in the rest of the view. This cemetery was unlike anything she had seen back home. In Salt Lake City the typical graveyard had mass-produced tombstones dotting acres of professionally tended lawns and trees. This cemetery was filled with family plots that the descendants tended themselves or paid others to care for in order to avoid costly fines for neglect. Each family plot was separated from the next by low fencing or shrubbery. It looked like a huge patchwork quilt because of the variety of flowers, plants, and statuary. Despite her reluctance to be there, Teira was both intrigued and impressed by the sight.

She opened the gate and felt her stomach clench. But there was no reason to turn back now. As she walked up the slight incline, she became increasingly tense. By the time she reached the plot her mother had described, she had started to shake.

Get a grip! Teira admonished herself. She took a deep breath and looked down at the headstone.

SOREN NIELS PEDERSEN

Sure enough, this was the right place.

Where did she begin? What did she want to tell her grandfather after all these years? Teira tried to put her jumbled thoughts in order, but still the words stuck beneath the lump in her throat.

"It's been more than sixty years," she said at last to the man who was buried there. "Sixty years since you made the decisions that put you here." Teira sighed. "They say time has amazing healing powers. It must be true. Somehow Grandma and Mom found the will to go on. They survived it all. They were lucky they weren't put into exile, you know."

Once she began talking, she couldn't quit. The next words came so fast they practically tumbled over one another. "Though maybe exile would have been more merciful. Do you have any idea how much they suffered? I'll be darned if I know how they did it. They obviously have stronger wills than I do because I can't seem to get past what you did to them."

Teira tucked her hands inside her jacket pockets and blinked away the moisture that had started to pool in her eyes. "I wish you knew what it was like for me growing up with stories of your 'brave' acts—only to learn later that my hero was a conspirator, a traitor. But that isn't the worst part. If you hadn't died of your wounds, you'd have been convicted of treason and probably executed." She sighed. "The king was your *friend.* He trusted you to help defend your country. How could you have turned on him—shamed and humiliated yourself and your family that way?" She swiped at the angry tears that flowed freely down her cheeks.

"Do you know what you did to Grethe? My mother was able to leave it all. She married an American, but Grandmother has remained loyal to you in spite of years of torment and ridicule. She still believes in you."

Teira looked away but was too lost in thought to see what she stared at. When she looked back at the headstone, her tears were gone, replaced by determination. "I'm taking things into hand. I'm taking *Mor mor* home with me when I leave here. She deserves to live the rest of her life with the peace and contentment she never found defending you."

Teira turned to leave, then reconsidered and turned back. "I'm angry, Grandpa. I'm sad and disappointed and I just don't understand. The whole thing doesn't make sense to me." She stared at the name carved into the stone. "Mother says I have to let it go. I wish I could. We've lived with your betrayal all our lives. I just wish I knew why you did it."

* * *

Teira flipped the signal to make a right-hand turn into the overgrown lane that had once been the driveway to her grandmother's home. Once she started to make the turn, if she punched the gas, she knew the car would make it over the tall, thick weeds at the edge of the drive and she could forge ahead from there.

"This is pathetic!" she moaned, repulsed once again by the sight of the run-down state of her grandmother's property.

She heard the thick brush scrape the bottom of the rental car ComTech had provided. That was the last straw. Furious with Magnus

Spelman for taking advantage of her sweet grandmother, she resolved to do something about this disaster site.

Just as she reached for the keys to go into the house, her cell phone rang. Checking the caller ID she noted it said *ComTech Wireless*. Instantly her heart skipped a beat. Maybe it was her boss. After all, she could see no reason for it to be anyone else.

In her friendliest voice she said, "Hello?"

"Hi, beautiful."

Teira's face fell. It wasn't Christian. She already knew his deep voice—had dreamed of it, in fact. "Who is this?" she asked hesitantly.

"It's Adam. Who did you think it was?"

"How did you get my number?"

He laughed. "You work for a phone company and you ask me that?"

"What do you want, Adam?" Teira sighed.

"I want to ask Cinderella to the ball."

Teira remained silent.

"Well? Do you want to go to the company party with me next Saturday night? I figure since you don't know anybody but me, it's the best offer you'll get."

"You're joking, right?" Teira was astounded that he had the audacity to ask.

"I would never joke about us."

"After the way you treated me today in front of our boss, you honestly thought you could ask me out on a date?" She almost sputtered. "And after what happened back in Salt Lake City, I—"

"We need to put the past behind us," he interrupted. "This is a good way to start."

Teira felt like a goldfish opening and closing her mouth. The nerve of the man! Was he insane or what? She took several deep, calming breaths. On the one hand, she had to work with Adam and didn't want trouble. On the other, she wasn't about to foolishly trust him again.

She gathered her thoughts and spoke evenly. "You're right. We should be on better terms than where we left things."

"I'm glad you see it my way. I'll pick you up—"

"However," Teira interrupted, "I'd planned to go solo so I can mix and mingle and get to know everyone. This time I'll have to decline, but thank you for the offer. I better go now. I'll see you at work, okay?"

Teira snapped her phone shut before he could reply. For a split second she was worried. How would he handle a second rejection? Then she put him firmly out of mind.

Turning to look back over the yard with disgust, Teira walked toward the front door and tripped on a stone, barely managing to keep from falling. She kicked the rock out of her way, wishing she was kicking the groundskeeper. It was time Magnus Spelman got over to this house and did exactly what he was contracted to do.

* * *

It was late Friday night by the time Teira plopped down on the couch. Next to her lay several brochures of various places for sightseeing around Denmark. The castles and palaces interested her most. Teira thumbed through these brochures first, glancing at the small photos and eagerly reading the travelogues.

A smile twitched at the corners of her lips. How could anyone be in Denmark and *not* have flashbacks of all those girlhood dreams of princesses awaiting their princes? Here was a land in which dreams came true. Castles of legendary beauty stood upon the shores of a sea that sparkled in the sunlight as though it was dotted with a million tiny diamonds. Moreover, there *were* princes and princesses here, and loyal subjects who loved them. She looked down at the pictures in her lap and sighed. Even the most unromantic person couldn't ignore this magic. In Denmark, it seemed, any dream could become reality.

Teira lay back, closed her eyes, and let her imagination take flight. It had been years since she had fantasized about finding Prince Charming, but it was an easy thing to do, here in this kingdom by the sea.

4

A week in Denmark passed by as quickly as a week in America. Working at ComTech during the day, visiting her grandmother each evening, and getting the inside of Grethe's home back in order consumed most of Teira's waking hours. It took no more than the sun rising over the tangled overgrowth in her front yard to convince Teira that the best use of her day off that Saturday would be to track down Magnus Spelman. She would have preferred using secret police and bloodhounds to do it, but there was an easier way. She worked for a phone company, after all.

By the time she was out of the shower and dressed for the day, one of the workers at ComTech had called back with Magnus Spelman's address and telephone number. The new acquaintance was reluctant to give it out at first, so Teira had to press and then casually allude to her new position of authority *and* personal friendship with Christian Tanner.

It turned out that Spelman wasn't the con man or petty thief she'd suspected. Rather, he was an influential man in the community whose son was now jockeying for political position—an appointment to Parliament to rub elbows with the upper echelons of Danish government.

Magnus lived some distance from her grandmother's run-down farmhouse on the outskirts of the city. His home was in the socialite area of Copenhagen, almost an hour's drive away. Despite the distance, Teira decided that a personal visit beat a phone call. It was harder to weasel out of one's responsibilities when the injured party stood in your foyer. And if he did weasel out, she could at least kick him in the shin on her way out.

* * *

Though her ancestral home was small, it was more enchanting than the gated estate that her grandmother's "yard man" lived in. Give her a quiet farming community minutes from the seashore anytime. The Vikings had been onto something when they settled in Blovstrod all those centuries before.

Teira peered through the gate. Not far distant, a well-dressed elderly man was using a gold-topped cane to navigate his way across a manicured lawn. The hat on his head shielded his eyes from the sun and kept Teira from seeing his face.

She called out to him. "Excuse me! I'm looking for Magnus Spelman."

Either the man didn't hear or chose to ignore her, so she tried again, this time louder. He looked over at her before continuing on his way. After a few steps, however, he stopped and turned back to face Teira.

"Magnus Spelman," she repeated. "Do you know where I can find him?"

The man said nothing, but stared at her as if beholding the Ghost of Christmas Past.

"Teira Palmer," she said, pointing to herself. *"Min mor mor Grethe Pedersen. Du Magnus Spelman?"*

Before the man could reply, someone tapped her on the shoulder. Teira whipped around.

"Is there something I can help you with?" a man with intensive eyes asked.

"I hope so," Teira said. "I'm looking for a man by the name of Magnus Spelman."

"What do you want of Mr. Spelman? Who are you?"

By this time the elderly man had walked up to the gate and was listening to the exchange. "My name is Teira Palmer," Teira began. "I'm—"

"You are an American," the man interrupted. "What could you possibly need to see my father about?"

Teira's eyes grew wide. She looked from the younger man to the elderly one and saw a resemblance. She'd bet the older one was Magnus Spelman. "This is your father," she said.

"He is," the younger man said, "but I see to all his affairs. How can I help you?"

Good enough, Teira thought. She didn't care who had the yard cleaned up as long as somebody earned the money her family had already paid. "My grandmother is Grethe Pedersen," she said. "I have a contract between her and your father that says he's supposed to have seen to the care of her property for the last several years. While you've received the money, I can assure you that nobody's been to that address in months and months."

Teira was proud of herself. Despite the fact that this man was older than she was—and very intimidating—she was standing her ground. While she waited for a reply, she sized him up in her mind. Frankly, he looked rather mean-spirited. This was surprising in a man who aspired to public office. Certainly, someone like that would never receive her vote.

His father, on the other hand, had the same piercing eyes but softer features on his weathered face. Teira wished he'd stop staring at her. His odd expression made her almost as nervous as the son's scowl.

"Ah, so Soren Pedersen was your grandfather," the younger Spelman said with false pity. "How unfortunate for you. Fortunately, we can easily clear up this misunderstanding. Won't you come in?"

It sounded more like a command than an invitation. Teira lifted her chin. Of course she would go in. If these two thought they could cheat her sweet grandmother one day longer, they'd better think again. She followed the man through the gate and into the house, Magnus a few steps behind. She could feel his eyes on her back and felt anything but flattered by his attention.

"Won't you have a seat?" Spelman said a few minutes later. "I won't be but a moment and then you can be on your way."

The words were all right but the tone was all wrong. It seemed almost as if he was threatening her. She sat up straight and assumed her best professional manner. "I'm sorry, I didn't catch your name, sir."

"Ulrike," he said as he turned to leave the room. "Ulrike Spelman."

Although she was glad the son was gone, Teira found the silence between herself and Magnus Spelman awkward. "Nice day," she ventured at last.

He didn't respond. He didn't stop staring, either.

"Beautiful home you have here."

More silence.

All at once Teira knew what it was. She leaned forward. "You knew my *bedstefar,* Soren Pedersen, didn't you? That's why you're looking at me—it's my eyes. *Mor mor* said I have his eyes. Do I remind you of him? Will you tell me about my grandfather?"

Just then Ulrike returned. His face was stony when he said, "Yes, he knew your grandfather. He's one of very few who will admit it. Most are too ashamed to say so." He walked over to where Teira sat and handed her a cardboard box slightly larger than a shoebox. When she took it, he brushed the imaginary dust from his hands. "There now. We Spelmans wash our hands of your family once and for all."

Magnus tapped his cane on the floor and spoke in rapid Danish to his son. Although she was seated right there, the words were spoken so fast and in such an undertone that she couldn't catch them. She could tell by the tone, however, that they were harsh.

Ulrike's only reaction to his father's outburst was to turn to Teira and say, "You may go now. We ask that you never return."

Teira was nonplussed. "I-I don't understand. What is in this box?" Ulrike took a deep, impatient breath.

"My father and Soren Pedersen were comrades on the Freedom Council during the war. Even though your grandfather betrayed everyone who loved him, my father still agreed to help his wife see to the farm while she had a child to care for. She insisted on paying him—with vegetables and milk at first. When my father married, your grandmother insisted on drawing up that ridiculous contract. She paid a pittance, but since the home was all your grandfather had ever provided, my father pitied her. He and I and my son kept it up until she left. After that, it was even more useless."

"Excuse me," Teira said, appalled, "but you could have at least let the family know you'd quit before the place fell to ruin."

"Family!" Ulrike scoffed. "All of Grethe's family have either died or abandoned her!"

"My mother did not abandon her! She left because she married an American, but half of her heart is still here with her mother and her native land."

He waved a hand as if shooing a mosquito. "The point is moot. The family is gone and the work is no longer necessary."

"But we've paid you!"

"Obviously, you have only supposed, not researched," he said. "If you had merely looked at your grandmother's bank account, you would see that the checks never cleared. In the box you will find unopened envelopes with her money still inside." While Teira was still looking down at the box in shock, he said, "Now, go. You've imposed on our family's charity and good grace long enough."

Teira stood, feeling foolish. He was right. She *hadn't* done her homework. She'd seen the contract, but she hadn't asked her grandmother about it for fear of upsetting the older woman. Her mother handled the bank account, but Teira hadn't wanted to bother her on her mission, either. She'd just assumed—and got exactly what she deserved for the assumptions.

"We owe you a debt of gratitude," she said at last. "Thank you."

"We don't want your thanks," Ulrike responded coldly. "My father is a magnanimous, forgiving man. He did not believe your grandmother and mother should have to pay for your grandfather's sins. Others, you should know, are not as generous."

This man was inexpressibly rude, but he was also right. She walked past him and slipped into a chair at the old man's side. Then she reached over and took his hand. "Mr. Spelman, thank you for being the only person who was truly kind to my mother and grandmother. I can't imagine what it must have meant to have a friend and protector like you."

Before Magnus could respond, Teira stood, walked back to Ulrike, and extended her hand. He shook it limply. "And thank you for your help," she said.

He tipped his head silently.

At the door, Teira turned to look back at Magnus Spelman. He still stared, but this time he was the first to look away.

Teira walked back to her car. She'd had high hopes of accomplishing much more from her visit with Magnus Spelman. Visions of green grass, blooming flowers, and beautiful foliage had danced in her head. Now all she could see were weeds, thorns, thistles, and crabgrass. The only things blooming in abundance in her grandmother's yard were the big, golden dandelions that would soon go to seed and multiply.

And who would have guessed she would end up walking away feeling begrudgingly indebted to the Spelmans rather than satisfied that she had taken them to task for cheating her grandmother?

Magnus may have looked at her like she was the Ghost of Christmas Past, but his son Ulrike was Scrooge. Leaving their estate, Teira decided she deserved a diversion before tackling the yard on her own. A slow smile crept over her face. She knew exactly where she would go.

* * *

A walk through the Rosenborg Museum was like a walk through Danish history.

It felt good to step away from the world and back into another time as she stood before the beautiful medieval castle. In 1606 the reigning king, Christian IV, had wanted a summer house built in the middle of a newly developed park called the King's Garden. But with extensions, turrets, and a drawbridge added, it wasn't until 1624 that the king referred to the castle as the House in the Garden for the first time. It looked every inch an enchanted palace, and Teira was overcome with a youthful excitement to explore it. This was exactly what the romantic side of her nature craved.

The first impressive sight upon entering the historic grounds of Rosenborg was the tree-lined walkway that led up to the castle. Beneath towering beech and oak trees, couples cuddled and families used the vast, manicured lawns to picnic. All around lay magnificent beds of fragrant roses, poppies, irises, and tulips. It was breathtakingly beautiful and serene. Teira wasn't surprised that so many locals came to the spot.

At the end of the long walk, guarding the entrance to Rosenborg, were two enormous copper lions, long since oxidized, but befitting a royal estate. Teira stopped momentarily to admire the magnificent sculptures before moving on in anticipation. After a couple of steps, she paused again and craned her neck to look up at the stately spires jutting heavenward from the fortress. The castle had been constructed of red masonry with a copper roof, which was now green with age.

A thrill shot through her. The pictures she had seen had not done this castle justice. Teira stopped again before setting foot on the drawbridge, lowered to welcome visitors to the palace courtyard. In another few steps she would be crossing an actual moat.

She walked to the edge of the drawbridge and looked down into the water. Carefully, she bent to touch the edge of the bridge, letting her imagination run wild. What stories in history this bridge could tell! How many knights on horseback had crossed this bridge to do battle for their beloved king? How many historical figures had stood in this very spot? Teira was filled with wonder. Within a few more minutes she had paid for her ticket and joined a tour group just entering the museum.

As she strolled from room to room, Teira looked at each costume, tapestry, and heirloom with wonder, scarcely believing that so many had survived and been so beautifully preserved. It wasn't the wealth that held her attention—though it was abundantly clear that everything here was truly fit for a king—but the authenticity of each artifact. Impressive didn't go nearly far enough to describe all she saw.

Entering the Rosenborg Treasury, the tour group passed through an outside door at which armed military guards marched back and forth with rifles in hand. Then the group walked down several steps, through an iron gate, and into a hallway lined with marble statues that led to the darkened exhibition rooms. The only lights were bright spotlights highlighting the rare jewels that only the Danish monarchy were commissioned to use. Standing there, so close to the crown jewels, Teira could hardly catch her breath.

Among the jewels other interesting pieces were displayed. Teira marveled at the golden goblets, kings' copies of the royal statutes and constitution, and a 17th century prayer book that had belonged to King Christian IV's wife, Kirsten, along with the king's scepter, and tiaras and hair ornaments worn by the queens. In the middle of the main room stood a glass case where King Christian III's Sword of State was displayed, along with the crowns of kings and queens from centuries past.

As she walked around the room looking over the treasures, only half-listening to the tour guide relate the history of each piece, Teira let her thoughts drift back to Christian. Somehow, she just couldn't stroll through the castle of a previous Christian without picturing her boss with the same name. Her mind wandered to thoughts of him. *Her boss.* Startled, Teira pushed the thoughts from her mind and hurried back to rejoin the tour.

"This small signet ring is a copy of one that belonged to King Christian X," the guide was saying. "It was given to him by his mother, passed down from his father, King Frederik VIII, on the day of Christian's coronation. From that day forth he always wore it on the smallest finger of his right hand. On it was the emblem of the Order of the Elephant, an emblem of knighthood and chivalry—the oldest, most prestigious, and highest order of distinction."

Teira leaned closer.

"The signet was made of gold, embedded in a stone of sapphire. It was the king's most prized possession," the guide continued. "Aside from its real and sentimental value, it reminded the king of his motto, 'My God, my country, my honor.' A few weeks before the end of the occupation in World War II, on May 4, 1945, the ring came up missing. Some say the king lost it, which was highly unlikely considering he never removed it. Others say he gave it in behalf of his country to aid in Denmark's cause. Either way, the royal administration refused to comment, and the king never spoke of it to his dying day. What you see here is a reproduction. The real ring has never been recovered. Surely if it were found, it would have an interesting tale to tell. Next, we move along to . . ."

Teira stopped listening. She couldn't explain the strange feeling that overcame her, but the hair on the back of her neck stood on end. What an eerie coincidence that the ring had turned up missing around the time her grandfather died. Teira tried to shake off the uneasy feeling and enjoy the rest of the tour, but her mind kept drifting back to the signet ring.

By the time the tour ended, Teira had so many questions about the ring that she didn't know where to begin. Her biggest concern was to not draw attention to herself to the extent that she would have to reveal her grandfather's story. It was, after all, uncomfortable having to explain to strangers that your grandfather was a traitor to their country and everything they held dear.

She approached the tour guide. After thanking the woman for sharing her knowledge, Teira asked about several other artifacts before bringing up the ring. "Why would anyone assume the ring was given in behalf of Denmark's cause if King Christian had no political standing?" she asked at last, hoping to seem like a clueless American tourist by speaking in her native tongue.

The guide glanced at her watch. "I'm sorry, I have another tour beginning. Why don't you talk to my boss, Olaf Jorgensen. He's head of security and can answer any further questions you have."

"Oh, no," Teira said. "That's okay. I was just curious."

Her protests fell on deaf ears. The guide had already motioned for a man to join them.

Jorgensen, a man in his early forties, wore a black suit, pale blue shirt, and red silk tie. It took little imagination to see the outline of a holster and gun beneath his coat. After a brief introduction, the guide went her way and left Teira facing a man whose eyes seemed to be able to penetrate her soul. He was so intimidating that she felt an irrational desire to turn and run.

In the next second Teira smiled at her own silliness. Looking the way he did probably made Jorgensen better at his job. With wealth untold sitting behind plate glass, the museum needed a man who could anticipate trouble before it occurred.

"My name is Mr. Jorgensen," the man said crisply. "How can I help you?"

"I don't want to waste your time," Teira said, "but I am curious about one of the artifacts."

"Which piece interests you?" he asked.

Was it her imagination or did his eyes narrow in suspicion?

Don't be silly, she told herself. *You don't look anything like a jewel thief or a traitor.* But neither had her grandfather, and he had been the latter. Probably the guard couldn't be too careful. Teira put the thought aside and said, "I'm a history buff. I was wondering about the story of King Christian X's ring. The guide said he might have given it in behalf of his country and I wondered how—I mean, if he didn't have any real political power . . ."

"It's speculation," Jorgensen said. "One theory. But if you are a real history buff, as you say, then you know that he was most concerned about Denmark's state of affairs and the desperate condition the economy would be in after the war." This time she was sure he had narrowed his eyes. "Is that what brings you to Denmark, your interest in our history?"

"No, I came here to work," Teira said. Going back to the subject at hand, she added, "I'm sure the king was concerned, but I still don't understand how a ring would help much. *Did* he give it to someone, do you think, or was it lost or maybe even stolen?"

"The rumor is he gave it to one he trusted who then betrayed him," Jorgensen said. "Either way, did the man not steal it by deceiving his king?"

"So you don't believe the king lost the ring or sold it for the country?"

"If we knew where the ring was, perhaps we would know a lot more than we do now."

"It's been missing for a long time," Teira said. "Maybe it really was lost. After all, why would anyone keep something like that hidden? Unless maybe because of its worth?"

"Everything has a price. One would only have to name it."

"Perhaps it wasn't about money."

Mr. Jorgensen made no reply, but he glanced at his watch.

Teira took the hint. "It's an interesting story. Well, thank you for your time Mr. Jorgensen."

He nodded once and Teira turned and walked away. As she neared the exit, she glanced over her shoulder. He was still watching her. She almost laughed. She'd been in Denmark only a couple of days and yet she'd already made a royal security guard's list of shady characters.

5

He wore a gray T-shirt, well-fitted jeans, and designer sunglasses instead of a business suit, but Teira would have recognized Christian Tanner dressed in anything. It was the two men with him she didn't know.

She pulled to a stop behind the small truck parked in the weed patch that had once been her grandmother's driveway. Then she stared in wonderment. What were those men doing? Well, they were hard at work cleaning up the mess of the yard, that much was obvious, but *why*? They couldn't possibly know how desperately she needed them. Christian had seen her yard, but he thought she was trying to locate Magnus Spelman. Little did he know she had found him.

Teira got out of her car and walked over to where Christian knelt in front of a greasy lawn mower. "You can pay homage to the beast all you want," she said, "but I don't think it's going to start. It looks like it gave up the ghost years ago."

"O ye of little faith," he responded. "Stand back and observe." Christian stood and pulled the cord several times, giving Teira the opportunity to enjoy looking at the ropy muscles of his biceps. As her eyes strayed, she noted that he had grease smeared across the front of his shirt and a little on his forehead where he had brushed away the sweat with a dirty, oily hand.

The machine sputtered to life before it died. Christian looked up proudly, ignoring the billowing smoke. "See? That's progress. I think the gas line is clogged."

"Uh huh," she agreed tentatively.

He chuckled. "You don't know what I'm talking about, do you?"

"Huh uh. But that doesn't make me any less grateful that you're here. I'm wondering, though, is this in your job description or do you have a small yard business on the side?"

"I'm taking pity on one of my employees. Come on, I'll introduce you to the crew."

As they approached the other workers, Teira asked, "So, did you threaten these guys or bribe them?"

"I merely told them I knew of a beautiful damsel in distress."

Teira laughed. "Is that supposed to be me?"

"Well, it certainly isn't me." Christian grinned. "However, I took the liberty of promising one of them a dance with you at tonight's dinner party."

"And what did you promise the other one?"

"That you wouldn't make lemonade." Christian burst out laughing and dodged her playful slap. "Not to change the subject, but this might be a good time for you to consider switching to another man to see to your lawn care needs—provided you still have a lawn beneath all these weeds."

"You don't know how good an idea that is. I finally located Magnus Spelman. Long story short—he's no longer on the job."

"It looks like he's been off the job for some time," Christian replied.

They stopped near a man who was whacking vigorously at tall overgrowth. Beads of sweat dripped from his auburn hair down the side of his face. Every few feet he had to stop to extend the string of the trimmer or pull a particularly well-anchored weed up by hand. He was making slow progress.

"Did I mention this is coming out of your paycheck?" Christian asked Teira as he tapped the man on the shoulder to get his attention.

The man turned off the trimmer and smiled as he removed a leather glove from his hand to extend it when Christian made introductions. His name was Lars and he was over maintenance and grounds care at ComTech.

Next Christian motioned for a dark-haired Dane with a goatee to join them. Erik was new with the company and hired to assist Lars. But recently Christian had learned that he had excellent computer skills and could fix almost anything that broke down, so he was considering reassigning the younger man. For that reason he'd invited Erik to the company party that night. Erik had been cutting away dead branches from bushes that had long been left unattended. He'd already dragged a large pile to the far corner of the lot.

Teira said, "I can't thank you enough for giving up your day off like this. Let me go inside and get you something to drink."

"No thank you!" the three said at once.

"We brought our own." Christian winked at the other two who chuckled.

"My reputation precedes me," Teira noted. Fortunately, she could take a joke as well as anyone. "Fine. I wasn't planning to open a lemonade stand anytime soon, but you guys don't know what you're missing. As for you Mr. Tanner, I can't believe you told! Remember, revenge is sweet!" With that she walked toward the house with her head held high.

Christian bounded up the stairs after her and followed her into the house. "Whoa there, Miss Palmer. We had a deal."

"What deal is that? I don't remember shaking hands on any deal. Are you perhaps referring to a previous conversation concerning mice?"

"I keep telling you—rats! What happened to that memory like an elephant? Besides, you're the one who brought vermin up in the first place."

"Women are *expected* to be afraid of mice," she said.

"We're talking rats," Christian repeated.

"I want my lemonade story added to the list of secrets we're keeping."

"Agreed. Except for those who have already heard it by way of the interoffice memo. Otherwise, I won't tell a soul. And while we're agreeing, I want a promise that that elephant brain of yours will recall that I dislike rats, not mice."

"Agreed."

"This time we shake." He held out his oily, dirty hand.

"Not a chance I'm touching that."

"I'll wash up. Try to remember what we're shaking on when I get back, will you, Elephant Woman?"

Christian found Teira sitting under a tree in the front yard. He was lucky to have found her there in all the weeds since he hadn't yet got the lawn mower to work. Still, the progress was amazing. She looked around at everything that had been accomplished while she was traipsing through Denmark's capital. For sure the yard was better. If not as beautiful as in her dreams, it was at least bearable.

"I can't believe you guys did all this for me," she told Christian gratefully.

"We've hardly begun," he said. "And as much as I hate to say it, we need to head out to get ready for the bash tonight. First, though, I ought to tell you a couple of things, starting with I was kidding about charging you."

"But I want to pay for the help!" Teira said. "Believe me, it's worth it!"

Christian held up his hand to stop her protest. "This acquisition is important to the company, and it's crucial that things go smoothly. Everybody is sacrificing to be here and I want to make it easier for all of you." He grinned. "You probably needed the most help. If I can lighten the load and help you focus on what you have to do at ComTech, it's a fair tradeoff."

Teira smiled. "Well when you put it like that . . ."

Christian continued, "But Lars really does have a small business on the side. So since this thing with Magnus Spelman didn't pan out, I would highly recommend him." Christian looked at the house. "If you're going to keep this place, it's going to need repainting and reshingling. Lars is quite a handyman." He shrugged. "No pressure. It's just an idea."

"A very good idea!" Teira said. "I'll take it. Thank you again."

Christian stood and offered his hand to help Teira up.

"And one last thing . . ."

"Yes?"

"Shake on our deal."

"Not a word." Laughing, she reached up and took Christian's hand.

* * *

Like any true princess, Teira Palmer was fashionably late to the ball. By the time she walked into the Copenhagen Marriott, most of the rest of the guests had already arrived and were enjoying cocktails. Christian watched her descend the staircase alone. In a word she was beautiful. Glancing hastily around, he knew he wasn't the only one who noticed. Every man's eyes had turned that direction.

A wave of protectiveness—and something else he didn't care to define—swept over him. Christian excused himself hastily from his group and made his way toward her. He halted, however, when Adam arrived first.

* * *

Everywhere Teira looked the men were in tuxes and the women in formal gowns from every designer in Europe and in every hue of the rainbow.

She paused at the bottom of the stairs next to a woman in a gold-sequined gown that revealed more than Teira's swimsuit. *Talk about being underdressed,* Teira thought. Now that she looked around, she realized that her gown must have taken more fabric than any two of the other women's. She shrugged. She might not be in style, but at least she was modest. Her black, form-fitting dress accentuated her tall, trim figure. Her only accessories were a small gold necklace and matching bracelet. To complete the sleek look, she'd pulled her dark hair into a chignon and put gold studs in her ears. Teira knew she was no raving beauty, but this dress gave her confidence.

A passing waiter stopped to offer her a glass of champagne. Teira smiled but declined. She had been glancing around the room for Christian, but saw Adam instead. No surprise there since he was standing right in front of her.

"Hello, Teira," he said. "You look fabulous."

"Thank you," she said. "How are you?"

"Better now that you're here. I hope you don't plan to blow me off again."

"Adam, please." Teira lowered her voice. "Don't do this. I need a chance to get to know everybody. I don't feel free to mingle if I have to stick to one person's side all night. Please don't take it personally."

"Fine," he said, "if that's what it is." He leaned close. "But it's in your best interest to stay on my good side." He turned and walked away.

Whatever that meant. Still, Teira frowned as she watched him leave.

Shortly afterward, Christian came up to greet her. Her worries over Adam melted away the moment he smiled. Unfortunately, a moment was exactly how long it lasted. They were interrupted by other employees, all vying for Christian's attention.

As she mingled throughout the room, people stopped her to introduce themselves and to welcome her to Denmark. She visited with several of the managers and discussed the new system, while others wanted to discuss anything but business. Teira found she was really enjoying herself.

Waiters had stopped several times, offering various drinks. She asked for soda water with a slice of lemon. From over her shoulder she heard, "Let me guess. Since you're from Utah, I assume you won't be drinking a lot of champagne tonight. Am I correct?"

Teira smiled and turned to see Christian. "Am I that obvious?"

"Not at all," he said. "I shouldn't have made the assumption. I'm sorry."

"Don't apologize. You assumed correctly."

"Have you seen the LDS temple they have here in Copenhagen?" he asked.

"No, not yet. I'd like to. Have you?"

"I have, actually," he said. "From the outside, anyway."

"Can I ask you a question?"

"Can I reserve the right not to answer?"

Teira laughed. "It's an easy one, and not too personal."

"Okay then. Go ahead."

"Your name is Christian—that's Danish. Do you have Danish ancestry?"

Christian smiled. "How do you know it's Danish?"

"You know that *C4* on every other building in Copenhagen?" She smiled. "That's for King Christian IV. Every other king in the monarchy is also Christian, so it's a given that Christian is a Danish name."

"My ancestors are from here," he said. "That's why I worked so hard to make this company in Denmark one of our first European acquisitions. I mean, it's a stable company in a techno-advanced area with great growth potential, but I can't deny I wanted to come here to see the area." He crossed his arms. "Am I to assume Teira is Danish as well?"

"It is, actually, but it isn't spelled correctly. The correct spelling looks like T-H-Y-R-A in English, and my mother was determined my name would be pronounced as it is here in Denmark."

As he was about to comment, a beautiful blonde walked up and put her arm through his. "Sorry I took so long," she said. "The line to the women's restroom is unbelievable."

The woman spoke English, Teira noted. She also saw the way Christian looked at her and smiled. "I'm Teira Palmer," she said, extending her hand. "I'm part of the American team."

Unless it was her imagination, this woman clearly looked down her nose. After a limp shake she removed her hand. "My name is Sophie," she said. "Christian, we should be mingling with everyone—there's quite a crowd to get through—and I'm sure everyone wants a moment of your time. Shall we?" She pulled Christian a step away. "It was nice to meet you," she added insincerely.

Christian turned. "I'm glad you were able to make it tonight," he said with a smile before he turned and walked with Sophie across the gleaming marble floor.

Teira frowned as she wondered who the woman was. Whoever she was, she exuded sophistication. Teira looked down at her simple black dress, the one that had made her feel so pretty at the beginning of the evening, and wondered if it was all wrong. Then she straightened her shoulders. Why assume she was the one lacking when it was Christian Tanner who had the reputation—professional and otherwise?

Who would have thought that someone so young (Christian was only thirty-two) could have achieved all he had in such a short time? Sterling Blackman, ComTech's founder, had already appointed him COO. Since then, Christian had led the company into increasingly profitable ventures. Now it was buying out a Danish telecommunications company and going global. It was widely rumored that Sweden and Finland would be next.

But that wasn't the only thing he was known for. According to office gossip—of which there was plenty—Christian Tanner was a ladies' man. He always had a different woman on his arm, and usually they were models. Obviously, he was successful and handsome enough to get away with it, but it irritated Teira just the same. She didn't care how good-looking he was. He could look like Crown Prince Frederik of Denmark, who Teira and millions of other women *had* noticed was handsome indeed, but that didn't mean he should flaunt his good looks. She didn't like the kind of man who wouldn't make up his mind and settle down.

A twinge of guilt struck. Was she perhaps being a little unfair at passing judgment on a man she didn't know? Besides, she was twenty-seven herself. How many times had she had to tell people she had *not* chosen her career over marriage? The truth was that nobody had ever come along who swept her off her feet. And, as painful as it was to admit, nobody had really tried. Her battered pride silently conceded that though she had had a boyfriend in the past, the relationship never amounted to anything more than companionship once the guy had found someone new. Teira snorted in disdain. Perhaps she found it easy to recover from the breakup because deep down she knew she too was never really in love.

Every day she listened to co-workers talk about their husbands, their wives, and their children. Every time it triggered a yearning so strong it was painful. She wanted to be cherished. She wanted her turn to be loved like that—and to love in return. Although she didn't consider herself a spinster by any means, Teira knew she was at an age to be settling down and starting a family. But with no prospects in sight, she had chosen to make do on her own. If and when her Prince Charming showed up, she was sure he'd prove worth the wait. In the meantime, wait, date, and wonder she would. If only she weren't so darn lonely.

* * *

Before dinner was served Christian stood to welcome everyone. He introduced the managing directors of the area offices and the American team that had come to help make the transition. Then he gave a short speech about ComTech and its outlook for the future. When he sat down, everyone applauded and soon dinner was under way. In no time it was over and the guests were directed to a large ballroom where an orchestra played. Teira's spirits lifted at the sight of everyone chatting and dancing.

A couple of times when Christian was in her vicinity, their glances met and they smiled or nodded. At least he acknowledged her, she thought. In fact, she added with silent satisfaction, she'd often caught him looking her way.

Teira danced with Adam. It was unavoidable. When the number ended, she tried to pull away, but he held her close and asked for another. With reluctance, she agreed. It was better than causing a scene.

On the third number they were cut in on by Erik, the man from maintenance who had worked on her yard earlier that day. He turned out to have quite a sense of humor and kept her on her toes mentally with his wit as he swept her across the dance floor.

When the selection ended, they walked together toward the refreshment table for a cool drink. Erik offered her a glass of wine. Teira smiled and politely declined, asking instead for a glass of ice water.

After awhile Adam and a woman named Tove from the Danish team joined them for conversation. Soon Teira grew tired and said her good-byes. As she walked away, Adam caught up with her and offered to see her home. Since she had her car, Teira politely declined.

Adam's jaw clenched. "Then I'll see you safely to your car."

Teira smiled on the outside while her insides screamed "No!" She said to Adam, "I appreciate your thoughtfulness, but it's in valet parking. I have my ticket in my bag."

"No problem. I'll walk out with you. I was about to leave myself."

Persistent little devil. "In that case, thank you," Teira mumbled politely. She walked toward the exit with Adam's hand uncomfortably at the base of her back. The faster she walked to get away, the more he picked up the pace. They walked up the grand staircase toward the massive double doors. At the top, she turned back for one last glance at Christian. He was on the dance floor with Sophie wrapped in his arms. A pang of jealousy shot through her as she walked even more quickly through the doorway and out into the foyer to claim her bag and wrap.

"Thank you," Adam said as they reached the door.

"For what?" Teira asked in confusion.

"For my new reputation. The whole office just saw us leave the party together. Their tongues will be wagging all week!"

"You set me up for office gossip?" Teira asked incredulously.

"It doesn't have to be gossip," he said, moving closer.

Teira stepped back. "We've been through this. The answer is still no!"

Adam didn't reply as she hurried outside and toward the valet attendant.

She made the mistake of glancing back over her shoulder to see the penetrating look he gave her. She hoped she hadn't made an enemy.

Overall it had been a wonderful night. The only dampers on the evening were meeting Sophie and dealing with Adam. Teira refused to dwell on either subject.

At least, she wouldn't dwell on them if she could possibly help it.

* * *

Late that night, after the party, Christian stretched out on his bed with his hands behind his head, lost in thought. Sophie had announced that night a sudden new desire to take a more active interest in her father's company. More accurately put, Christian knew, she had decided to take a more active interest in *him.* Sophie had no role with the company other than to represent her family at the company functions. So far. But recently, Mr. Blackman had said it would be comforting to know his company would stay in family hands when he retired. It didn't take a rocket scientist to catch the innuendo and understand that he hoped Christian would soon be part of that family with Sophie at his side.

Sterling Blackman's retirement wasn't far into the future. He already left all the travel and most of the business decisions to Christian. Sterling had worked hard building an empire and had molded Christian to fill his spot.

Tonight Sophie had come on too strong, Christian thought, especially when he'd been talking to Teira Palmer. He hadn't known what to say to either woman at the time, so he'd let it go. Now he wished he'd gone to the dinner alone. After all, he and Sophie weren't dating, though they attended most company functions together. It seemed natural that as head of the company he often escorted the family representative. But that wasn't the same as dating her, was it? Whatever happened to the old-fashioned kind of dating where the guy called up the girl to ask if he could take her out for the evening?

Whatever Sophie's or her father's plans were, Christian didn't have any romantic feelings for Sophie. And he didn't appreciate the way she'd snubbed his employee, either. He'd been talking with Teira and had hoped to talk with her more. He'd also wanted to dance with her, but with Sophie hanging on his elbow, his hands were, quite literally, tied. There was no way he could have made that happen.

Adam had been at Teira's side for most of the party. He shouldn't have been surprised. Teira had mentioned the language course they'd taken together in Salt Lake City. Obviously, Adam was interested, and Christian had the unwelcome suspicion that the interest might be reciprocated. Teira looked as if she had been enjoying herself.

Isn't that just great? he thought, before quickly dismissing the sarcasm. Really, what should it matter? He barely knew Teira.

There was something about her, though. She wasn't as gorgeous as some women he'd dated, though she had a natural beauty Christian found appealing. Besides, he'd never been one to be impressed by clothes, jewelry, or elaborate makeup and hair. What did impress him were spunk, intelligence, and a great personality—things Teira had in abundance. But she also had an imaginative, almost childlike side that she wasn't afraid to show and that he found incredibly refreshing after all the jaded businesswomen and ambitious debutants he'd dated. In short, Teira possessed rare qualities that, while difficult to quantify, added up to make her the most intriguing woman he had ever met.

Christian bolted upright. What was he thinking? There was too much going on in the company for him to get involved with anybody right now, especially an employee. Besides, if tonight was any indication, she already had a boyfriend—Adam Carson.

Christian ran his fingers through his hair and groaned.

* * *

"Now that we have determined who she is," the man said, "I had her followed—"

His employer nodded. "And?"

"As far as we can tell she's here on a work visa, but today she went to the castle." He paused for emphasis. "She was particularly interested in the ring." The fierce reaction the man might have expected didn't come.

Instead, his employer's face remained expressionless, although his voice lowered. "Keep an eye on her. I want to know her every move." Once his employee left, he couldn't help but think that if he had it in him, he would follow the girl himself. There was a time when he was known as one of the best in covert operations. But that was then . . .

6

Teira went to church on Sunday. One of the first people to greet her was the branch president's wife, Zella Hansen. Zella wrapped her arms around Teira upon introduction and then immediately began to introduce her to the other sisters. It was soon obvious that nobody in the branch could resist the charming, petite woman with the vibrant personality. Though in her early sixties, Sister Hansen had energy to spare.

The missionaries were happy to sit next to Teira to translate. They seemed almost disappointed to learn that she knew Danish well enough to get by. One whispered that they always looked forward to speaking with Americans and hearing how things were back home. Not only that, it was a good excuse to speak English again, if only for a few minutes.

At the end of sacrament meeting, Sister Hansen joined Teira again and asked if there was anything they could do to help her.

Teira explained that she had moved into her grandmother's house while she worked at ComTech and was mostly settled.

The expression on the older woman's face changed measurably when Teira told her where the house was, but she hesitated only briefly before offering to drop by for a few minutes for a longer visit so she could welcome their visitor and get to know her better.

Embarrassed by the condition of the property, Teira asked if they could chat in the building after the meetings since she'd planned to visit her grandmother before going home. Zella was more than willing. They met in the Relief Society room, where Zella asked if they could begin with prayer. Though surprised, Teira welcomed the idea. Zella offered a prayer. Afterward, they chatted about ComTech and Teira's work there. Zella asked about the education required to assume such an exciting position.

Teira smiled. "I got a business degree in college, but when I first started working for ComTech, I was in the marketing department. From there I advanced to where I am today."

Teira went on to tell Zella about her parents and the mission they were serving in Canada.

She felt a twinge of homesickness as she talked of her parents' home in Holladay, overlooking the Salt Lake Valley. At one time she had an apartment of her own, but when her parents left for their mission, she moved back home to care for the house. Then they talked about Teira's grandmother.

At last Zella said, "Perhaps I should tell you who I really am."

Teira's eyes widened in surprise.

"What I've told you about myself is true," Zella explained. "But I haven't told you everything. It wasn't until you told me who your grandmother is that I knew who you were. I knew your mother. We went to the same schools when we were children. Our parents knew each other for years, Teira, and I am afraid that at one time they were good friends. Then your grandfather was accused of treason. After that, I am sorry to say that many friends turned against your family, and some of that hatred rubbed off onto their children."

Zella drew a shaky breath while Teira waited in stunned silence for her to continue.

"I won't make excuses for my actions," Zella said with troubled emotion. "I gave your mother and grandmother a terrible time. I was among the townspeople who wanted to drive them away."

Teira couldn't believe what she was hearing. "What did the people do to them?"

Tears streamed down Zella's cheeks as she recalled some of the ugly memories from the past. It took several moments for her to pull herself together. At last, with deep sorrow etched on her face, she said, "They burned a swastika on the front lawn. Many times their home was ransacked—windows smashed, doors broken in. That was right after the war, and I had nothing to do with it. I was much too young." She looked up at a framed picture of the Savior before quickly turning away. "But to think of that poor woman and what happened to her after she lost her husband, and with such a young child to care for." Zella shook her head sadly.

"But you said you were among the persecutors," Teira said. A lump rose in her throat and tears glistened in her eyes.

"I don't know if I can properly explain," Zella said. "It took years for people to recover from the war. So many lives were lost. It's almost impossible to define a fear so tangible—a fear that caused one to wake screaming in the night years after the war had ended."

Zella leaned forward. "At the time, sirens sounded each night. Everyone who was not in their homes risked being gunned down. Sometimes people were shot in the streets at random, and even within the walls of their homes in the middle of the night. Food and clothing were in short supply and coal was almost nonexistent." She sighed. "As you know, Denmark was not the only place that suffered, some suffered so much worse. War is ugly for all involved, is it not? But let me tell you, there was mortal fear for one's life during this time. There was so much bloodshed. And it's difficult to describe the haunting cries of those who mourned their many losses."

Tears blurred Teira's vision and spilled down her cheeks.

"I believe," Zella continued quietly, "people simply could not tolerate those who had helped the enemy in any way. We sought to punish everyone who played a part in our country's loss."

"What part did you play?" Teira asked. Her mother had told her of her grandmother's torment, but without details. She had a clearer picture now. A terrible picture.

Zella opened her purse and took out a small package of tissues. She offered one to Teira before using another herself. Shame overcame her bravery and she could no longer meet Teira's eye. "I participated in the gossip. I called her names, made fun of her. I—" Tears rolled steadily down her cheeks but she forged on. "I hurt that dear woman so many times I couldn't name them all. Never once did I try to befriend her when I knew she needed a friend. I can't tell you how many times I saw her sitting or walking alone and I did nothing to change it. No matter what your grandfather did, his wife and daughter should not have been forced to pay for it. I am so very sorry. It was a hateful thing for me to do. This has weighed on my conscience for years." Zella reached for another tissue, wiped her eyes, and finally looked at Teira.

The younger woman didn't know what to say. She covered Zella's hand with her own but couldn't speak.

"I moved away," Zella said. "I only returned to the area a few months ago. When I came back, both your mother and your grandmother were gone. You are my only chance to seek their forgiveness. They may not be willing to talk to me, of course. Who is to blame them? But I have to try."

The tears that had gathered on Teira's lashes fell. What should she say? What would her mother want her to say if she knew what was happening at this moment half a world away?

Teira knew her mother well. She knew how her mother would respond. It gave her the wisdom to speak with conviction. "I'm sure my mother already has forgiven you, Zella," Teira said. "But I know she'd love to speak to you and I can help you get in touch. As for my grandmother, if you'd like to go with me sometime to visit, I'm sure she'd never turn away a new friend."

Zella smiled her relief. Then she grabbed Teira and hugged her tightly.

* * *

Zella's words weighed heavily on Teira long after she had left. She didn't trust her ability to keep her emotions in check if she visited her grandmother, so she changed her plans and went instead to the place she loved the most—the seaside.

As Teira sat on the beach that Sunday afternoon, a myriad of emotions played foursquare in her heart.

With the smell of saltwater filling her senses, Teira removed her shoes, stood, and walked to the water's edge. The shock of the cold water thrilled her, as did the sensation of sand shifting beneath her toes. She stood and watched the water and earth repeatedly changing places, lost in thought.

Finally, with sand sticking to her feet, Teira returned to the blanket she had set out and watched the waves crash onto the sand with a fierceness that matched the tangle of her emotions. Though her mother hadn't related much of the cruelty she and her mother had endured, she'd always been willing to answer Teira's questions. Thus Teira had learned it was difficult for her mother growing up, but until today she hadn't realized how harsh and terrifying her life had been.

Teira's mind drifted to what she knew of Danish history. Before war broke out, the Danish Nazi party had already formed. It went from being a group with very little influence to one that tried to exercise its so-called authority by turning against its own countrymen. They were constantly recruiting and their ranks had actually begun increasing. It wasn't difficult to understand why, really. People who are frightened often take irrational courses. Others seek for power, while still others long for strong leaders to follow blindly and blame when things go wrong.

Teira also knew that on April 9, 1940, a day her grandfather was off duty, German troops invaded Amalienborg Square in Copenhagen. Rifle fire was exchanged with the Royal Guards. The Danish government had to concede and the Danish Occupation began. Later, Teira knew, independent resistance groups formed. Most were small; some developed into sabotage units. Within three years, Denmark's Freedom Council was organized. This group gave direction to the countless smaller bands assembled throughout the country. The council had seven leaders, each from a different resistance force, and one special operations executive.

Under this new leadership, acts of sabotage against the Nazis increased. By the time the Americans staged D-day, there were more than 20,000 members of the Resistance movement in Denmark. Despite the executions of Danish saboteurs, resistance activity increased. The Germans retaliated. Things became, in many cases, gruesome.

Teira sat on the beach and considered it all as she never had before. Characters in history books were very real individuals to her: they took a stand for what they believed in and gave their lives for the liberty of their country and the safety of their families. People Teira knew and loved—and their contemporaries—had fought in this very spot for the survival of their people.

Her grandfather had been a hero in the Resistance movement working with the Freedom Council. He had worked tirelessly smuggling

Danish Jews to safety in Sweden. He'd headed countless missions to blow up the railways to impede the German troops and supplies upon which railways Danish citizens would have otherwise been deported to concentration camps. He'd risked his life a thousand times over . . . and *then* became a traitor? It didn't make sense. How could a man who loved his country so deeply one day, turn his back on it the next?

But the council, Teira knew, believed that he had. Moreover, an extensive investigation left little doubt that Soren Pederson had betrayed king and country. As the story went, a few weeks before the war ended, Soren and one friend went to sabotage a train filled with enemy officials. The timing was crucial. The officials must not reach their destination. However, according to later testimony, Soren was never given the order to sabotage the railway in the first place.

On the day of the mission, Soren and his most trusted ally set the explosives. While his friend took cover several yards back, Soren told him he would go light the dynamite. Moments later a tremendous explosion ignited the car, killing everyone onboard. But as it turned out, the car was filled with Danes. Not a single German officer or soldier was found.

Soren Pedersen, badly burned and near death, was returned to Grethe to care for. The doctor said they didn't dare take him to a hospital because he was a wanted man. The gestapo would execute him on sight. Soren died at home in the early-morning hours without regaining consciousness.

The treason, according to Soren's friend, occurred just before he lit the dynamite. He said he'd seen Soren address enemy officials through the window of the car. Those officers quickly exited the train and got into a car only moments before the grisly explosion. Because of this, the key officials had escaped, while thirty-eight Danish men, women, and children lost their lives.

A sudden question came to Teira's mind: Wasn't it awfully convenient that there had been a car waiting? Obviously, her grandfather hadn't worked alone. Had his co-conspirator ever been identified? Shouldn't Soren's friend have been able to identify him?

The more she thought about it, the more questions began to swirl around in her mind. Her grandmother had always believed in her husband's innocence despite evidence to the contrary. Now, Teira wondered just exactly who had conducted the investigation that brought all that evidence to light. Members of the Freedom Council?

Then a thought struck Teira that chilled her to the bone. Zella said her grandmother's house had been ransacked several times. What if those hadn't been acts of retaliation from the townspeople, but rather incidents of somebody looking for something?

Mr. Jorgensen at Rosenborg Castle's treasury had said that one theory behind the missing ring was that the king gave it to someone he trusted who then betrayed him. Her grandfather had known the king, and his traitorous act certainly would constitute betrayal. But if the king had given his most prized possession to a trusted friend, meaning her grandfather, surely her grandmother would have known. Wouldn't she? Teira considered. What if for some unknown reason her grandfather had kept it a secret? Wouldn't that explain the break-ins to his home?

If *the king had given Grandfather the ring*, she reminded herself. According to Mr. Jorgensen, the other theory was it could have been lost. Still, she remembered the way he'd said one would only have to name their price for its return—as if he suspected the first theory were the more probable scenario.

This line of thought only filled her with more questions.

Did her grandfather know something about the ring? *If he did*, Teira thought regretfully, *the secret was buried with him.*

The sun was beginning to set, but Teira couldn't bear to leave. She rose and walked along the mostly deserted beach. It was isolated but beautiful.

Isolated. The word echoed in her mind. It described very well how Teira felt. She finally gathered up her things and headed for home.

7

By Monday morning Teira had determined to push all thoughts of her family's history aside to better focus on her work. She had a little extra time to get organized. A midmorning board meeting had been postponed until late afternoon since Christian was at the hospital seeing to ComTech's night security guard.

According to the office grapevine, the man had been in a near-fatal accident on his way home from work that morning and was now in surgery. His internal injuries were serious enough that he might not live through the day. Although Teira had never met the man, she could see by the Danes' concern that the regular staff was very fond of him.

Teira used the extra hours to go over a proposed training program she had prepared in Salt Lake City. She had dedicated a lot of time to it and hoped it would inform ComTech's employees, new and old, about the technological breakthroughs that loomed on the horizon, while exciting them about their prospects within the ever-changing world of telecommunications.

Mid-morning, Adam stopped in to say hello. As if that weren't bad enough, he brought Christian's ball date with him. Adam leaned against her desk. "Teira, have you met Sophie Blackman?"

Blackman? Teira thought. *As in the Blackman-who-owns-the-company?* She forced a smile. "I have, actually. We met at the party the other night. But it's a pleasure to see you again."

"I'm sorry," Sophie said airily. "I don't recall the meeting. There were so many people. It's hard to keep them all straight."

Adam smirked. "I don't think it was all those new faces that held your attention, Sophie. I'd say by the looks of it that you had eyes only for the boss man."

"Mmm." Sophie sent Adam a charming smile. "My man did look rather dashing, if I do say so myself."

"Judging by the looks he got, I'd say most of the women there agreed with you," Adam said. "Doesn't it bother you when they make eyes at your guy?"

"Heavens no, I find it rather cute," Sophie said. "If I was insecure in my relationship with Christian, I suppose I might worry, but we have an understanding. They can look all they want, but they can't touch. He's mine. I expect we'll make the formal announcement after the merger is complete." She smiled at Teira. "That's confidential information, by the way."

"Certainly," Teira said uncertainly.

Sophie headed for the door. "Excuse us, but since Christian's gone, Adam's introducing me to all the new employees. We'd better get on with it." She took his arm. "And you're right, Adam. Teira's a real gem."

Adam winked. "I'll be back."

Teira slumped in her chair. Adam's words were both a promise and a threat, but it was what Sophie had said that disheartened her. Was she crazy to think the woman was establishing territory? Why announce engagement plans to a stranger, after all? Surely she didn't think there was anything between her and her boss. She hoped that she and Christian were friends, but despite the daydreams, she never expected it to go any further than that.

Well, so much for his reputation as a playboy at least. She'd been misinformed when it came to that. Clearly, Christian *could* choose to settle down. Sophie had seen to that.

But Sophie? Although Teira would be the first to admit she had nothing to go on but first impressions, the girl seemed so . . .

And Christian was just so . . .

At a rare loss for words to describe what she was thinking, Teira gave up and went back to work. She had almost finished when Erik came by her office to ask her to lunch. Although she wanted to decline, he *had* spent his Saturday cleaning her yard. Besides, it was a good way to avoid Adam and maybe lift her dragging spirits.

Her spirits did lift, right up to the time when she spotted Magnus Spelman dining at the same restaurant Erik had chosen. The good news was that he was with another man his age instead of Ulrike.

Better, they were seated across the room where she could avoid having to greet them. Still, their glances met and Teira nodded her head in friendly acknowledgement. Magnus's friend looked at her for a few brief moments before turning back to continue the conversation.

The first thing Erik ordered was a bottle of wine.

"I don't drink alcohol," Teira told him.

"Never? Not even with a meal?"

"No."

"Well, this once won't hurt you," he said with a smile. "In fact, maybe it will help loosen you up a bit."

Teira tried not to take offense. "I'll settle for ice water."

"Would one glass of wine be so bad?" Erik was no longer smiling.

"It goes against my religious beliefs," she explained. "If you'd asked me before you ordered, I would have explained." The waiter returned to the table. "They haven't opened it. Can't you change your mind about buying it?"

"You may not appreciate a good wine, but I certainly do," Erik said. To the waiter he added, "I will have it with my meal and take the remainder with me."

Teira could tell that Erik was offended, but she didn't know why. Nor did she know what to do about it. She certainly wouldn't apologize for her beliefs. They sat in uncomfortable silence until their meals were brought to the table.

After a couple glasses of wine, the old Erik seemed to return. Teira didn't know if the alcohol or passing time had made the difference, but by the time they returned to ComTech they were chatting like old friends. It was with some reluctance that Teira thanked him for lunch and excused herself to prepare for the meeting.

* * *

Christian began the board meeting with an update on Kort Madsen's accident. He'd been driving home from work when, according to witnesses, he ran a red light and slammed into a cement barricade. Luckily, no other vehicles were involved. Kort, unfortunately, would not be returning to work any time soon. The office Kort worked for would provide his replacement.

After the brief report, he turned time over to the Danish team. Key members took a few minutes to introduce themselves and welcome the Americans. Then they explained their respective positions and what they hoped to achieve in their individual areas of expertise. After each of the Americans had had the same opportunity, Christian took over again.

Teira watched him closely. It was no wonder Sterling Blackman had brought him onboard to build the company. Christian had a gift for conveying his passion for the work and his belief in his co-workers. His excitement for ComTech's future was contagious. Teira was impressed by him, professionally and personally.

Another thing in Christian's favor was that he knew how to be brief. As Teira exited the room, sooner than expected, she paused by Christian's side to hand him a file.

He turned toward her. "Do you have a minute to meet in my office?"

"Sure," she said. "But I hope I'm not in trouble already."

"No. I have a favor to ask."

She smiled. "Great. Having you in my debt is much better than being in the unemployment line after working barely a week."

Teira followed Christian to his office. He got right to the point. "I need better-trained employees at the Roskilde office. A few of them are barely getting by. I'm doing all I can to see that the acquisition doesn't cost them their jobs—they're a good bunch of people—but the way their numbers are going, my hands will be tied."

"Do you want me to go there and see what I can do?" Teira asked.

"Unfortunately, we can't lose ground on this end, so I need you here. I'm asking if you'd be willing to put in overtime in evening training."

"Of course," she said with a smile. "By the look on your face in the boardroom, I expected worse."

"I knew I could count on you," Christian said. "I'll get them here for classes. It'll be easier on them in the long run than losing their jobs."

"When do you want me to begin?"

"As soon as you can."

"I gave you my proposal," she said. "Once you approve it, I'll be ready." His face showed his appreciation so well that Teira almost swooned. She was relieved when he thanked her again and then dismissed her to look at the file.

* * *

That night after work, Teira made a phone call to her mother. She didn't want to bother her parents, but she was confused on several points. Most of all she needed to let her mother know what she had learned from the Spelmans and to let her know she had hired Lars. After all, it wasn't her money, so it wasn't her decision to make.

"Hi," Teira began. "It's me. I'm finally here! Denmark's as beautiful as I remembered! How are you and Dad?"

After several minutes of excited chatter, Teira told her mother about the state of the property and how she had been to see Magnus Spelman. "I wasn't trying to interfere," Teira added hastily when her mother expressed her shock. "I thought he was taking advantage of Grandma, and I wanted him to do the work I thought he'd contracted to do. The last thing I expected was for them to return payment of all those years of service. But it's a good thing, right? I mean, it's bound to help her financially."

"Ulrike was very selective of the facts he shared," her mother said. "He left a few things out. For one thing, your grandmother and I did most of the work ourselves. We were very self-sufficient. We had a few chickens, an old milk cow, and a pig. We also had a large garden. Mother sold eggs, vegetables, and what little milk she could. She also took in sewing. As you know, she was a wonderful seamstress. Magnus would come to mend the fences or do other heavy work and Mother offered him food in exchange. He offered to marry her a couple of times, but I don't know if he loved her or pitied her. At any rate, when she turned him down a second time, when I was ten, he married Ulrike's mother. That's when we started paying him so even the appearance of his help would be proper."

"And Grandma could afford to pay?" Teira asked.

"That Ulrike was correct about," Hanne said. "It was very little money. But it was also very little labor. He came around less and less. Before long my mother got rid of the animals and took a job in a factory stuffing cigars in boxes." She paused, then added, "You wouldn't believe how grateful we were that someone hired her. We were outcasts for such a long time."

"I know it was so hard for you," Teira began.

"We didn't have much in the way of material things, but I was my mother's life and I knew it. She made me feel safe and secure and would have given me the world if she could." There was a long pause before Hanne said softly, "I guess she did exactly that when she allowed me to go to America. She must have known I'd never return—that I would meet and marry someone like your father."

Hanne cleared the emotion from her throat. "The point is, the arrangement with the Spelmans was never solid and the work was sporadic. I expect she knows they didn't take her money, but in offering it she had kept her end of the bargain."

Teira told her mother she had thanked the Spelmans on the family's behalf and then hired Lars to put the property back in order. Then she changed the subject to her experiences at Rosenborg Castle. "Do you know anything about the theory of the ring?" she asked.

"Only that after the war some men from the Royal Guard, men who worked with my father, visited my mother one day and asked if she knew anything about the ring. Of course, she denied having any knowledge, and she never heard from them again that I'm aware of."

Teira took the plunge. "Mom, I met Zella Hansen. I don't know what her maiden name was, but you knew her as a child. She told me your house had been ransacked several times. Are you sure they believed Grandma?"

"My, but you have been busy!" Hanne exclaimed. "There's something you need to understand about the king back then. He was highly revered, an honorable man. He wouldn't send thugs to do dirty work. That's not how the monarchy dealt with things. They wouldn't send people to break into our home because they didn't believe her."

"Another thing," Teira said. "Who drove the car the enemy officials escaped in?"

"Nobody knows," her mother replied. "The driver wore a hat. Nobody saw his face."

"But it stands to reason that *someone* must have been working with Grandpa."

"Not necessarily, Teira."

"Who went with him on the mission that day?" Teira pressed. "Who testified against him?"

Hanne was quiet.

"Mom? Are you there?"

"Yes, I'm here."

"Well? Do you know who it was?"

"Yes," she said. "There were two who testified against him—the one who went on the mission and one other witness."

"Who were they?"

"Magnus Spelman—and your grandmother."

8

Her *grandmother?* She must have misunderstood. Teira clutched the cell phone and lay back against the couch. "What did you say?"

"It's true," her mother said through the receiver. "I think the reason Magnus first volunteered his help was guilt over testifying against your grandfather. I think it in some way made him feel responsible for us."

"Maybe he lied," Teira said. "And how does Grandma come into all this?"

"That's the saddest part of all," Hanne said. "Everything had to be kept secret; the less she knew, the better. Remember, Teira, at this time people were being executed and sent to concentration camps for the kind of work my father did. Still, there were times my father had to use her. She concealed documents in the bottom of my old pram and acted as though she was taking her baby out for a walk."

Teira marveled at her grandmother's courage as her mother continued. "That morning, on the day of the explosion, he asked her to meet a man in the Amaliehaven royal gardens behind Amalienborg Palace. She recognized this man from times she had been with my father at the palace, though she never knew his name. She only knew he was one who worked closely with the royal administrators. They never spoke a word. The man bent over to peer at the baby and something fell from his sleeve. He tucked it under the blanket beneath the doll, then tipped his hat and walked away. My mother never saw what it was. She left it in the pram and took it home where my father waited. By the time she'd retrieved me from the neighbors, Father was gone. His military uniform was thrown on the bed and drawers were left open. All she knew for sure was that he'd changed clothes because the ones he had been wearing were left in a heap on the floor. Later that day she made one other delivery for him."

"Did she recognize that person also?"

"No. She had no idea who it was."

"But you said she did that for him at times when she was needed. How can that incriminate Grandpa?" Teira asked.

"The Freedom Council says there were no deliveries or missions that day. Your grandmother knew nothing more, of course. I don't know what was going on, but I don't believe he turned against his country. My father was not a traitor."

"So what do we do?" Teira asked in frustration. "Our name is ruined, Grandma is still heartbroken, but we just smile and move on?"

"Justice will come," her mother replied. "I believe that and so does your grandmother. If you want to help her, embrace her loyalty. Let her talk about him. She has wonderful stories to tell. I came to love my father through her."

"It's just so tragic that it ended that way," Teira insisted. Her mother changed the subject, but Teira didn't hear much of what she said. By the time the call ended, she had resolved to do as her mother suggested. She would find out who Soren Pedersen really was—and who he had been to deserve so much love and loyalty.

* * *

Christian leaned his elbows on his desk and used his fingers to massage his temples. It had been a bad evening. Sophie had left the office furious, and he was exhausted from yet another scene with the drama queen.

After most of the employees had gone for the day, Sophie had sauntered in. Christian's nose, twitching in response to the overpowering fragrance of her perfume wafting through his office, told him in advance she was coming.

Her dinner invitation would have seemed innocent enough, but the gleam in her eyes warned Christian she wanted him for dessert. He put aside a report and sighed.

"I think we need to talk . . ." he began.

To say it had not gone well was an understatement. When he'd tried to explain that he didn't want a serious relationship with her, she'd accused him of using her and leading her on. That caught him off guard. He'd never even asked her on a date, for crying out loud. As for the other, there was no doubt in his mind that he'd earned his position at ComTech. *Her* only contribution to her father's company was to show up at social events on Christian's arm, looking pretty.

Still, the accusation stung. And it worried him. If that was how she saw things, might others see them that way as well?

Christian knew it was only a matter of time before Sterling called. His shoulders felt stiff and tight. He hoped this thing with the owner's daughter wouldn't spill over into the boardroom. ComTech needed him, Christian knew. Sterling Blackman needed him. But did *Sterling* know that? Christian had built his own standing in the field, but Sterling had given him the chance to do it. Besides, he admired the older man for his work ethic and integrity. He hoped that integrity would hold fast even where his daughter was concerned. Christian hated to envision everything they had worked for together tumbling down because of a woman scorned.

* * *

If she had one really nice physical attribute, Teira thought, it was her hair. It was long and thick with just enough natural curl to work with. There was almost no style she couldn't pull off. However, get it wet and it looked like bad carpet. The natural curl went up and out instead of down and under, resembling nothing more than a rat's nest.

Wouldn't you know it would have to rain on Tuesday morning? Teira ran in from the ComTech parking lot sopping wet—with "run" being a relative term, since she'd worn a navy pencil skirt that day. Running was not something a girl did in one of those. Of course, the parking spots closest to the door were taken, so she had to traverse most of the lot with rain pelting her in the eyes. Her waterproof mascara proved faulty; she knew because the makeup stung her eyes. She knew too that she must look like a raccoon. Blinking rapidly, she never saw the pothole until she stepped into it, soaking her high-heeled shoes and nylons up past the ankle.

Once inside the lobby, Teira didn't even try for dignity. She had none left.

With the day beginning so well, it came as no surprise that the first person she encountered was Christian. His lips turned upward as he asked, "Is this your new let's-get-to-business look or are you going Goth on us?"

Teira rolled her eyes, "This is my new don't-mess-with-me-I'm-having-a-bad-day look." She chuckled in spite of the humiliation.

"It's about to get worse," he said sympathetically, but seriously. "I've called an impromptu board meeting."

"No!" Teira gasped, horrified. "Give me two minutes."

An eyebrow rose. "Trust me, you'd need a lot longer than two minutes."

Teira put her hands on her waist. "It's true what they say about chivalry being dead. You're a real gentleman, you know that?"

He held up a hand. "Kidding. There's no meeting. Come see me when you have a minute, though." He smiled, but the smile didn't quite reach his eyes.

Teira wondered what was bothering him. When he turned to walk away she reached for his arm. "Are you okay?"

Christian looked down at her. She was a frightful mess, yet she was so sincere he was touched. Her teeth chattered from the cold and wet, but she wanted to know how *he* was? Just her asking eased his tension. "I'm good. But come see me, okay?"

"I'll be right there," she promised.

Teira made a beeline for the ladies' room. Once inside she realized how awful she looked. Mascara ran down her cheeks and her hair was plastered to her head in wisps of wet curls. She looked like the drowned rat who lived in the rat's nest she had been thinking about. She hated rats. Most of all she hated that Christian had seen her at her very worst.

While her nylons dried under the hand drier on the wall, Teira used paper towels to absorb as much moisture from her hair as she could. Thank goodness the curls were already starting to reveal themselves. She wiped the makeup from her face and did what she could with the few cosmetics she carried in her purse. At last she straightened her clothes and wiped the mud and water from her heels.

Just as she was ready to leave the ladies room, the door swung open. To her dismay, a beautifully dressed, not to mention perfectly dry, Sophie walked in and burst into a laugh that sounded to Teira's ears like a witch's cackle.

"Good heavens, you look positively dreadful," Sophie smirked. "What did you do, swim here from Utah?"

Teira smiled tightly. "Well, I certainly feel like I've been playing with mermaids. But, this *is* the home of Hans Christian Andersen, and you know what they say, 'When in Rome . . .'"

Sophie rolled her eyes. "You do know you're not in Rome, don't you?"

Teira pushed open the door as she muttered under her breath, "Neither are the mermaids."

Back at her desk, Teira removed her suit jacket, grateful that it had kept her blouse from getting soaked. She found an elastic band and pulled her hair into a ponytail. A mass of stray curls framed her face and neck, but at this point there was nothing she could do about them.

A few minutes later she stood in the doorway to Christian's office, looking at the top of his head as he bent over some paperwork, reading intently.

When she rapped lightly on the doorframe, he looked up. He didn't look any happier than he had in the lobby.

"You wanted to see me?" she asked.

Christian forced a smile as Teira walked in and sat in the chair facing his big mahogany desk. "Yeah. I read your proposal. I'm impressed with how extensive your research is, and the training log looks great." The smile broadened. "In other words, you've got my approval. Did you get a chance to talk to the Roskilde manager?"

"I did," she said. "Let me know when you want me to start."

"Monday, then. I'll have my secretary make arrangements to get them here." He leaned back in the chair, twirling a pen between his fingers. "I appreciate you getting right on this."

"I guess my social life can take a hit for the team," she teased. When he didn't reply, she sobered and leaned forward. "You're not really okay, are you?"

"Why do you ask?"

"You look stressed. Anything I can do to help?"

"You're saying I don't have a great getting-down-to-business look?" He smiled weakly.

"Is that what it is?"

"Well, I'm trying to make this takeover go as smooth as possible. Maybe I'm putting in too many hours doing it."

Teira shrugged. "If that's the story you're sticking to, okay. Just know you've got a friend if you need one."

Christian considered Teira's offer. It would be nice to unload on a friend. And even if Teira couldn't fix it, she seemed like somebody who would definitely make him feel better. Besides, how could he explain that for someone who seemed to have it all, something was definitely missing?

At the most successful time of his life, he had never felt more alone. He had friends to keep him company, a business that kept him almost too occupied at times, and he had many successful investments. He knew what he wanted in life. There was just no one to share it all with.

His dating—the little he did—left him feeling empty. He wasn't about to get married just for the sake of having a wife. He had almost made that mistake once back in college when he was working toward his MBA. Luckily, they had both realized before it was too late that neither one of them was what the other was looking for.

No, he didn't want just anybody. He wanted to find *his* wife. The one meant for him. Unfortunately, since a boss confiding his love life—or lack thereof—to a new employee just didn't make good business sense, Christian refrained. Still, it was nice to have been asked, and he had to admit that he really liked having Teira around.

"I have a lot on my mind and it's starting to show," he said. "I'm worried about Kort Madsen, the security guard. He's a good guy. The accident is under investigation. Plus, the Roskilde office is going under where they once had the best customer service center going." Christian laid the pen down on the desk. "And, frankly, there are some personal issues weighing on me. So until the merger is complete and I see some positive numbers, I don't think I'm going to be doing much in the way of relaxation."

Teira nodded. "Since you gave me such great advice, can I return the favor?"

"I don't recall ever giving you any advice."

"But you did. You suggested Lars for my yard."

"Your yard is the least of my problems," he joked.

"Mock me if you will," Teira said playfully, "but I can help."

Christian was intrigued. "Give it your best shot."

"You have a big melting pot of problems," she said, forming a cup with her hands. "It's too overwhelming as a whole; you have to break it down. For example, we're on top of the problems in the Roskilde office, so check it off your list of worries. Kort Madsen *is* worth worrying about. I don't know if you're religious, but I'm a big believer in the power of prayer. It's often the only thing we can do to help somebody." She leaned forward. "As for the merger, forget the numbers for now. Worrying won't change them. All you can do today is your best and expect the rest of us to do the same." She smiled. "I hope you know I'm not trying to minimize your problems. I know you carry heavy burdens. I'm just saying it helps me to prioritize, worry about the important ones first, and then tackle them each in turn whenever possible."

All Christian could think was how incredible the woman seated in front of him was. She made it sound doable. Believable. Maybe even easy. He'd never worked that way. He'd taken the proverbial bull by the horns and wrestled it to the ground. But it wasn't working this time. Maybe her way would.

She was right about Kort being worth worrying about. The latest report on his prognosis was devastating. The latest word on the ongoing investigation was alarming. But he couldn't tell Teira Palmer that.

Sophie Blackman was a problem that seemingly wouldn't go away no matter what he did, but he couldn't tell Teira that either. He had hoped that when he told Sophie that they had no future together, she would leave Denmark. Instead, she'd sauntered into his office and leaned over his desk. The pose was calculated. She spoke in her most alluring come-hither voice and said, "I've thought about what you said last night. Right now I think it's hard for you to devote much time to building a relationship with me. So, I'll be right here waiting for you."

He knew then that he'd wasted his breath the previous night.

And then there was Teira. She was intriguing. Above all else he wanted to get to know her better. Obviously, there was no way he could tell her that.

But, boy, he wanted to.

She stood. “I hope I wasn’t out of line.”

He rose as well. “Not at all. I appreciate your giving me something to think about.”

“Is Kort Madsen married?” Teira asked from the door.

“Married with three kids—all under the age of five.”

“Does he have any income? Workman’s compensation of some sort?”

Christian took a deep breath. “He works for the city, not for ComTech. I hope so. At least medicine here is socialized. I hope that means he’s getting what he needs.”

“I’ll keep him in my prayers,” she said.

* * *

The letter was delivered by a courier. It had no return address on the envelope that came tucked inside the delivery packet. Stranger still, the label on the outside had a false name and address. Teira knew because she checked it through phone company records. Next she called the courier and learned that a blond man had walked in, given the information, and paid cash for the delivery. There was no way to trace the sender.

The letter was short:

> *Teira Palmer,*
> *Go back to where you came from.*
> *Never return here again.*

If it was meant to scare her, it failed. But she was frustrated. If she’d offended somebody at work already, she wished they’d confronted her so they could work it out. It was a silly game to play in a company like ComTech.

There was also a part of her that was hurt. Teira wasn’t in the habit of making enemies. Besides, she was by nature a mender and resolver. But, as far as she knew, there wasn’t anything here to fix. That bothered her more than anything.

* * *

He found the older man in a dark, cold room, staring at a fireplace that had long since turned to embers.

"You wanted to see me?" he asked. Several moments passed. He wondered if the man had noted his comment.

At last the other answered. "She's up to something. She may be onto us."

The younger man didn't reply. It wouldn't be wise considering his companion's state of mind. Instead, he stood quietly and listened.

"She's asking too many questions, talking to too many people. She should never have come here."

9

On Wednesday a pop-up appeared on Teira's computer screen announcing that on Friday afternoon a group from the office was getting together to go see Kronborg Castle. It was a friendly outing designed to welcome the Americans.

At first Teira worried about whether she should decline because of the anonymous note she'd received the day before. She didn't want to spoil the occasion for anybody else, and she certainly didn't want to welcome a confrontation. But on further thought she decided to go. This might be exactly what she needed to make friends and let everybody see that any offense she might have given was unintentional. Besides, she was dying to see the famous castle that Shakespeare had used as the setting for *Hamlet.* Teira sent an immediate response, signing up.

She was happy for exactly twenty-four hours. But when she arrived at the office on Thursday morning, another white envelope marked CONFIDENTIAL was on her desk. Teira's heart sank as she opened the flap. This note was different in tone.

> *You may have found success in coming here, but your days may be limited if you are not careful.*
> *Watch yourself.*

What was that supposed to mean? She slapped the letter down on her desk in frustration. How was she supposed to watch herself if she didn't know what it was she was doing to offend this person in the first place? Ready to tear up the letter, she stopped herself and looked at it again.

Threatening? Maybe. But whoever it was would not get the better of her. She would continue to try to be her best self. That would have to be enough.

Teira slid the letter back into the envelope. Then she pulled out her key ring to unlock a drawer in her desk. She dropped this letter on top of the first, shut the drawer, and locked it back up. If only she could also lock it up in the back of her mind where she wouldn't have to wonder and worry about it.

* * *

Late Friday afternoon the small group from ComTech boarded the last tour bus of the day headed to the northernmost corner of Zealand where Kronborg Castle guards the entrance to the Oresund and Baltic Seas. They shared the bus with a group of senior citizens from Australia.

On the way up Riviera Road to Elsinore, Teira sat next to a kindly man who was not a minute younger than eighty. His suspenders and the handkerchief in the top pocket of his plaid shirt made him the picture-perfect grandfatherly type. Only his extremely flirtatious behavior ruined the cameo. Christian was seated across the aisle next to one of the secretaries named June, whose overly bright smile and flirtation rivaled that of Teira's bus partner. She had seen June hanging around Christian quite frequently, so seeing her sitting next to him now came as no surprise, though Teira wondered why Sophie opted not to join them on the outing.

"I'm spending my children's inheritance," Paul Sandstrom told Teira with a playful jab to her ribs.

Teira chuckled politely. "I'm sure they're happy to see you having a good time."

"I think they're worried I'll bring me home a Scandinavian wife as a souvenir. I will, too, if I find me one. They're awful pretty. You're not Scandinavian, are you?" He grinned as he raised and lowered his bushy eyebrows.

Teira scooted toward the aisle. "Only half. Sorry. The rest of me is American."

"Well, half is good. Are you married?"

From the corner of her eye, Teira saw Christian try to suppress a grin. He was obviously more entertained by her conversation than his own with June. "No, not yet," she mumbled.

"Do you want to be?"

"Well, yes, certainly. Someday."

Paul put his arm around her shoulders. "When should we tie the knot, sweetheart?"

She pulled her face as far back as her neck would allow. Paul laughed heartily at his own humor. Teira laughed weakly. "My, you are a clever one, aren't you?" She turned to Christian, who was laughing himself. "Are we there yet?"

"Not yet," he chuckled. "But why hurry? This is entertaining."

"I'm so glad you're amused!" she hissed.

Teira removed the man's arm from around her neck and gently laid it back in his lap. Then she patted it for good measure. "I hope to know my fiancé longer than eight minutes before we wed, but you keep looking," she said. "I'm sure your Scandinavian 'souvenir' is out there somewhere."

The man laid his hand on her knee. "You think on it and you might change your mind." He winked. "I'm a rich man. I could make you happy."

"Gosh, I haven't had a better offer in . . . well, my whole life," she said. "But I still have to decline." Teira removed the man's hand from her knee, firmly this time. Then she skillfully changed the subject. Soon he was telling her about his children back home.

When they were twenty minutes outside Copenhagen, the tour guide stood to call their attention to a small town they had just entered called Rungstedlund.

"It was here that the famous author Karen Blixen, who wrote under the name Isak Dinesen, was born," the guide said. "After seventeen years in Africa, she returned to this home until her death in 1962. She wrote her greatest works here, including *Out of Africa.* Her estate still stands and has a museum and large bird sanctuary that is open to visitors. Near the end of her life the author was asked the most important lesson she had learned from life. She said, 'Three things: courage to live, ability to love, and a sense of humor.'"

Karen Blixen's words touched Teira deeply. They were goals she would like to emulate in her own life.

Upon arrival at Elsinore, one could see the stately walls and towers of the majestic castle. It was only a few minutes later that the tour bus rolled to a stop outside the grounds of Kronborg Castle.

The tourists exited the bus, excitement evident in the way they pushed toward the palace. Elsinore had been built in the 1400s to collect taxes from ships passing through the narrow straits to the Baltic Sea. In the sixteenth century, King Frederik II transformed the crude bastion into a magnificent castle with richly decorated ceilings, marble fireplaces, and the finest of tapestries. Yet to Teira this place looked more like an intimidating fortress than the fairy-tale variety of castle.

As the group made their way toward the castle, the tour guide explained that the seventeen large cannons facing the sea were kept in pristine condition by a special unit in the King's Artillery Regiment since they were still used on special days or upon the visit of a foreign dignitary. And, she said, the royal family still used Kronborg Castle from time to time for various celebrations.

They passed through the castle doors, and Teira listened with interest as the guide described this perfect setting for *Hamlet*. From the outside the castle looked like a magnificent military stronghold, but inside it was filled with art popular during the Baroque and Renaissance periods. Though daylight still came through the thick-paned windows, lights also burned in the broad rooms filled with tapestries and hoards of treasure.

Room after room delighted her as she looked at armor worn by knights, antiquated furniture, clothing, and other artifacts. The tour guide had told them they could wander and look at their leisure or follow her. Either way, they would meet back at the bus at the appointed time.

Teira walked through the Knights' Hall, one of the longest halls in Europe, then on to the separate chambers of the king and queen and the magnificent castle chapel.

Recalling her literature class, Teira let her thoughts wander. She tried to conjure up images from *Hamlet, Prince of Denmark.* Standing in the back of the chapel, she thought that it was here that the body of Polonius was laid to rest. He had been killed after hiding behind a tapestry like the many that still adorned these walls. Gertrude and Hamlet had met in the queen's chambers, and the fencing match had taken place in the great hall. Meanwhile, Hamlet's father roamed the parapets.

As the others wandered on, Teira stood off to one side of the room and closed her eyes. She took a deep breath. The pungent aroma of salty seawater, mingled with the musty scent of old wood and mortar, filled her lungs. With her eyes shut tight she could almost feel medieval history radiating from within the ancient walls and floors.

After a few moments of daydreaming, Teira opened her eyes to see the last group of elderly tourists pass through the far doorway. Hurrying after them, Teira found herself on a steep, circular stairwell that led round and round farther down into the depths of the castle. With each level they descended, the air grew more cold and damp. She inched through the crowd until she was standing next to Paul, her seatmate from the bus.

"Are you sure the rest of the group came this way?" she asked uncertainly. They were in the lower chambers now, but they hadn't caught up with the guide or others from ComTech.

"My dear, I have read extensively about this castle," Paul said. "Even if we don't catch up, I'm certain I know where we're going."

Teira would have to take his word for it. She was hopelessly lost. "Where are we headed?"

"Why, to see the famous Holger Danske of course!"

"And it's this way?" Teira asked. "It seems to me they wouldn't put a famous statue down in such a damp, musty place as this."

With a glare Paul continued the march into the depths of the catacombs. After rounding another bend, Teira stopped in her tracks. The woman behind her stumbled into her, causing a chain reaction.

"Paul!" Teira exclaimed. "What have you done? This isn't the way to Holger Danske! You've led us to the dungeons! I don't think this is part of the tour."

"If it's not, it ought to be!" he said stubbornly. "Look at the cells! And there's information on that plaque on the wall."

"It says only one person ever survived the torture," a lady near the sign called out.

"Why is that?" another asked as she walked down into the cell.

Teira followed. She had to stoop almost double to get into the cave-like area. The cell was wide in front, but narrowed dramatically farther in. She took the lady's arm to escort her back out. "I don't think we should be down here. We—"

Her words were interrupted by a loud, metallic bang. Teira turned to see Paul on the other side of the bars, grinning from ear to ear.

"Depending on the severity of punishment, they allowed less and less room to move around," he said. "It would eventually drive a person insane."

"Paul, open up right now," Teira ordered. "This isn't funny."

"I was just showing you how it worked," he pouted. "Hey, Joseph, give me a hand, will you? These bars are a lot heavier to lift than they are to lower."

Together the two elderly men struggled, but the bars wouldn't budge.

"It's rather unpleasant in here, isn't it?" the woman asked Teira. She was short enough to be barely bent over, while Teira felt like an ape with her knuckles dragging the ground. She was about to sit down to ease her aching back when a mortifying thought crossed her mind. *Rats.* It was a perfect breeding ground for them. She looked around nervously. It was times like this she wished she had never read any rat facts, let alone remembered them. Hadn't she recently warned Christian that not even a moat could keep them at bay?

Although Teira drew a ragged breath to forestall panic, fear nevertheless crept up the back of her neck and sent shivers down her spine. Still she spoke slowly and clearly. "Everybody who can, help grab a bar on the cell. Now, on the count of three, lift!"

It was hopeless. One man had arthritis, another had a heart condition, and a third said he was too cold.

Too cold? "What do you mean you're too cold?" Teira demanded.

"Well, it says here the place is six to seven degrees centigrade. Now, I don't know where you come from, but where I come from, that's cold! I'm going back."

"Wait! We should stick together," Teira said quickly.

"We're all cold," another man pointed out.

"Group hug!" a jovial lady sang out, and everyone gathered together for warmth. Meanwhile, Teira stood inside the torture chamber and wondered how long it would take for their respective groups to notice they were missing. She wanted out of the cell immediately. According to Shakespeare, this castle was haunted. She wasn't surprised. Hundreds of people had probably died right here. Teira shivered at the dreadful thought and cursed her overactive imagination. The only thought worse than that of tortured medieval souls was the one about rats.

"This place is most unpleasant," Teira's cellmate observed once more. She peered longingly out at her group of traveling companions.

"My thoughts exactly," Teira murmured. She glared at Paul, who was now testing his best pickup lines on other women instead of helping the two he had imprisoned. Teira's dander rose. *If I ever get out of here, I'll kill him,* she thought. Surely Danish law would never convict her.

* * *

Outside by the bus, the tour guide counted heads for the second time. Almost a fourth of her group was missing. It was strange. Castle security had been unable to turn up anyone in the castle or on the grounds.

Christian joined her. "I'm missing one," he said.

"Male or female?"

"Female. Long, dark hair, beautiful brown eyes, about five foot seven, twenty-seven years old. She has dimples and—"

"I'm sorry, sir," the guide interrupted. "That's more than I need to know."

"Well, if it helps any, the elderly gentleman she was seated next to on the way here is also missing."

"Thank you. We'll find them." But the guide looked at the sky when she said it—a sky that was growing darker by the second.

* * *

"Who knows the legend of Holger Danske?" someone in the group called out.

Teira did. It was her favorite bedtime story. From where she now sat cross-legged on the floor she said, "My mother told it many times."

"Do tell!" a woman encouraged. "If we can't see the statue, at least we can hear the story!"

"Well, Holger Danske was a mercenary at the court of Charlemagne. He never lost a battle. However, he became exceedingly homesick, so he walked all the way from the south of France back to Denmark. When he arrived, sometime in the eighth century, I think, he's said to have fallen asleep immediately and still sleeps today. Supposedly, if Denmark should ever have its sovereignty threatened, Holger will wake and defend his country."

Anxious to show off his knowledge, Paul added, "He sits in what were the stables back when the garrisons were active. Not even pounding hooves could wake him." He chuckled. "But he's not many meters from the brewery. That might have had something to do with it. You know the soldiers got eight liters a day?"

"Maybe that was to help them forget they were living in a dungeon!" one of the crowd called out.

Teira smiled. "Hans Christian Andersen wrote the myth into a fairy tale," she said, "but it originated in French literature." She leaned forward, smiling mischievously. "The most interesting thing is that in a sense the legend came true."

"What do you mean?" Paul asked.

"Well, Holger was supposed to awaken and defend Denmark should the need ever arise. During Denmark's occupation in World War II, one of the most important Resistance groups operated under the name of Holger Danske."

In the distance they heard someone calling out. As a group they returned the cries as if they had been lost for days.

Two unhappy security men came around the bend. The first lecture was for moving the rope barrier aside and entering a forbidden area.

Roped-off area? Teira wondered. In her haste to catch up with the group she hadn't noticed it. But it was soon clear that Paul had moved the rope aside to lead the group on a "shortcut" to see Holger Danske.

Anxious to remove the group from the dungeon, the security men didn't notice Teira and her chamber partner. The two ladies had to call out to be rescued from the freezing cell.

If the two security men were unhappy when they first found the group, seeing Teira and the elderly woman "playing" in the cell made them furious.

Teira tried to smile. "We seem to be stuck in here."

"The cells were built to keep people in, not let them out," one of the men muttered. "At least not alive."

"Can you make an exception this one time?" Teira asked hopefully.

"We'll see what we can do, but these bars are old. They aren't meant to be tampered with."

The elderly woman pushed Teira aside. "Could you hurry with that please? I need to visit the ladies room something terrible."

* * *

The group was escorted back to the bus. To Teira it felt as if they were being marched to the guillotine like the criminals they were. The welcome they received seemed to bear it out. They were met by scowls and grumbles from those who had waited more than forty-five minutes for their rescue.

Teira sank down on her seat, relieved to finally be on the way home. Christian leaned over. "I hear you spent time behind bars. This will have to go on your employee record, you know."

"And it's not the first time," she said, returning his grin. "The same thing happened to me when our family went to Alcatraz. I need to stop visiting historical sites with bars."

Christian's laugh relieved much of Teira's tension. At least it did until the bus started and she overheard someone comment that they should have left them down there. She hoped the person was talking about Paul, but she wasn't counting on it. So much for using this outing in her quest to win friends and influence people at ComTech.

10

Teira was excited to pick up her grandmother the following morning. Lars had done wonders with the front yard, so the older woman wouldn't be too disappointed when she returned home and saw the condition it was in. After Grethe knew it was all right, Teira would break the news that the Spelmans hadn't cared for it in the two years she'd been in the care facility. But before any of that, they'd have a wonderful time together seeing the sights of Copenhagen.

First stop was the bakery. Teira's biggest weakness when it came to Danish pastry was *smorkrger.* There was nothing like it in America—bread that was fluffy and cakelike, with a creamy brown sugar-and-butter icing. Her mouth watered at the thought of eating it freshly made, warm from the oven.

As they stepped out of the shop with their purchases in hand, another customer held the door for them. Teira looked up to thank the gentleman and smiled into the eyes of Christian.

"Great minds think alike," he said.

"Do we have great minds or weak willpower?" she asked with a smile. Then she said, "Do you have a minute? I'd like you to meet my grandmother. She doesn't understand English, so it's Danish all the way."

"I'd love to meet her."

Grethe had already scuttled ahead down the cobblestone sidewalk without noticing that her granddaughter lagged behind.

"It's like running a marathon keeping up with her," Teira said. "She's a spry little thing!" In a couple of quick paces they had caught up. Teira put her arm around her grandmother and pulled her to a stop. *"Mor mor,"* she said in Danish, "I'd like you to meet my boss,

Mr. Christian Tanner. Christian, this is my grandmother, Grethe Pedersen."

"I'm very pleased to meet you Mrs. Pedersen."

Grethe shook his hand and patted it with her other while she craned her neck up to smile at him. "Thank you for bringing my granddaughter home to me."

"I don't think I can take credit for that," he said. "She earned her way here. We're happy to have her on the team. She's a real asset to the company."

"You seem so young to be the boss of a big company," Grethe observed. "Do you have family here?"

"I have a few distant relatives in Denmark, but most of my family is in California."

"No wife or children?" There was a twinkle in Grethe's eye.

"No," Christian said.

Grethe made "tut-tut" noises with her tongue as she looked from Christian to Teira. "What's the matter with you young people?"

"Uh, Grandma, we should be on our way." Teira took her arm and tried to move the older woman along. "It was nice running into you," she told Christian. "Have a good weekend."

"Mr. Tanner," Grethe said, turning back, "would you like to ask my granddaughter out?"

Christian laughed good-naturedly while Teira turned ten shades of red. "You don't have to answer that!" she said. "Grandma, let's go." Then she muttered, "Thanks a lot for the help, but you don't need to take care of my social life. I'm doing just fine."

"You're still unmarried so I wouldn't say you're just *fine*." Grethe smiled and patted Teira lovingly on the cheek. "And perhaps he *wants* to ask you!"

"I would rather ask *you* out," Christian teased. That earned a hearty laugh from Grethe, the kind Teira hadn't heard since she arrived.

"Mr. Tanner, you're a charmer!" the older woman said. "If you have no plans, please join us on a boat ride. I know some wonderful stories."

"Okay," he agreed quickly—and unexpectedly. "Thanks."

Teira was horrified that her grandmother had spoken so bluntly. She leaned closer to Christian and said in English, "I am so sorry about this! I truly am. Use any excuse and bow out now. She'll understand."

"Are you kidding? This will be great!"

Teira hoped it was true.

* * *

Fortunately, Teira had thought to borrow a wheelchair when she'd picked up her grandmother from the senior center in Copenhagen that morning. Christian lifted it from the trunk and helped Grethe get seated comfortably. When he bent down to slide the footrest into place, she bent over and slapped him on the shoulder. "Are you looking at my legs, young man?"

"What?" he choked, as bright streaks of color highlighted his cheekbones.

"I saw you looking at my legs!"

"No! I wasn't! I was trying to—" Christian stopped the horrified stammering when he saw the twinkle in her eye.

"No need to be embarrassed," Grethe said. "I happen to think they're my best feature. Why, Mr. Johansen looks at them every chance he gets. Opened his mouth so wide he lost his dentures last week when he saw me walking in the garden, he did! But I have to tell you, sir, you're much too young for me. You should be looking at my granddaughter. They say great legs are hereditary, you know. Hers could look like this when she's my age if she takes care of them."

Christian almost choked on his laughter. This little lady was going to keep him on his toes. She'd called him a charmer, but she was a tease.

"Mor mor!" Teira admonished in humiliation.

Their first stop was Amalienborg Square.

"You could say it all started here," Grethe said to begin the story she had promised.

Teira turned toward her uncertainly. From what she had heard, the story *ended* here. She glanced at Christian, who stood admiring the stately palaces. He had no idea what he was getting himself into when he had agreed to come. Perhaps she hadn't known either. She'd expected a little matchmaking and perhaps a few fond reminiscences, but she hadn't expected her grandmother to reveal their family secrets—secrets she didn't want Christian to know. Nevertheless, she held her tongue and remembered the promise she had made to get to know her grandfather through her grandmother's eyes.

If only she didn't have the feeling that what they were about to embark on would be the ride of all time and would have far-reaching effects on her own life. She looked at Christian once more. If anybody could change her life, he was the one. He was captivating and handsome. He was intelligent and hard working. Teira caught herself in her reverie. He was way out of her league. Besides, they didn't share religious beliefs and nothing was more important than that. Still, she looked at him and felt—

"Teira?" Grethe nudged her granddaughter.

"I'm sorry!" She'd been caught daydreaming. She hoped she hadn't been staring as well. "What did you say?"

"That kind gentleman is offering us a better view of the changing of the guards." She pointed to an officer who was trying to get their attention.

"Oh, I didn't hear him," Teira said.

"Yes, I saw your mind was on other things."

Teira looked at the ground and silently implored it to open up and swallow her. Then she guided the wheelchair to a spot toward the front of the crowd that had gathered around the octagonal courtyard known as Amalienborg Square. Ringing the courtyard was the castle that still served as the royal couple's winter home. Every day at noon the replacement troop marched in to commence the ceremonial changing of the guards.

Pale cobblestones paved the courtyard. High above their heads the Danish flag, the *Dannebrog*, waved brilliant red and white in the cool breeze. Puffy white clouds drifted in the sky over the nearby ocean while overhead the sun shone brightly.

It was easy to determine in which of the four palaces the queen, Margrethe II, and her husband, the prince consort, Henrik, stayed. Near the top of their residence, the Order of the Elephant hung from an enormous gold chain. It was near there that the Danish flag, the oldest national flag still in use in Europe, was raised.

And it was here, beneath the king's window, Teira thought, that gunfire was exchanged the morning Denmark was occupied. She wondered again how her grandmother's story could possibly *begin* here. In the next moment she asked her grandmother.

Grethe blushed and held her fingers to her lips as a twinkle came into her eye.

"Although I knew your grandfather for years, we didn't date until I was in high school," Grethe explained. "He graduated before I did and was accepted into the Royal Guard. He was gone for training for a long time. I didn't know if he cared for me as much as I cared for him. He had only asked me out a couple of times, and while he had held my hand, we had never kissed."

Teira raised her eyebrows at the look on her grandmother's face. "Let me guess. He was moving a little too slowly for you, Grandma?"

"Too slow? My dear, a tortoise ran faster than my Soren when it came to making his move."

Christian groaned. "You women make it sound so easy. Since he isn't here to defend himself, I feel the need to make a stand on his behalf. You bat your lovely eyelashes at us unsuspecting fools, draw us to our knees, and when we *make our move*, as you so eloquently put it, we know the odds are in favor of our being rejected. We men are scared to death of first kisses."

Teira and Grethe looked at Christian and laughed. "Well, we are!" he said defensively.

"Oh, poor you," Teira said, tongue in cheek. She found it hard to believe he'd ever experienced rejection of any sort.

"You mock our pain," he said, acting affronted.

Grethe watched the interchange between Christian and Teira with a grin. "Anyway," she continued, "I wanted to know if Soren truly cared, so I went to stay with my aunt and uncle because my uncle was a friend of Soren's. On a dare, my uncle and another of the guards helped me sneak into one of those little guardhouses outside the palace. In fact, it was that one, right over there." She pointed toward a red-painted station that was big enough for only the guard to stand in.

"Every two hours," she continued, "the guards are relieved by a replacement. Late that night the queen wasn't in residence so the guard told me where Soren stood watch. Then he let me into the guardhouse Soren would be stationed at. Inside each house hangs a red coat in case of bad weather, so I hid behind the coat. Once the changing of the guard was complete, I got Soren's attention by whispering his name as he marched past. The Royal Guard are under strict orders to speak to no one but their colleagues, so you can imagine his surprise when he found me hiding in there. His eyes grew as large as saucers!" Grethe whooped with laughter. "I've never seen Soren at such a loss!"

"Was he angry?" Teira asked.

"Not so much angry, but he took his job very seriously and I *was* breaking the rules."

"What did he do?"

"Once he saw that the officer was nowhere in sight, he smiled. But he still told me I had to leave. Not that I blamed him. I would have gotten him into so much trouble. But love makes you do crazy things! So, it was very dark outside, but the palace was well lit. I could see to get away. Just as I started to leave, he grabbed me by the wrist, pulled me back, and kissed me. It wasn't long, of course, but he *took the risk* as you so eloquently put it, my dear Mr. Tanner. Then he whispered, 'Meet me here when I'm off duty tomorrow.' I shall never forget the look in his eyes as he brushed my cheek with his finger and sent me off into the night. My life changed forever. There were many kisses after that, and I will remember the feel of the tingle in my toes from every one of them until the day I die."

Teira sighed. "That's a great story, Grandma."

"I will agree with Mr. Tanner," Grethe said. "The most difficult part of a first kiss is the approach. There is an air of uncertainty. But when it is with the right person, someone you care for deeply, the anticipation outweighs the risk. There is nothing more exciting or amazing than a first kiss when you are in love." Grethe looked over at the guardhouse and smiled as her mind drifted to those days long ago. Her eyes grew misty.

Moments later the crowd hushed as the steady rhythm of marching feet came down the street from Amalienborg. Marching uniformly into the square, the guards wore "the bear"—bearskin headgear known to be so hot that some fainted during extreme heat or longer marches and drills. Their uniforms were dark blue jackets with light blue trousers, a design that dated from the 1800s. Each carried a rifle steady and sure.

As they watched the ceremonial changing of the guards, Teira noticed an officer look into the guardhouse behind the red coat that hung there. She looked at her grandmother, who winked. "He's checking for girlfriends. A habit from long ago that I am sure is still in practice." Grethe smiled while Christian chuckled.

11

The threesome stopped off at a sidewalk café for lunch. While they ate, Christian's cell phone rang. He slipped it from his pocket, apologized, and turned it off.

Grethe's eyes rounded. "What is that contraption?" she asked.

Christian held the phone toward her so she could look at it. "It's amazing what modern technology has done with these," he said. "I can get on the Internet, record a video, or even use it as a digital recorder. Look, by pushing this and this, I can record what we say. Here, you try it."

Christian put the phone in Grethe's hand. He was pleased to see she could do it herself as easily as he had.

When she handed back his phone, Christian showed her more features. "I can text message. I can tell who is calling by the tone of the ring. That helps screen calls. I can take pictures." He held up his phone, snapped a picture of Grethe, and turned the phone around so she could see it.

"Yes, but can you call anybody?" she asked.

Christian laughed good-naturedly. "Yes. And once I know the number, I can program it into the memory and call that person by hitting just one button."

"Show me how to do that." Grethe turned to her granddaughter. "Teira, do you have your phone?"

"I always have my phone, why?"

"Let Christian put your number in so he can show me how this works." Grethe winked.

Teira's face turned crimson. "Grandma, you are so obvious. Let's go catch that boat ride." Maybe the ocean would swallow her up since the ground hadn't. Teira feared she might die of humiliation before this day ended. She began to clear the lunch trays.

"What if I want to buy a cell phone?" Grethe asked innocently. "How will I know if that is a feature I want to have?"

Teira couldn't help but laugh at her not-so-subtle grandmother.

Christian winked at Teira. "You're turning away a potential customer. That's bad for business. Give me your phone number."

Without looking him in the eye she gave him the number.

"Okay, turn your phone on," he said as he programmed her number into his phone. Then Christian leaned over and said to Grethe, "Next, I go into my directory, pull up her name, and find that her number is twelve."

"Twelve?" Grethe asked, appalled. "Why twelve? My granddaughter deserves nothing less than number one. I want that changed or I am not buying a cell phone."

Teira groaned and laid her head onto her folded arms. *Could this get any worse?*

"I'm not sure my mother will be too happy about that, but you're a tough customer. Sold. Mom moves to number two and Teira is now in the number one spot. Which plan are you interested in?"

"The forever kind. Nothing else is good enough for my Teira," Grethe said sternly.

Yep, it definitely got a lot worse, Teira thought with despair.

"Well, we've barely met, but she's moving up the list fast!"

"I'm going home!" Teira declared, not facing either one.

"That was a compliment," Christian said.

"Aren't you feeling well?" asked Grethe.

"I meant to America." Teira rose and walked away.

Christian caught up with her. "Don't go."

"I am so sorry she is doing this," Teira said, turning. "I sincerely had no idea she would play matchmaker. I hope this won't make things awkward between us at work."

Christian smiled reassuringly. "I like your grandmother. She has your best interests at heart, and it's flattering that she would consider me worthy. I'm having a good time humoring her."

"You're not offended or embarrassed?"

"Are you kidding? It's a challenge keeping up!" He looked at her doubtfully. "You're not really leaving, are you?"

"Yes, but only to the ladies' room." Teira grinned.

* * *

Grethe, Teira, and Christian next stopped at Nyhaven. There a large anchor mounted in stone had flowers and mementos at its base, honoring the 1,700 Danish sailors who died in World War II.

Christian helped Grethe into a large boat for the harbor tour while Teira stored the wheelchair at the side of the dock. When she joined them, she sat on the other side of her grandmother.

Grethe looked from one to the other. "I get seasick very easily," she said. "I need the aisle seat."

"Should we find you a seat at the side?" Christian asked.

"No, no. An aisle seat will be fine. Just trade me places, will you?"

"But if you become ill, you'll want an outside seat," he argued. "That way—"

"Okay!" Teira interrupted. "We get the picture." She tossed her hands up in the air and stood. "Christian, my grandmother wants you to sit by me, although she's about as subtle as a nuclear bomb. Grandma, scoot over closer to the side." After everyone exchanged places, Teira said, "Now, if we're through playing musical chairs, we can enjoy the ride." This day, Teira knew, would be one for the books.

"Thank you, dear." Her grandmother patted her on the knee.

"Wow, she's good," Christian whispered in Teira's ear. "I didn't catch that one."

As the tour began, Teira's thoughts drifted from the narration. What were the chances of running into Christian today in a city the size of Copenhagen? Surely he must live somewhere near the bakery where they'd met. And what were the chances that he'd have the day free to spend with them at the drop of a hat? It was awfully nice of him to escort them this way. Physically, it was making things easier on her having someone to help with the wheelchair. Emotionally, it was a nightmare.

Her grandmother was laying on the cupid stuff pretty thick. As much as she wanted to run and hide from her embarrassment, Teira loved her grandmother for trying so hard. She bore little resemblance to the introverted, cautious woman her mother had described. Teira suspected that once Grethe knew someone, she felt free to be her true self—an adorably fun, mischievous, loving woman with a heart of gold. She had taken an instant liking to Christian. Teira only hoped her playing matchmaker wouldn't have a negative impact on their working relationship. Away from the office, it was easy to forget that Christian had a girlfriend. But within the walls of ComTech, there was a constant reminder that Christian was taken.

Not that Teira didn't daydream anyway. When Grethe described her first kiss, Teira had found herself wondering how it would feel to kiss Christian. The thought thrilled and excited her. Of course, she would never know, but daydreaming had always been her favorite pastime.

"Penny for them," Christian said.

Teira looked over at him and smiled. "They're worth a lot more than that."

"Now you've got me curious."

"I was thinking it was nice of you to escort us today. But I'm not fool enough to think you had the entire day free. This must be one of those ways you're trying to make things easier for an employee. I thank you for that—and for being such a good sport."

"That's not what you were really thinking," he said, "but I'll let you off the hook. I may not have had this on my agenda, but make no mistake, I'm where I want to be—and without any sense of obligation, either."

"It's not easy for my grandmother to be so trusting. I do believe you have captured her heart."

"I take it that's not an easy thing for the women in your family to do," he said. "But she may change her mind when she sees how hard I make you work."

As the tour progressed, Teira shot picture after picture with her digital camera. They saw the home that once belonged to Hans Christen Andersen; the royal yacht docked near Amalienborg; a statue of Absalon, the founder of Copenhagen; the new opera house; and, of course, the world famous bronze statue from the Hans Christian Andersen fairy tale "The Little Mermaid," which sat on a granite stone at Langelinie Pier.

Grethe turned to Christian and Teira and said, "People are always surprised at her size. They tend to forget she is called the *little* mermaid."

Teira looked at the statue. "That story always made me so sad. I guess I'm a dreamer and always wanted her to get her prince."

"What do you mean?" Christian objected. "She marries the prince, the sea witch dies, and Sebastian the crab gets to keep his job. I saw the movie."

Teira rolled her eyes. "That's not how Andersen's story goes. And for the record, her name isn't Ariel. In the original fairy tale, the prince never knows all she sacrificed for him, or how much she truly loved him. In the end, she dies."

Grethe turned to her granddaughter. "You know the story well. Do you think she regretted her decision? Might it have been worth it to her to have been with the man she loved for even a brief time?"

Teira considered the mermaid who would forever gaze wistfully toward the enchanted, illuminated world of humans. She realized that the question Grethe asked was far more soul-searching than it appeared. In light of the life that Grethe had lived after sacrificing everything for Soren, how could Teira answer? She had never known a love like that, only dreamed of it, hoped, and even prayed for it. But Grethe's story had ended in tragedy, too. That was perhaps her greatest frustration with her grandparents' history.

Grethe waited for her reply.

Teira smiled a little uncomfortably. "What can I say? I'm a romantic at heart. I still believe that love can conquer all. Do I think the mermaid regretted her decision? Probably not. But was it too high a price to pay? In the end, probably. She never got her prince and lost her life in the process."

Grethe grabbed Teira's hand. "It's not too much to hope for a prince. That's a wish every girl should be granted." She motioned to include Christian. "There is something I want you both to remember—life does not guarantee happy endings. You must make your own happiness with what life gives you. Otherwise, you will be miserable, always wanting more and never recognizing the happiness and satisfaction you already have. Be grateful for what you have before you now, and the rest will come."

Seeing how intently they were listening, Grethe continued. "You may think I am a poor old woman, but I tell you, I am not. My life is rich because I had the love of a good man who gave me a wonderful daughter and a beautiful granddaughter. What more can a woman ask for than such a family—such a wonderful posterity—as this to love? I miss my Soren every day. He brought me so much joy. I am lonely for him, and though we were only together a short time, his love was worth all the lonely days since. I would do it all again. That kind of love is *not* too high a price. It is worth every sacrifice and more."

Teira blinked back the moisture that had gathered in her eyes. Christian sat silently as Grethe turned and looked out to sea.

* * *

Back on the quay of Nyhaven, Teira could see that Grethe was getting tired, but she asked for them to stop and visit one last place. The three strolled along the busy cobbled walk to the Church of Our Lady, the Lutheran cathedral in Copenhagen. They entered from the back. There stood an original sculptured statue by Bertel Thorvaldsen.

Teira said in surprise, "The Christus?" She could scarcely believe she was seeing the original upon which replicas in many LDS visitors' centers around the world were based.

Grethe nodded. "I knew you would recognize it."

As Teira marveled at the beautiful statue, Grethe stood from her wheelchair and walked quietly to a pew and sat. Moments later Teira and Christian joined her. Both noticed the single tear that slipped from Grethe's eye.

"I married my Soren here. Not a single day goes by that my heart doesn't ache to be with him again," she whispered. Then gathering her emotions and wiping her tear, she took a deep breath and smiled. "We should always be grateful for the time we have together."

* * *

As much as she hated to part with Christian's company, she knew it had been a full day for her grandmother and it was time to head back home. They walked to Teira's car, where Christian loaded the wheelchair once again. Then he hailed a taxi so Teira wouldn't have to return to the bakery where he'd left his car.

As Grethe said good-bye to Christian, he bent over and kissed the back of her hand. "Lovely lady, it was a pleasure to share this day with you."

Grethe blushed like a schoolgirl. "You really are a charmer! I knew it from the moment I met you. But I see in your eyes you are also a good and sincere person." She craned her neck to whisper conspiratorially, "You have my granddaughter's phone number. I think you should use it."

Christian smiled as he closed her car door. Then he walked over to Teira, who stood waiting to thank him. Before she had a chance, he said, "From what I heard on the boat, I gather that your grandmother's wonderful story has a sad ending."

"My grandfather passed away a few weeks before the war ended in 1945," Teira replied.

"And she never remarried?"

"No, never. She wanted only him. She said she had already given her heart away once."

"Wow," Christian replied, clearly touched. "She's quite a woman. Thank you for letting me join you today. It was very enlightening. I can't think of a better day I've had in Denmark."

"I'm glad you came. I guess I'll see you at work on Monday."

"You're doing it again," Christian said.

Teira looked at him, confused. "Doing what?"

"You're thinking. Before, they seemed pleasant thoughts, but now you seem troubled. Care to unload?"

"What makes you say that?" Teira chuckled uneasily. Was she that easy to read?

"You have expressive eyes. I may not be able to tell what you're thinking, but they reveal your emotions. Right now you seem troubled. So let me ask you honestly. Is there something bothering you that you need help with?"

Teira smiled uncomfortably. "No. I was thinking about my grandfather and the story she told about him today."

"She has a tremendous love for him, doesn't she?"

"She sure does."

"I want that myself one day," Christian confided.

"I do too. I suppose everyone does."

Their gazes locked for a moment, and then Christian took a deep breath. "I guess I better let you get her home. Thank you again for inviting me to join you both today."

"I'm glad you could come. I hope my grandmother didn't make you feel uneasy."

"Not at all," he assured her. "No worries."

After saying good-bye, Christian climbed into the taxi. Thinking over their adventure, he had been amused, enlightened, curious, and even inspired. The day had given him much to think about. Mostly about a girl who was stealing his heart.

12

"All I'm saying is you can't force Christian to like me," Teira told her grandmother. They'd gone from their adventure around Copenhagen to home for a sleepover. Teira had rolled her grandmother's hair and was now giving her a manicure at the kitchen table. "Besides, he has a girlfriend."

"*Ni,* his heart does not belong to another, child. I know what I see."

Teira tried to smile. "And what do you see?"

"He sees you. This much I know. And you see him. So what is the problem?"

Teira's heart took flight. "I wish you were right, but you, dear heart, are a romantic. It must run through our veins. He is my boss and my friend. There can never be anything more. Grandma, he has women flocking around him by the dozens. I don't want to be one of a crowd."

"Have you noticed that some of the things we get most worked up about are things that matter the least?"

The question came so out of the blue that it threw Teira off. "I hate the thought of wanting to marry a man who already has so many women falling at his feet."

"So you want to marry Christian?" Grethe asked.

"You're twisting my words." Teira smiled awkwardly.

"In a universe of brilliant stars, don't you ever look up and see one shining brighter than the rest? Do you not suppose that you have something about you that makes you shine brighter than others? He looks up and sees you, my dear Teira. This I know."

"It's an awfully big universe, Grandma," Teira replied.

"Shouldn't a man be in the company of women to discover the traits he wants in a future spouse?" Grethe asked. "Otherwise, how will he know what he's looking for?"

"It's not okay when he's playing games with other people's feelings."

"Are you saying that because Mr. Tanner has dated many, his intentions have been unkind or anything but honorable?"

"I wouldn't know," Teira said. "But he has a reputation for being a ladies' man."

Grethe spoke sternly. "My dear, sweet granddaughter, *my* husband has the reputation of a traitor and I assure you he is not what his reputation suggests." She settled back against the chair. "Now, I am too old to know exactly what being a *ladies' man* entails, but if it means he has dated many women, it does not mean he is a bad person who has intentionally beguiled any one of them. Why draw and quarter a person without hearing their version of the account?"

Teira found herself momentarily speechless.

"It seems to me that if many women like him, there must be something worth the attraction," Grethe concluded.

"I haven't known him long, but I have yet to find anything dishonorable about him," Teira admitted.

"You have my Soren's eyes. I can see you are falling for Mr. Tanner in your heart, even if your head tells you not to."

"Please tell me you're the only one who can see that," Teira pleaded.

Grethe smiled. "Don't worry. He doesn't see it. He is too worried about looking within his own heart for what he might find there."

Teira fell silent as she massaged cream into her grandmother's hands. "Grandma, is it difficult for you to talk about what happened to Grandpa all those years ago? Do the memories make you miss him more?"

"It is my favorite pastime to talk about him. You never knew him, but he was so handsome. You have seen pictures, yes?"

"A few. He was handsome. Tell me more about him."

"You have heard much, but you never ask me about what happened. Hanne called and said you had been to see Magnus Spelman. My dear Teira, you can ask me anything. What do you want to know?"

"Everything, I suppose. I love your stories. They make Grandpa seem more real. But I don't want to bring up hurtful memories. Share with me anything you will."

"First, you should know that your grandfather loved the king," Grethe said, taking a deep breath. "He had great admiration for King Christian X as a man, not only a monarch. He knew many people from the royal administration from working with the Royal Guard and with the Danish Army as well. He was good friends with many of them. The accusations about him turning against the king were preposterous. Thank goodness the burns and the bullet wound he sustained killed him. Otherwise, he would have died of a broken heart."

Teira looked up in shock. "Bullet? What bullet? I thought Grandpa died of burns from the train car explosion."

"That's what it says on his death certificate, but he was also hit by a bullet in the ribs. He had many abrasions all over his body, too. The doctor told me how to tend his wounds through the night, but in the end, I'm afraid they were just too severe."

"What did you do after you went home and found Grandpa's uniform and things thrown about?"

"I straightened up after him. Then I met your grandfather once more that day."

"Where?"

"Behind a market. He gave me a note to deliver to someone who he said would know what to do with it."

"Did you know who it was?"

"No. Most of the time I didn't know who anybody was. It was for their protection and mine. The less I knew, the better we all were. I met the man Soren told me to meet, delivered the note, and left with the baby pram."

"Magnus was there that day with Grandpa," Teira said. "Does he know who he had you give the note to?"

"Once Magnus gave his report, I never spoke to him about Soren again. I wasn't there when he testified. I never heard what he said. If he had questions, he didn't ask them of me. He knew I would never have said anything to incriminate my husband."

"Who brought Grandpa here?"

"The doctor told me about Soren's injuries and then two men carried him in on a homemade stretcher. Magnus stayed out in the truck and kept watch."

"He was the driver?"

"Yes," Grethe confirmed. "Hanne stayed with the neighbors that night. It wasn't until a few days later that word broke as to what he had supposedly done. Then everyone started acting out their anger."

"I know if there is anyone who knew him, it was you," Teira said tenderly. "But with all this evidence stacked against him, why are you so convinced that he might not have been working for the other side—for whatever reason?"

Instead of anger, Teira saw sadness in Grethe's eyes. "It is the same lesson I have been trying to teach you all day long. Listen to the convictions of your heart and not your head. What does your heart tell you?" Grethe got up from the table and walked into the front room.

Teira sat alone in the kitchen. She hadn't meant to hurt her grandmother. She had been invited to ask anything and it was a fair question. Wasn't it?

Teira joined her grandmother on the couch moments later. "Grandma, I never knew him. I don't know what to believe. My head tells me the evidence is accurate or somebody would have figured it out by now. My heart wants to believe something is missing. The only thing I know for sure is that I believe in you and know you live by your convictions. Can that be enough?"

"It is enough for me," Grethe said, "but we both know it's not enough for you. You need more answers for your peace of mind, and I will help you find them. This week, when you have time, look for a beautiful old trunk in the attic. It has some of my most prized possessions in it. They are practically valueless, but to me they are priceless. I give you permission to search in there and see if you can find anything that will help you in your quest for the truth."

"What is in there?"

"Your grandfather's uniform, pictures, letters—simple treasures of my heart."

"Grandpa's uniform? I thought he was buried in his uniform."

"He wasn't allowed a military burial, but I saw to it that he wore his best suit."

Teira grew silent. She knew her grandmother was watching her face intently. "I hope I haven't hurt you by my questions. I don't understand. I want to believe in him, if that helps. It broke my heart when I learned my hero had been accused of being a traitor."

"One thing about a broken heart: it opens wide for new possibilities to enter in to mend it—or destroy it—depending on how it is cared for. The choice is yours, Teira. Care for your heart wisely."

* * *

He thrashed about on his bed, caught in the nightmare that had tormented him for years.

But this night was different. This time there was no escape.

The blankets twisted about his legs, enslaving his sweat-soaked body in manacles from which he struggled to free himself. All around, haunted groans of the tortured and dying echoed eerily through the air.

He could not get free. There was nowhere to run, nowhere to hide.

The demons of the past had caught up with him at last.

13

Bright and early Monday morning, Teira waited until the car pulled away from the driveway before she drove closer to the house and parked across the street. She got out of the car and looked both ways before crossing the road, not only to avoid oncoming traffic but to be sure the car that had pulled away only moments before was truly out of sight. Quickly she walked to the gate of the Spelman home.

Knowing Ulrike had just left, she had eliminated the worry about confronting him again. She was in high hopes of talking with Magnus without the interruption of his rude, intimidating son.

She walked up the path and rang the bell. Nervously she brushed away the invisible lint on her skirt as a maid opened the front door. “Greetings. My name is Teira Palmer. I’m here to see Magnus. Is he in?”

“Wait here a moment,” the housekeeper in the starched uniform responded. “I will see if he is accepting visitors.”

Teira hadn’t seen the woman before. That was a good thing. If she hadn’t been in the house on her first visit, she couldn’t have heard Ulrike tell her never to return. Magnus was another story. He could certainly refuse to see her or have her escorted from his property.

Teira was both surprised and relieved when the maid returned and ushered her into the same room she’d been in a week earlier. Magnus waited to see her.

When she crossed the room to thank him for seeing her, she met the same piercing eyes. He nodded and told her to have a seat. “You took a risk coming back when my son told you never to return,” Magnus said.

“I wanted to talk to you alone.”

"My son does not tell me who I can and cannot visit with. I am glad you returned."

His comment came with so little emotion it was hard to believe, but Teira was grateful for any graciousness offered. "I hoped you'd say that. Your son can be quite intimidating."

"He didn't scare you away as he had intended. Here you are," Magnus said with no hint of a smile.

"What does he have against me?"

"You threaten his peace of mind."

"Yes, but why? Did he hate mowing my grandmother's lawn so much?" It was apparently such a poor joke that Magnus couldn't manage a smile. He was a tough audience.

"You represent a dark and painful part of my past," he said. "That is why you are here and what you want to see me about, is it not?"

"Yes. I hope we can be friends. I don't understand anger after so many years, especially your son's. He wasn't even alive during the war. What grudge does he have?"

"You are a threat," the old man repeated.

"How? How can I possibly threaten him?"

Magnus shook his head. "You did not come to talk about my son. You came to talk about your grandfather, did you not?"

"Yes," Teira said, leaning forward. "I've heard a couple of accounts of his last day now. I hoped you would tell me yours."

"Why are you doing this?"

"Doing what?" Teira asked, confused.

"Bringing up the past. Tearing open old wounds that have taken years to heal."

"Is that what you call it, Mr. Spelman? Have you taken a good look? I'd say no one has healed from anything. Questions have been left unanswered. My family is still hurting and my grandmother is existing on memories." She frowned. "And your family isn't any better. Your son banned a stranger from your home just because you can't bear to look me in the eye. Have you healed?"

Magnus glared at Teira. The only other evidence of emotion was that the grip on his cane was so tense his knuckles whitened and his hands shook. Finally, he released his cane and let it fall to the floor. He looked away. "What do you want from me? I don't know what I can tell you."

"I never knew my grandfather," Teira said, her head bent low over her lap. "I'm trying to understand why he brought dishonor to everyone he cared about when every story I was ever told about him proves him to be a man of integrity. What made him do it?"

"I loved him like a brother," Magnus said. "He was a good man. A leader. I don't know what went wrong that day, why he would do such a thing. He told me he had sent for help, but help never came."

Teira's head jerked up. "Who did he send for?"

"He never said, only that it would come. Later we learned that nobody had talked with him that day but me."

Teira thought of her grandmother's second mission. "Is it possible somebody lied to cover themselves?"

"Of course it's possible, but I hate to think that of another comrade as much as I hate to think it of Soren. We were united in purpose."

"How was my grandfather shot?"

Magnus's eyes narrowed. "I know nothing of Soren being shot. He was burned in the fire. Maybe some debris pierced him."

"After the explosion weren't you with him until—"

A firm hand grabbed her shoulder from behind, cutting off her words. Teira whipped around to meet Ulrike's fierce glare. "I thought I told you never to return here."

Teira wrenched her shoulder from his grasp. "Don't touch me."

"I insist you leave," Ulrike said through gritted teeth.

"Enough!" Magnus yelled. When he had their attention he said to Teira, almost sadly, "Miss Palmer, I'm afraid I cannot help you. I believe it is time for you to go. Ulrike, I would like you to see my guest to the door and show her the respect we usually show our guests." It was an order.

"Wait!" she pleaded. "My grandfather was shot!"

Magnus said, "There was debris raining all around. There must have been a misunderstanding—"

"Oh, there has been! That's for certain!"

Ulrike took her firmly by the arm and pulled her toward the door. He wasn't fazed by his father, only further infuriated.

Teira looked back at Magnus. He was turning away, refusing her the help she sought. What was he afraid of? Was he hiding something? Could he have been part of a conspiracy her grandfather knew nothing about?

Teira yanked her arm from Ulrike's grasp. She had no idea where to turn for the truth if Magnus wouldn't help. He was her only chance. If only Ulrike hadn't come back. What was it with him? Teira felt discouraged and rejected.

"You said you loved my grandfather like a brother," she said from the door. "Yet you do nothing but sit by, content to have his name dragged through the mud. I know you believe he doesn't deserve it. What are you afraid of?"

"We are afraid of your filth rubbing off onto us," Ulrike said smugly.

"My grandfather may or *may not* have been a lot of things, but he was never a coward," Teira shot back.

"Stop!" Magnus demanded.

"I'll see myself out," Teira conceded angrily. "I know the way well." She turned and walked from the room.

At least Magnus had revealed more information than she'd had before today's visit. Magnus hadn't known Soren was shot. And he'd told her about a plea for help. Teira was willing to bet the second message her grandmother delivered that day was it. If she accepted what her grandmother believed, the man to whom the message was given was the one who failed the mission.

As she walked to her car, Teira's heart felt lighter. Just knowing there was another reasonable explanation for the day's tragic events was enough for her to believe her grandfather wasn't the evil man others had labeled him.

* * *

It was after ten by the time Teira made it in to ComTech. She plunged into her work immediately and didn't stop until almost lunchtime when someone tapped on her door. She turned to see Adam leaning against her doorframe.

"Hey, hey. How was your weekend?" he asked, straightening up to enter her office.

"It was good."

"Nothing bad or unusual happened?"

"What do you mean?" Teira asked, frowning. She thought of the letters locked neatly away in her desk.

"Rumor has it you got lost in a castle."

"Oh, that," Teira sighed. "That was nothing short of mortifying."

Adam sat down in the chair near Teira's desk and made himself comfortable by leaning back and putting his hands behind his head.

"I'm sorry I missed it. If it weren't for those last-minute network emergencies that cropped up, I would have rescued you myself. From what I hear, you were down in those dungeons quite a while."

"Don't remind me!"

"Turns out I spent some time going over a few things with the boss's girlfriend after I took care of the other work, so I guess it was time well spent. Still, I hear there's a day trip planned for Tivoli Gardens coming up. I'm not missing that one. You'll be there, won't you?"

"I'm not sure my ego can take any more company parties."

"Maybe it'll take a little convincing," he said slyly.

"Who knows, maybe my bruised ego will be healed by then." Teira glanced anxiously at her computer, thinking she was falling further behind with every passing minute.

"What are you working on?" Adam asked.

"My training classes start tonight and I need to finish preparing. Despite my rush order, the workbooks still haven't come in yet. Now I need to prepare work sheets—among a million other things."

"I stopped by to give you this." Adam handed her a file that had been sitting on his lap. Teira took it from him and looked inside as he continued speaking. "It's a list of temporary passwords for your class members to access the computers they'll be training on. Remind them to log in with their corporate ID numbers and they'll be good to go."

"I appreciate you getting this to me."

He shrugged off her thanks. "Several of the workers have headed over to a nearby pub for lunch. I told them I would grab you and catch up with them. What do you say?"

Put like that, what *could* she say? The hunger pangs in her stomach told her it was time to eat. The little voice in her head warned her to be on guard, as she never knew what Adam had up his sleeve.

Showing up to lunch with Adam might fuel the fires of gossip, but if things went as she hoped, this might instead be her chance to put out the few fires that had started after their departure together from the company party.

* * *

The group of employees met at a pub within walking distance of ComTech. They'd chosen it because it offered a variety of soups and sandwiches. Teira recognized a few faces among the fourteen gathered at the long tables. Adam was on one side of her. The chair across the table was taken by Christian. Up until that point he had been talking to Sophie, who possessively kept one hand on or near Christian at all times. Was it just Teira, or did the woman's giggle affect everyone's nerves like fingernails grating on a chalkboard?

At first the conversation around Teira was general and focused on ComTech and the acquisition. But by the time the food arrived, conversations had become more personal and friendly. Down the table, a few of the guys talked sports and deep-sea fishing while the girls nearby discussed shopping. It turned intensely personal when someone at the far end of the table called out, "Hey Christian, how do you feel about intraoffice dating?"

The question came when he was drinking from his glass of ice water. So, whether it was the ice that lodged in his throat, the question itself, the look he and Teira shared, or a combination of all three, Christian practically choked.

14

"Excuse me?" Christian croaked.

"You've never sent out a memo on the office dating policy," somebody said to general laughter.

"Why would I care who you date?" he asked, confused.

"Just making sure. We wouldn't want to put our jobs in jeopardy," someone else said as he looked at the girl across the table. She smiled shyly back at him.

Earlier Christian had noticed the looks that passed between them. "Okay, okay, I get the picture. There are obviously a few office romances going on. There's a time and a place for that. I can't dictate what you do with your private lives, but I expect things to be kept professional in the office. I also have to remind you about the company policy that no one in management who is in a personal relationship with another employee can advance or promote said person. Fair enough?"

"Well, that should eliminate you dating anybody in the company," somebody else said.

"No, it simply means they won't be promoted," Christian smiled weakly.

"From what we hear, you date your fair share of gorgeous women."

Sophie snickered loudly. Christian glared at her before turning back to the group.

"The rumors are only that. The reality is quite boring." He then looked at Teira, but she turned away and reached for her glass of water, avoiding eye contact with him or Sophie.

"I saw you two at the company party," Adam said indicating Sophie and Christian. "By the looks of things, you won't be on the market long. Come on, boss man, spill the beans."

"Sorry, folks," he said. "There's no news I plan to share with you. I think discretion is an underused virtue. So with that, my private life is a closed subject."

"Speaking of the company party, we saw who you left with, Adam," one of the guys at the end of the table said.

Adam's pleased look irked Teira. She spoke up immediately to quell the rumor. "Things weren't as they appeared. He walked me to valet parking."

Teira noticed that the eyebrows of a few of Adam's closest associates shot upward. She had a sneaking suspicion he had done nothing to clear up any misconceptions about what had happened that night. In fact, he might have started a few more. It gave her great satisfaction to have just squelched them.

The conversation shifted when Christian said, "I think we've exhausted the topic. Time to move on, don't you think?"

Teira was relieved, but Adam obviously wasn't pleased with what she'd said. He glared in her direction and didn't say another word the rest of the lunch break.

On the way back to the office, Teira walked with the women, keeping her distance from Adam. He lagged behind the crowd, still fuming.

* * *

Later that afternoon, Teira heard a light tap on her office door. She spun around to see Adam standing there. "I just want to know why you would embarrass me like that in front of everybody," he asked aggressively, his voice grating.

"I don't see how telling the truth was so embarrassing," she replied. "All I did was set the record straight."

"You tried to make a fool of me in front of all those people I work with!"

"Don't forget, Adam, I work with them too! You want them to believe there is something going on between us and there isn't. All I did was stop the rumor mill, which by the way, *you* started at my expense. And I did it without humiliating you. You just didn't like the truth coming out. Let's be honest, that's why you're really upset."

Adam paused for several seconds before he said coldly, "He's taken, Teira."

"Who?" she asked, momentarily knocked off balance by the abrupt change of subject.

"You know who. I saw the way the boss kept looking over at you. Don't think for one minute I'm the only one who noticed. Sophie was sitting right there."

"You're imagining things," she said. "We're just friends."

"So you say, but he wasn't the only one doing the looking," Adam said meaningfully. "Just remember, he's taken. I was standing right here the day Sophie Blackman made it very clear he belongs to her." Teira looked at Adam but made no reply. Finally he turned to leave. "You're a fool if you think you can go up against her."

* * *

A half hour before her evening class was due to arrive, Teira was setting up when Christian walked into the room.

"Have you got a minute, Teira?"

"I have thirty, actually. What's up?"

"If it's okay with you, I'd like to sit in on your class tonight."

Teira hesitated. "Of course. Is there a problem?"

"No. I was hoping to see where things stand with this group."

"You're welcome anytime, of course."

Christian cleared his throat before changing the subject. "I hope the lunch conversation wasn't too awkward for you."

"Actually, I was glad for the opportunity to clear up a few things," Teira said.

Christian nodded before excusing himself. "I need to do some work in my office. I'll be back when class begins. I didn't want to throw you by walking in unexpectedly." At the door he turned back. "Teira?"

She looked up from what she was doing. "Yes?"

"About lunch—clarification is a good thing." He smiled and walked out the door.

* * *

Two and a half hours later, Teira watched the van pull away. The class had not gone well at all. She could safely say it was her worst training experience ever.

Christian had stopped in to observe the class, and at first Teira felt confident that things were going according to plan. She had done so many training meetings that it was second nature to her by now. Although having Christian there made her a little nervous, once the meeting started she got right down to business. She played the introductory DVD and couldn't help but smile when Christian appeared on screen, introducing himself and the program this time in Danish. Afterward she handed out the training pamphlets that ComTech had paid a fortune for because of the rush order.

Relief had flooded her when the pamphlets were delivered in a brown box only minutes before class started, but when they were in the employees' hands, her relief turned to dismay. The entire case of books had been printed in English rather than Danish. Teira apologized profusely for the mistake. It was bad form to blame somebody else for the mishap, but she knew she had been very specific in her instructions to print them in Danish.

She looked at Christian sitting at the back of the classroom, his expression unreadable. Teira floundered for a minute and tried to make a smooth recovery, promising the booklets would be available the following night. She went instead to the dry-erase board only to find the markers that she had put there before class were missing. She did the only thing she could think of—she stood before the class and held a group discussion. Surprisingly, many questions were answered and problems were solved by explaining and clarifying facts. All in all, the time was still productive.

After class Teira assured Christian she would get to the bottom of the problem with the pamphlets the very next morning. If the mistake had been hers, she would cover the cost of the new printing order herself. He assured her kindly not to worry and said that mistakes happen.

But you are wrong, Teira thought. *There was no mistake, at least not on my part.*

One thing in her favor was that the employees weren't quite as far behind as she had thought. She had hooked her computer into the screen, allowing them to follow along from their individual workstations. They easily picked up on the correct method and followed the procedure. If they hadn't followed along so well, tonight would have set them back another day. As it stood, she felt confident they would be caught up by the end of the week.

Christian left after their brief discussion, but Teira still had another issue to contend with—the new security guard. What was up with him? She had caught him peering through the classroom window periodically throughout the class time. It was odd to look up at the most unexpected times and find him standing there, watching her every move. But when it came time for the class to end, he was nowhere in sight.

Teira walked with the class members to the front doors of ComTech and told them all good-bye as they loaded into the van. When the van pulled away, she turned back and ran smack into a large body. "A-ah!" she hollered and bounced back.

The security guard looked at her and grinned. "Scared you, did I?"

Teira saw nothing funny in his approach. "Not scared," she said, a little breathless. "Startled. I didn't hear you come up behind me." She took a moment to study him. He was a big bear of a man with a bristly beard and mustache. A man of his size could put a scare into anyone. He wore his mousy brown hair in a ponytail tied back with a leather cord. Unlike the day guard, he looked messy and unfit. "I was just seeing the class off for the night," she said. "I need to straighten up the room and get my things. Then I'll be on my way."

The guard nodded and muttered as Teira headed back into the building and down the hall.

A few minutes later she returned to find him sitting at the security desk near the door. "Good night," she called out.

"Good night. Be cautious," he warned.

Teira's brows creased in confusion. "What do you mean by that? Copenhagen is a safe enough city."

"I only meant that being new here, one can never be too careful."

"Oh, of course," she mumbled. "Thanks."

His words hung heavily as she walked out the door.

15

It was raining by the time Teira pulled into the driveway of her grandmother's home. It wasn't any wonder things were such a luscious green in Denmark with all the precipitation. As far as Teira was concerned, it could rain all it wanted at night as long as she had the sunny days she loved. Besides, tonight the rain fit her mood perfectly. It had been a long, miserable day.

Making her way into the house, she turned and locked the doors without bothering with the lights. Since dinner was the last thing she wanted, she walked slowly up the stairs without first detouring into the kitchen. A good long soak in a hot bath might soothe away the tension.

Crossing the cream-colored carpet in the bedroom, she reached into her closet for a terrycloth robe. Then she walked over to the bedroom door and turned off the lights. Looking back at the inviting bed, Teira considered sinking into it right then and forgetting the soak in the tub altogether. The burdens of the day seemed overwhelming.

Raindrops splattered against the window. Peering through the glass, Teira saw the moon peeking through an equally small break in the clouds, giving the earth below an eerie, distorted glow.

Teira looked down the road that led to the neighboring farm. Trees dotted the path, but the farmhouse was too far distant to see. Her gaze shifted closer to home. She watched the bushes that lined the street directly across from the house as they swayed in the wind.

The moon had ducked behind another cloud. She looked away and gathered up her robe. Exhaustion was taking over. When she glanced back toward the window, however, her heart slammed against her chest. Someone was out there.

All she could see by the dim glow of the porch light was the outline of a person standing near the bushes, watching her house. A second later, whoever it was turned and headed down the road out of her line of vision. Teira ran downstairs to peer out a larger window, but by the time she got there the figure was gone.

Were her overwrought nerves driving her off the deep end, or was somebody really watching her?

* * *

On Tuesday morning Teira stopped in at the print shop on her way to work to find out what had happened with her order. A clerk confirmed that the original order had been for pamphlets printed in Danish, but at the last minute the order was changed. Someone, she was told, had paid an exorbitant fee to have a rush order done in English to be delivered in time for her training meeting.

Fortunately, luck was on her side this time. The original order had already been completed in Danish. For yet another fee she was able to retrieve them. She now had the correct pamphlets in hand and could keep her promise to Christian.

Teira stepped unsteadily through the door of the print shop deep in thought.

The bright sunlight assaulted her senses, making her see red.

Once outside she leaned against the red brick building with the box of pamphlets held tightly in her grasp.

In silence, she stared ahead as she felt the first throbs of a stress headache coming on.

Someone had tried to make a fool of her in front of the boss during her class. But that didn't make sense. Who could have known he would even be there? And what of the stranger outside her window? Was all this connected to the letters?

"Why?" she asked aloud.

Passersby looked at her strangely before hurrying on their way. Teira never noticed. Instead she took a deep breath and sighed. She shook her head in frustration, unable to fathom why anyone would do this to her.

Slowly she pushed herself away from the wall to continue on her way. Teira felt angry, confused, and even somewhat violated.

However, there was one thing she did know for certain. She wouldn't break that easily.

* * *

Since she was near Christiansborg Castle where the Danish Parliament offices were located, Teira stopped there next. She looked up at the imposing building, the third castle to be constructed in that very spot since the first one had been built by Bishop Absalon over eight hundred years ago. Knowing she was in the same place that Ulrike Spelman worked made Teira's stomach clench with nervous tension.

As she neared the large wooden doors to enter the building, they suddenly swung open and out walked two gentlemen with familiar faces. The first she recognized instantly as Olaf Jorgensen, head of security from the Rosenborg Treasury. The other she couldn't place at first. Then she recalled having seen him dine with Magnus Spelman the previous week when she'd gone to lunch with Erik.

It was easy to surmise that Mr. Jorgensen had an office at Christiansborg Palace, but she wondered about the elderly gentleman. Was he also a member of Parliament?

Walking up to the receptionist at the large front desk, Teira cleared her throat. "Excuse me," she said. "I was wondering if you could help me. I'm visiting your country and am interested in its history. Could you help me find a place to research information on the Resistance movement during the occupation?"

"Certainly," the woman said with a smile, "if you'll wait one moment."

"Yes, thank you." Teira smiled gratefully.

The woman excused herself and walked away. While Teira waited, Ulrike Spelman walked through the front doors, briefcase in hand. When their glances met, he stopped abruptly and his eyes narrowed.

Teira turned away. She wasn't there to see him. She hoped the cold shoulder she'd just given him would convey that message.

After a couple of seconds, she noted his passing through her peripheral vision. He called, "Good morning, Eva."

"Good morning, Mr. Spelman," the receptionist replied with a smile.

Ulrike paused in front of the receptionist's desk. He looked toward Teira. She couldn't miss his frown. "It's a fine morning after so much rain," he said to Eva.

"It certainly is."

Teira took a step forward. "I don't want to rush you, but I must be on my way or I'll be late for work."

Eva offered her a pamphlet. "The Danish National Museum maintains the Museum of Danish Resistance here in Copenhagen. I believe if you begin your search there, you might find what you're looking for."

"Is there a way to find out if any of the prominent members are still living?" Teira asked.

"I'm sure the people at the museum could answer that question," Eva assured her.

Teira gratefully accepted the brochure and thanked Eva for her assistance.

Ulrike stood by listening, his brows hanging low and a scowl covering the lower portion of his face.

* * *

Teira entered Christian's office with the heavy box in tow.

"What's that?" he asked.

"The study guides I promised my class for tonight—signed, sealed, and delivered. I want you to know I'm not incompetent." She winced. "Though you'd never know it by last night's example."

"You have nothing to prove," he said. "Your record speaks for itself. Otherwise you would never have been put on the team. So what gives?"

"What do you mean?"

"I know those weren't printed this morning. I also know you had dry-erase markers because when I first went in to tell you I'd be sitting in on the class, I saw them there." He frowned. "My guess is you were ambushed."

She nodded gratefully. "Any guesses why or by whom?"

"I was hoping you could tell me," Christian replied. "At any rate, nice recovery."

"Thanks. As for who did it, I don't have a clue, but I plan to find out."

"Keep me posted, will you?" he asked seriously.

"Sure thing, boss. Can I ask a favor?"

"You can always ask." He grinned.

"Can I leave these here until class tonight? I have a feeling they'll be safer."

"Sure," he said. "No problem."

After stowing the workbooks in a corner of Christian's spacious office, Teira returned to her desk. There was an e-mail from her mother waiting.

Hanne had received a letter from Zella Hansen. As Teira had suspected, her mother was not only thrilled to hear from the woman, but extremely touched. She said it was a letter she would always cherish, and the two planned to stay in touch. The rest of the e-mail was entertaining, but at the end she left an inspirational thought for her daughter as always and sealed it all with love.

Teira loved letters from her mother.

While reading the first e-mail, a pop-up had appeared to let her know another message had just been delivered to her mailbox. After carefully filing away her mother's letter with the rest, Teira automatically opened the next without looking to see who had sent it.

> *Teira,*
> *You shouldn't play these games.*
> *You CANNOT win.*
> *Your days could be numbered.*

Time seemed endless as Teira stared at the screen, rereading the lines over and over. At last she swallowed around the lump in her throat. There was more than one way to interpret the letter. There were so many ways, in fact, that they left her confused.

It wasn't an actual threat, but it was worded carefully enough that it could certainly be construed as one. On the other hand, no one had done anything to endanger her. Everything that had shaken her up so much thus far could be a product of her imagination, a misconception, or even borderline paranoia. She looked back down at the e-mail. On the other hand, the danger might be very real.

Teira had no idea where the e-mail had come from or how to trace it. She tried sending a reply to the address only to have it come back "undeliverable."

No shocker there, she thought. Next she tried contacting the Internet service provider to file a complaint about the e-mail content. Later that day, she received a message that the contact person was nonexistent in their accounts. No other information was available. It was another dead end.

Teira thought of the people in the office. The first to come to mind was Adam. He seemed the most logical suspect. He certainly had the computer know-how. He had been pretty upset with her on a few different occasions. He angered easily—mostly when he didn't get what he wanted, which just happened to be her. On further reflection, however, she ruled him out. Adam was trying to *start* a relationship, not *end* one. Why would he encourage her to go back to the States?

Then another thought struck. Erik had been standoffish since their lunch date. Though nice-looking and possessed of a good sense of humor, Erik wasn't her type. She had assumed he felt the same way about her. But maybe she'd offended him more than she'd realized. On further introspection, she very vividly recalled Christian telling her he was also a genius with computers. He could be behind the e-mails. It was unlikely, but possible.

Teira rubbed her temples with her fingers. Her head pounded from frustration. Accusing *anyone* was out of the question. She would be more cautious from here on out and watch her colleagues more carefully, but she would keep her thoughts to herself. She couldn't risk appearing suspicious or paranoid, even if she felt that way from time to time. Teira printed the letter and placed it under lock and key with the others.

* * *

This time the security officer was at his desk by the door at the end of class when the students walked out to the van. Once they left, Teira turned to him. "We didn't introduce ourselves last night. In fact, we may have got off to a bad start. My name is Teira Palmer. I see yours is Rolf Tycksen. Can we start over and be friends?" She extended her hand.

He nodded and they shook. "I wasn't trying to scare you or anything," he said. "I was just trying to say you ought to be more concerned about your safety."

Teira was willing to give him the benefit of the doubt. He had a strange way with words, but she didn't like the way things had been left last night. "I appreciate that, and I will," she said.

"You're ready to go now?" Rolf asked.

"I need to clean up the room and get my things first. Then I'll be ready."

"Fine."

To Teira's surprise, by the time she'd finished cleaning up, Christian stood in the doorway. His expression looked strained.

"Hi," she said, straightening up after shutting down yet another computer.

"Teira, we need to go somewhere to talk," he said. "Can we get some dinner?"

"Sure," she said uncertainly.

"We'll take both cars. I don't want to leave yours here in the lot."

"Lead the way," she said. "I'll follow."

At the restaurant, Teira broached the subject first. "What's wrong, Christian?"

He rubbed his eyes before leaning across the table. "What I'm about to tell you needs to be kept in the strictest confidence, okay?"

"Of course."

"Kort Madsen, the security guard who was in the accident?"

"I know who you're talking about," she said, "but I've never met him."

"Well, the results of the accident investigation are in. His brake lines were cut. It was no accident."

Teira drew in a deep breath. "Does he know who? Why?"

"Not a clue. Neither Kort nor his car were supposed to survive like they did."

Christian told Teira how authorities had come to talk to him about the accident and the investigation results. He answered all their questions the best he could, but with Kort working the night shift, he was afraid he had been very little help. Someone had cut the brake lines in such a way that the brakes would have worked a couple of times, but then lost fluid fast. By the time Kort reached the red light, he'd picked up speed. With no brakes to stop him, he'd flown through the light and hit the cement barricade. Whoever had tampered with his car had probably assumed he would hit head-on. In a last-ditch effort to save himself, Kort had managed to turn to the left enough to prevent the engine from bursting into flames upon impact. It had saved his life—and preserved evidence.

Christian had come from seeing Kort Madsen at the hospital earlier that evening. With tubes and wires everywhere, the man was still heavily sedated. "The authorities assume it was done while he was at work," Christian said. He could only wonder if someone was trying to sabotage the acquisition. If so, who? And why?

"Do you think it's in association with ComTech?" Teira asked.

"I hope not, but I can't rule it out."

"Has anything else happened to make you think someone might be trying to destroy the company?"

An eyebrow rose. "Somebody tried to cause mayhem in your training last night."

"The two are hardly comparable." Teira was convinced the words were true until she remembered the e-mails. The one she had received today *had* seemed a bit darker and more ominous than the others. Deep in thought, Teira fell silent.

"What are you thinking?" Christian asked.

After an inner battle she gave in. "There's more," she said quietly.

"Why was I afraid you were going to say that?" Christian groaned.

"I've made an enemy since coming here," she confessed. "For the life of me, I can't figure out who I've offended."

"What makes you think you've offended anyone?" he asked in concern.

Teira told Christian about each of the notes and what she'd done to try to trace the senders. Then she told him about the person she'd seen outside her bedroom window the night before.

Concern showed on his face. "Why didn't you come to me?"

"I thought I could figure it out before it became a problem for you or for ComTech. Besides, I'm not convinced it's connected with ComTech."

"How could it not be? Under the circumstances, I mean."

"Kort isn't directly associated with ComTech. He doesn't even work for you. If I remember correctly, he's hired by the city. Not only that, but his accident happened before I had a chance to meet him."

Christian leaned back. "Maybe there's no connection. Think, Teira. Is there anybody else who might have a problem with your being here?"

"Well, yes," she said. "He works for the city, too. Well, I don't know if that's true—for the government, at least. But I didn't cross him until after Kort's accident. So, that doesn't make sense, either."

"Who is he?"

"Would you believe Magnus Spelman's son, Ulrike?"

"The guy who is supposed to do the yard work? What did you do? Threaten his dad with that guillotine?"

"No, it's a lot more complicated than that. I—" Teira paused. Did she really want to tell him all this? While it would be good to have someone to talk to, she had never told anybody her family history because she was ashamed of it. But now that she was becoming more and more convinced her grandfather may not be guilty, perhaps she could unload a little of the burden and let Christian help her put things in perspective. She suspected he wouldn't judge her family as everyone else had. He'd already been taken in by her grandmother's lovable character, after all.

Christian raised an eyebrow. "Yes?"

"I'm related to my grandfather," she said quickly.

Christian laughed. "That was anticlimactic. I was expecting something revealing—at least another secret to add to the list. I'm related to my grandfather, too."

Teira rolled her eyes. "There's more. Trust me, I won't disappoint you in the secrets department. The family skeletons are going to come flying out of the closet at such an alarming rate, you may want to run for cover."

For the first time ever, Teira told someone about her family in Denmark. After relating the whole story, she finished by telling about the price her grandmother and mother had paid, according to Zella, and then relating her meetings with Magnus and Ulrike Spelman. By the time she had finished and answered Christian's questions, it was after ten. They had finished dinner and ordered dessert.

At last Christian said, "Let's walk off some of the dinner. The waiter seems to be getting a little antsy to have us out of here." Teira agreed, and he left a generous tip before they walked out of the restaurant. The weather was perfect for a walk. Stars shone brightly in the darkened sky as the two weaved their way in and around people on the cobbled walk.

"You were reluctant to tell me about your grandfather. Why?" Christian asked.

"I guess it's because I've always been a little ashamed," Teira admitted. "I'm twenty-seven years old and just now finding out that all the resentment I've felt toward him may have been unjustified." She looked up at Christian. "Or maybe it's that I'm finally tired of judging a man I never knew."

"What do you mean?"

"Well, let me tell you a story," she said rather mischievously. "Once upon a time in a land far away there was a beautiful little girl." She winked and Christian smiled. "She loved her grandfather very much. To her he was the bravest knight in all the land. She believed he lived in a magical world filled with castles and kings where everything was golden. Then one day her beautiful kingdom came crashing down—because of the supposedly brave knight. The end."

"That's it?"

"In a nutshell. I gave you the *Reader's Digest* version."

"Who's the author of that rotten story?"

"Reality," she said. "It has a way of sneaking in. You see, it wasn't all that long ago and not all that far away that the story took a drastic turn. The beautiful little girl needed braces and her fairy-tale dreams suddenly had a realistic ending." Teira smiled sadly at Christian. Then she looked ahead as they continued to walk. She went on. "For as long as I can remember, I wanted the fairy-tale life. I wanted to be the princess and I wanted the prince to exist as well. In my little fantasy world, the king was real and so were the castles. I mean, look around you!" Teira twirled with her arms spread wide. "This kingdom is full of them." Sobering, she continued, "There was even a brave knight at one time. That was supposed to be my grandfather. And, you'll think I'm crazy, but I felt close to him even though he had passed away long before I was born. There was little doubt in my mind that Prince Charming would someday ride along to sweep me off my feet."

"There's still that," Christian said with a smile.

"Okay, I know it's silly," Teira said. "What can I say? I was a little girl in a little girl's dreamland."

"Dreams are noble things," he said seriously. "They're what we base our ambitions on. I wasn't mocking you."

"But my dream turned into a nightmare when that brave knight—my grandfather—became a traitor. His countrymen were killed because of him and he died without first explaining why he would turn his back on everything he believed in and once loved."

"And with him the dream died, too?"

"I guess I stopped believing in the dream the day I stopped believing in him. Nothing turned out quite like I imagined it would. Life rarely does, I guess." She shrugged. "Anyway, I am his granddaughter, the spitting image of him, according to my grandmother. His history is part of me. It's who I am. I lost a little part of myself the day I learned the truth about him. Now it's like I'm on a quest to prove it was all wrong, that someone has made a horrible mistake, because I want to believe again." She considered. "But it's more than that. It just doesn't make sense that he would do what he did, Christian, and I can't accept the version of the 'truth' everybody tells me. Everybody but my grandmother—now there's one who believes in him. I feel driven to find out what really happened and make it right again if I possibly can."

By this time they had stopped walking. Teira was so caught up in her tale that she didn't notice where they were. She noticed now. They were standing in front of the Copenhagen Temple.

16

The temple was more magnificent than any castle in Demark.

It took her breath away. Or maybe that had already been accomplished by the tall, dark, and heart-stopping man at her side.

Christian led her toward a magnificent statue of the angel Moroni that stood to the side of the temple—rather than atop it as it does almost everywhere else in the world. "Moroni is looking particularly good tonight, don't you think?"

Teira looked up at Christian in surprise. His dark eyes seemed to catch and reflect back the angel's golden glow.

"Y-you know Moroni?" she stammered when at last she could speak.

"Not personally," he admitted with a teasing smile, "but I know quite a lot about him thanks to a couple of local missionaries." Before Teira could recover, he added, "In fact, Moroni was the one who told me if I'd read the Book of Mormon and pray about it I could come to know it was true. I did, I do, and I'll be baptized a week from Saturday. Want to come?"

The next breath Teira drew seemed to be filled with all the hope and promise in the world. "Yes!" she said. "I would *love* to come. But how . . . when . . . who . . . how . . . ?"

"You're repeating yourself," Christian said, clearly pleased at her surprise and gratified by her joy. It had been a hard secret to keep as they grew closer. It would have been impossible except that, with her living outside of Copenhagen, they lived in different ward boundaries. "It's a long story," he said, "one I'd love to tell you sometime. But that's not why I brought you here tonight." He took her hand and led her a few steps to the reflective pool. "I just thought I'd toss that out first because I've heard that some of you good Mormon girls don't date men who aren't of your faith."

Gazing into the pool, Teira saw a vision she wanted to preserve forever—that of herself at Christian's side. And he was joining the Church! She was still trying to compose a coherent sentence when he abruptly changed the subject.

"I happened to be going through your file at work today," he said, running his thumb along the top of her hand. "You aren't up for promotion or a raise anytime soon."

Or maybe, Teira thought, remembering what he had said at lunch about intraoffice dating, it was the same subject. Her breath caught in her throat and she shook her head. Then, fearing it was an incorrect response, she nodded.

"Plus, I really like your grandmother," he continued. "I'd love to make her happy. If there was something I could think of to—"

"Yes!" Teira cried. When his eyebrows rose, she faltered. She almost fainted. He'd been hinting that he was about to ask her out.

Or had he?

She saw the exact moment when the look of faux surprise on Christian's face was replaced by something rather smug and mischievous. Now she knew for sure: he *was.* Her heart soared.

"Yes, what?" Christian asked, feigning ignorance.

Teira smiled. Two could play this game. In fact, it took two *to* play it. "Yes, I know you love my grandmother, and yes, I know I'm not up for promotion yet," she said sweetly. "But how nice of you to look it up today. I know my grandmother will be thrilled when you write a letter of commendation to add to my file for all the after-hours training I'm doing."

Christian's eyes widened. "That wasn't exactly what I had in mind," he said. Then he added quickly, "Not that you don't deserve it, Teira. I will, of course—write the letter, I mean. But I brought up your file and your grandmother because I . . . well . . ."

"Yes?" He was so sweet and boyish she felt weak in the knees. Then she remembered that this boy was a man—and a man of the world as she'd heard tell. Baptism washed a person clean, but it didn't wash the spots off a leopard. Christian would still be what he was come Saturday afternoon. Her head cleared and her heart came back to hover a little closer to earth. When she'd told her grandmother she didn't want to get involved in all the competition for her boss's attention, she'd meant it.

Teira looked up at Christian in all seriousness. "Before this conversation goes any further, may I ask you a question?"

This time his surprise was genuine. "Sure."

"Sophie."

His brow rose. "That isn't a question. I think it's a noun." But he took her elbow and led her gently toward a bench where they could sit in the soft glow of the Copenhagen Temple. "Despite what you might have heard," he said quietly, "I have never asked Sophie Blackman on a date. Our appearances together are just that—for the sake of appearance."

Their game had ended. Teira saw it in Christian's eyes. The truth was there. It gave her the confidence to confess. "I-I won't be part of a . . . a . . . harem!"

He leaned back as if the words had pushed him away. "Now you've lost me."

She sighed. "I know you date. A lot."

"You need better informants," Christian replied dryly. "All I do *a lot* of is work. I attend various and sundry public functions as part of that work—the worst part, I might add—and I often escort the owner's daughter or someone the host has arranged for me." He shrugged. "When left to my own devices, well, let's just say there are Buddhist monks who see more women than I do." He reached over to tuck an errant curl behind Teira's ear. "And I've been okay with that until recently." He leaned a little closer. "Very recently, in fact."

The tingle of happiness that had begun at the top of Teira's head had worked its way down her spine and now made her toes curl. She grasped the hand that had just left her temple and held it in both her own. "Will you go out with me?" she asked breathlessly.

Christian grinned. "I thought you'd never ask."

* * *

A few minutes later they agreed it was getting late, so Christian walked Teira back to her car. On the way he again brought up the topic that had induced him to ask her to dinner. "I'm worried about what's happening. I can't figure out *how* or even *if* it's all connected, but I appreciate your openness with me. Let me see what I can come up with. Maybe we can start with this Ulrike Spelman character. Even if he's uptight about your grandfather, it doesn't make sense for him to be so angry. I'll see if he has any connection to city security. That will narrow our field. The incidents may be coincidental. In the meantime, play it safe and keep me posted. Will you do that?"

"Yes," Teira assured him. "Thank you for trying to help me figure this out."

"Thank you for joining me tonight and trusting me with your confidence," he said. "I think for now it might be best if we keep as much of this under wraps as we can. Does anybody else know?"

"No. I haven't said a word."

"The fewer people who do know, the better. People tend to talk too much. One last thing—can I call so I know you've made it home safely?"

"Okay." Teira smiled. How thoughtful. She could get used to this kind of chivalry very quickly.

* * *

Sometime during the night something startled Teira awake. She sat up and saw the bright green screen of the television. A soft hum indicated that the station had gone off the air for the night.

She had fallen asleep on the couch. Her work clothes were wrinkled and the light was still on. Drowsily she turned off the TV and the lights downstairs as she made her way toward the bedroom.

Then she heard it—the unmistakable noise of something, or *someone,* outside.

Probably a dog out wandering around, Teira tried to reassure herself. The neighbors lived about a mile up the road. Their farmland connected to her grandmother's. She knew from driving past that they had cattle. Most likely they also had a dog.

Knowing she would need to get up for work soon, Teira went into the bedroom to get ready for bed. She heard a car door slam and then the sound of tires crunching the gravel before speeding away.

Someone *had* been there.

The hair rose at the nape of her neck as Teira stood motionless, listening to the sounds of silence and willing another noise that would give her reason to call the police. The house remained silent. Whoever had been there was gone now.

She inched her way across the room to the front window. Crouching down, she peered over the window edge to look outside. The moon cast enough light that she could see the front yard. Nothing seemed out of the ordinary. Her car, still there in the haunting stillness of the night, looked unharmed. If it had been disturbed at all, the alarm would have gone off.

Nothing looked any different, but someone had been there. *Who was it, and why?*

Teira, still staying low, crossed to her bed and knelt to pray. By the time she finished her prayer, she felt calm. Without undressing, she lay on top of the down comforter and closed her eyes. Sleep evaded her. She used to love the peaceful calm of the night; now it filled her with apprehension.

It would be another two hours before the alarm would ring. Rather than lay awake and worry, Teira got up and changed out of her work clothes into slippers, her favorite sweatpants, and a T-shirt. Then she grabbed a flashlight from the kitchen drawer and went into the upstairs hall. There she pulled on the latch above her head to release the door and reveal the folding stairs that led to the attic.

Teira climbed carefully up the wobbly stairs. At the top she flipped on the flashlight and shined it into the darkness. The narrow beam of light allowed her to see a string hanging from a single light bulb in the center of the room. When she pulled it, a dim light cast long shadows.

Dusty marked boxes were stacked in one corner alongside an old rocking chair and mirror. A sewing mannequin was in another far corner, but it was the old wooden trunk in the third corner that caught her eye. That was what she'd come looking for.

In anticipation, Teira hurried across the attic toward the trunk. In her haste she didn't see the nailhead that protruded from the wooden floor. It caught on her slipper and she tripped, fell to the floor, and hit her knee. The flashlight flew from her hand and rolled under the trunk.

She picked herself up, dusted off her sweats, and walked more cautiously to the trunk. First she reached beneath it for the flashlight.

When her fingers proved too short, she slid the trunk aside. Tired from the exertion, she sat down in front of the trunk and reached for the lid. Surprised at how heavy it was, she lifted it carefully until it was all the way back, straining its hinges.

Inside the cedar box she found a world of treasure. Her eyes glowed with excitement and her fingers itched to dig into the depths of the trunk to see what cherished mementos she would discover.

The first thing Teira pulled from inside was something she recognized right away—her grandmother's wedding dress. She'd seen a picture of her grandmother wearing this dress, but it was even lovelier than it had looked in the photo. Wrapped in tissue paper and folded on top of the other items, it had turned from white to a beautiful ivory. Discounting the wrinkles, the dress was in perfect condition.

Teira's fingers ran lovingly over the silky material. Lost in a time long since past, Teira stood and held the dress up to herself while she walked across the attic to the old-fashioned oval mirror. There she admired the reflection of the long gown. It had sleeves that puffed at the shoulders before tapering at the wrists, and a tight-fitted bodice with a high neck. The lace formed an A-line that flared into a trumpet hem and dragged behind, forming the train. On the back, a gathering of lace and a small bow comprised the bustle. Holding the dress with one arm, Teira gathered her hair with the other and held it high up from her neck. When she turned this way and that, the dress swished from side to side.

If she remembered right, there was a long, lacy veil that matched. She returned to the trunk. Sure enough, the veil was tucked inside more tissue along with a picture of her grandparents on their wedding day—the same photo her mother had displayed back home in America.

Teira studied the smiling faces. Looking at her grandfather, she felt as if she was looking at herself. They had the same face shape and practically identical eyes. Funny she had never noticed the similarities before. Perhaps she'd never wanted to. She had always been told she looked like her mother, but that had been by people who never knew her grandfather. She did indeed look like her grandfather, too. That she had his smile was evident in the photo that she now held in her hand.

Teira gasped when she saw the next item in the trunk. It was her grandfather's uniform. Her hands shook as she reached in and pulled it out carefully. The medals he had earned were still pinned in place, almost as if the jacket had been gently slid from his shoulders and placed into the trunk.

A shiver shot through Teira as she ran her fingers lightly over each medal, wondering what they signified. He had laid out his uniform that last day, but never donned it. Why? Had he merely been looking at it, considering what it meant to him?

In America, a uniform was worn as a symbol of pride, duty, and honor. Teira was sure it was the same in Denmark. Sadness filled her at the sight of her grandfather's uniform, creased now from years of being folded away in a cedar-lined trunk. The medals were tarnished—as if the deeds that were done to earn them were as useless as the material onto which they were pinned. Teira was overcome with emotion. Tears ran down her cheeks.

The medals *did* stand for something, she assured herself. Her grandfather had done great good for his country. Surely he wouldn't have thrown all that away at the end.

Teira didn't know how long she sat deep in thought, but it was long enough for her toes and heels to start tingling with pinprick sensations. She switched positions to allow better circulation to her feet.

No matter what had happened all those years ago, her grandfather had clearly done a lot of good in his life. If he *had* made bad choices, he'd paid dearly for them—with his life. Burning was a horrible way to die. Now, more than ever, she wanted to know the truth about the end of the story. Teira carefully folded the uniform and set it on top of the wedding dress. She would take them both downstairs. Later, she would find someone who could clean and preserve them.

Next she pulled out an old photo album and carefully opened the cover. Inside was her heritage. Black-and-white photos pasted to yellowed pages showed images that were still proud and serene. In some cases, names and dates, faded with time, were written beneath the pictures, recording information that would soon be lost if not restored. Many of these photos were pictures of ancestors, Teira knew, as she lovingly turned each page. There were even pictures of her grandparents as children. What heirlooms!

Teira determined that with her grandmother's help, she would get as many names, dates, and memories recorded as possible. Then she would move everything into a book with acid-free paper to better preserve the priceless photos. Finally, she would return it all to her grandmother as a gift.

Deeper in the trunk Teira found a small bundle of letters tied with a faded ribbon. The scrawled penmanship was clearly that of a man. Immediately, Teira knew these were love letters written from her grandfather to her grandmother. Feeling they were too personal to read, Teira tucked them back into the trunk.

Teira then pulled out a small leather box and flipped it open. Inside was a gold pocket watch with two gold chains of different lengths. One was for a vest and the other for a suit. Engraved on the back of the pocket watch were her grandfather's initials. On the front was a delicate, intricate pattern.

Teira lifted the watch from the case and opened it. She wound it a couple of times. As she held it to her ear, the watch ticked rhythmically. It was beautiful. She laid it gently back in its case, glanced at her own watch, and noted the time. She hadn't realized she'd been up in the attic so long. If she didn't hurry, she'd be late for work.

In the bottom of the trunk was a handgun; beside it, a box filled with bullets. Teira shuddered. She didn't blame her grandmother for packing something like that away in the bottom of the old trunk and placing it in the corner of the dusty attic where no one would ever come close to it.

There were still a few more belongings in the trunk Teira wanted to inspect. She was eager to discover any clues hidden inside. She pored through the contents, searching for anything that would divulge secrets to the past. Soon disappointment overcame her.

She'd found only a few odds and ends: aged newspaper clippings about the town, stacks of old documents pertaining to the property, and a couple of obituaries of family members. She tucked these remembrances into the photo album, hoping to better preserve them along with the pictures. Teira had finally reached the bottom of the trunk. Despite the treasures, she'd found nothing that would help her understand the circumstances that had led to that fateful day so many years before.

She stood and shut the trunk lid. Then she gathered the dress, uniform, and photo album. She tugged on the light string and plunged the room into semidarkness before realizing she'd left the flashlight by the trunk. She'd come back after work to retrieve it. For now, light filtered in from the hallway. Coupled with the first rays of morning light streaming through the small window, it was enough for her to see her way across the room and down the stairs.

* * *

Teira was running late and rushing out the door when she figured out what had happened the previous night. The reason a mysterious visitor had paid her a call lay on the step in front of the outside door: a silver DVD disc with a typed letter on top of it.

Teira's heart hammered in her chest as she read the few lines.

> *Teira Palmer*
> *I'm watching your every move.*
> *I want you gone. Now.*

Returning to the house, Teira slipped the DVD into her laptop and turned it on. Then she watched in horror as she saw herself pull up to the house late the night before. She watched herself lean over to pick up her briefcase before getting out of the car and walking into the house. There she saw herself pull her blouse from the waistband of her skirt before shutting the blinds on the big picture window. At this point the screen went fuzzy and the recording stopped.

Someone had recorded her every move. While she was sleeping he must have used a laptop of his own to transfer the footage onto the DVD. Finally, he'd walked right up to her door to deliver it.

Teira's fingers shook as she turned off the computer. How could she not have sensed she was being watched? From the camera angle, it was apparent that the photographer had been hiding in the bushes across the street. Realizing that she hadn't sensed his presence frightened her even more than the actual recording.

She ejected the disc, stuck it in her briefcase, and pulled herself together before walking out the door and locking it behind her.

* * *

The room was dimly lit by flame-shaped bulbs set into crystal wall sconces. The creak of a door being opened alerted the man to the fact that he was no longer alone. He didn't need to turn to see who it was. He'd been standing, waiting.

Always waiting.

"Your pathetic scare tactics are useless," he growled.

"What will you have me do? You have only to say."

"Does she have what we want?"

"We don't know."

"Not good enough! If we're not careful, she will destroy us!"

Shaking his head, the man sank into his chair. Too much was at stake. After all that had passed, he could not, would not, allow the young American woman to demolish all he had achieved.

17

In her office that morning, Teira prepared for the next group of people she would train—the local Danish management team. She knew there was much to do to get ready and it would take all her concentration to work with her pounding headache.

She sat down at the computer and turned it on. Her inbox showed a slew of messages. A couple of them were from friends back home in Salt Lake; she'd put them off until later. Suddenly, an instant message came in from Christian.

> GOOD MORNING
> Teira grinned and typed:
> GOOD MORNING TO YOU, MR. TANNER
> Christian wrote:
> COME AND SEE ME
> Teira responded with:
> IS THIS PERSONAL OR PROFESSIONAL?
> Christian typed:
> YES
> Teira finished with:
> I'M ON MY WAY

Teira finished up an e-mail, closed the message box, stood, and straightened her skirt. She made a quick stop at the ladies' room to check her appearance before heading down the hall toward Christian's office.

* * *

Christian shut down his computer with a satisfied smile. He leaned back and sighed. Lost in thought about the previous evening with Teira, he was brought out of his reverie when the door to his office opened. He looked up, expecting to see Teira, and then had to try to hide his disappointment when Sophie entered instead.

The boss's daughter sauntered over to his desk and draped herself over its edge.

"Sophie, come on. I'm trying to work," Christian said with exasperation.

"That's not what I saw. You were miles away." She leaned forward. "And speaking of being missing, I went by your place last night. You weren't home." She waited for an explanation. When none came she said, "So where were you?"

"I was out. Now would you kindly remove yourself from my desk, please? Now." Knowing she wouldn't comply, Christian leaned back in his chair to widen the space between them.

"Out?"

"My private life is my business and, as I said the other day, I choose to keep it that way." He frowned. "Off my desk, Sophie."

"Your private life?" she repeated with a well-rehearsed pout. "You make it sound as if you were out with another woman."

"I was."

Sophie's eyes narrowed. "Who was she?"

"Am I speaking a foreign language?" Christian asked, rising from his chair and circling the desk. "Let me repeat it slowly. One, none of your business. Two, get off my desk." He glanced at the clock, then scooped up the black silk tie he'd tossed over the chair when he'd first arrived. He looped it around his neck and began to tie it.

"Was this a first date or have you fooled yourself into thinking you care about this person?" Sophie rose in one graceful, fluid motion and walked over to where Christian stood. Then she pushed his fingers out of the way so she could finish tying his tie for him.

"Sophie!" Christian tried to step back again, but she tightened her grip.

"Daddy taught me how to tie the perfect knot." She looked up into his eyes. "And whoever she is will never be as good for you as I can be."

Sophie had just wrapped her arms around his neck and kissed him when Christian heard a gasp from the doorway. He tried to pull away, but Sophie's arms, like a boa constrictor, only grew tighter. At last he grabbed her wrists and managed to yank her arms from around his neck. Then he looked toward the door. Teira had just turned to leave.

"Teira, wait!" he called out.

She stopped but didn't turn around.

"I'm sorry," she mumbled. "I should have knocked. I didn't think."

"This isn't what it looks like," Christian said.

"What is it then?" Teira asked quietly.

"Bad timing on your part," Sophie inserted. "So if you don't mind—"

"I asked her here," Christian interrupted. "So you're the one who's leaving, Sophie." Her mouth was still open when he added in a low voice, "And if you ever pull another stunt like that, one of us is leaving this country. I seriously doubt your father will want it to be me."

"I know why you're acting this way," Sophie said as Christian ushered her toward the door. "You don't believe in public displays of affection in front of your employees." She cast Teira a dazzling smile. "We'll finish our . . . conversation . . . a little later."

When Sophie was finally gone, Christian turned toward the window and ran his fingers through his hair while he regained his temper. At last he turned, glad to see that Teira was still there.

"I'm sorry you had to see that," he said. "That woman has a sixth sense about knowing when to stage the most dramatic scenes at the most inopportune moments."

Christian stepped around Teira and closed his office door. She hoped no one had seen or heard the "demonstration." Talk about setting the office gossips' tongues to wagging. Her second thought as she turned to look at Christian was that he was worth fighting for. Even if the adversary was Sophie Blackman, the boss's daughter. After all, Christian was so handsome. In his dark gray, pin-striped suit and white shirt, and with his dark hair and dark eyes, he looked irresistible. Those dark eyes were looking at her intently, trying to assess what she was thinking.

What *was* she thinking? She wasn't sure. When she first entered his office and saw the two of them kissing, she'd wanted to cry. Last night had filled her with such hope; she felt alive with excitement like she'd never before known. Then, when Christian pulled away instantaneously—and possibly before he'd had a chance to see her standing there—she wondered if perhaps the kiss was something else. Perhaps it was a ploy by a woman desperate to capture the attention of a man who didn't return the affection.

One could always hope.

She forced her brightest smile and said, "Let's start again." Then she carefully opened the closed door, slipped out behind it, and shut it behind her.

After hearing a soft rap, Christian called out with a grin, "Come in."

"Good morning. You look very dapper today, Mr. Tanner."

"Thank you, Miss Palmer. Since I have a meeting in Sweden later today with a board of directors, I thought I'd better clean up. May I say you look beautiful yourself?"

"Thank you." Teira blushed. "So, you're headed for Sweden?"

"I'll be gone for the rest of the day. Tomorrow I'll be in Aalborg. I was thinking it would be good if you came with me to introduce the training program to the managers there. Can you prepare a half-hour presentation?"

"I'll work on it today."

"Great. I'll have Siri get us on the commuter flight in the morning. I was thinking that if we finish in time we can rent a car and have our first official date afterward. We could drive up to Skagen for dinner. There's some beautiful scenery there. How does that sound?"

Teira smiled. "It sounds nice."

Christian smiled back. "Good. Okay, now one last thing. I stopped in at Köbenhavns Radhus, the town hall, to check out the situation with the security guards. Then I went over to Christiansborg Palace to see what position your friend Ulrike Spelman holds."

"Were you able to find out anything?" Teira asked anxiously.

"It was very easy actually," Christian assured her. "Different ministers of the Danish government report to Parliament. I simply asked the woman at the reception desk in what department I would find Ulrike Spelman. She told me he worked for the minister of education and ecclesiastical affairs. Evidently, one person holds both positions."

Teira's face fell. "So there's no connection with security?"

"Not at first appearance," he conceded. "But I bet the officials run in the same social circles, so I'm not discounting anything yet. Setting that aside, is there anything else you can think of that might have set somebody off?"

"Not a thing. I haven't done anything here besides work, visit the cemetery, and sightsee." Teira recalled the uncomfortable meeting she'd had with the head of security in Rosenborg Castle and the stirrings in the pit of her stomach upon hearing the story of King Christian X's missing ring.

Christian noticed the change in Teira's demeanor. "Did something happen when you were seeing any of those sights?"

Teira told him about the ring and the questions she'd asked the head of security during her visit to the castle. She also told him how the ring had turned up missing around the time her grandfather died, and about the story Zella had told her of the suspicious break-ins at her grandmother's home. She still thought it odd that the break-ins occurred just after the Royal Guard had come to inquire about the ring.

"Did you ever ask your grandmother about the ring or the vandalism?" Christian asked.

"No. I asked my mother, and she said that the monarchy doesn't work that way. Of course, she's right, so I left it alone. The townspeople *were* angry at the time."

"That doesn't explain the mystery of the ring," Christian said, deep in thought. "Maybe we should see what more we can learn about it from another guide."

"Okay. Let's storm the castle," Teira agreed. She was about to tell him about the mysterious visitor and the DVD when Christian looked at his watch.

"Sorry, but I've got to go," he said. "I'll get back as soon as I can. Then we'll see what we can figure out."

"Maybe this will all blow over," Teira said hopefully.

"I'd like to hope."

"You don't think that's the case, do you?"

"Not if it's connected to Kort's accident."

"Great," Teira mumbled.

"I'm sorry. I was going for honesty. Be careful, and I'll talk with you later today, okay?"

"Okay." She turned to leave and then turned back. "Christian? Thanks again. It means a lot to me to have your help."

"Don't worry," he said. "We'll get to the bottom of all this."

This would be a perfect time for a good-bye kiss, Teira thought. Little did she know that Christian's mind was running in the same circles. Instead, they both smiled as Teira walked to the door, turned the handle, and exited the office in disappointment.

Teira returned to her office and found Adam sitting at her desk. "Where have you been?" he asked without preamble.

"Talking to Christian."

"I should have known," he muttered.

Ignoring the jab, Teira looked at Adam curiously.

"What?" he asked.

Teira hesitated, debating whether she should ask the questions that plagued her. She and Adam had been friends in Salt Lake before he had gotten the idea that he wanted more than friendship. What would it hurt to ask? Finally, she went for broke. "Are you getting along with everyone you've met so far?"

His brow creased. "Yeah. Why would you ask that?"

"I mean, there's no one here that's upset about the acquisition, is there? Anyone who doesn't want us Americans here?"

Adam shrugged. "Not that I've heard anything about. This is a big move for both companies—classic win-win. Why?"

"It's nothing," she said. "Maybe my imagination has just mounted a runaway horse."

Seeing Adam's quizzical expression, she reconsidered. "Do you know any reason why someone would want me gone?"

"I can't think of one. Why?"

"Adam, think about it. With us stepping in and taking over the old company, plus being foreigners and all, are any toes being stepped on?"

"Come on, things like that happen in the corporate world all the time. You know that." He shrugged. "I haven't heard anything. The Danes have been genuinely good people. Everyone I've met has been helpful and ready to learn so they can take over when we leave. These are strange questions you're asking. Did something happen?"

"I've made an enemy out of someone," she confessed, "but I don't want to point fingers. In fact, I have no idea who it is. Forget I mentioned it. I guess I just wanted to know if you'd experienced the cold shoulder too."

He looked interested. "How do you know you've made an enemy?"

"Really, it's nothing." Teira couldn't believe she'd confided in him of all people. "But if you hear of anything, let me know."

"Not if you don't tell me what's happening."

Teira frowned. Adam irked her to no end. Making her look like an incompetent professional was embarrassing enough, but the letters, the man at her house, and now the DVD had upset her, and yet he sat there treating the situation as if it was nothing more than light banter. To his credit, he had no idea to what extent she was being harassed. Still, she wanted to wipe that attitude from him.

"It started with some silly letters—" she began.

"What do you mean silly letters? How many?"

"Well, if you count the e-mail and the one on the DVD this morning, four."

"What DVD? What are you talking about?" Adam's face filled with alarm.

Although it was the reaction she'd sought, it didn't fill Teira with the satisfaction she thought it would. Instead she felt sick. "You know what," she said, "I don't want to discuss this anymore. I'm already upset. All I'm asking is that if you hear of any reason why someone would want me out of the company, or know that someone is unhappy about the acquisition, will you please let me know?"

Adam nodded. "Yeah, of course I will. But let me ask you this. Do you have any idea why someone would do this—or who it could be?"

"No," she said, "but I intend to find out."

* * *

Thankfully, Teira didn't see Sophie for the rest of the day. Teira wasn't in the mood to cross paths with her again.

Class that night went smoothly too, and she was deeply satisfied to see that as she'd promised, the group would be up to speed after Friday's class. Even Rolf watching her through the glass window hadn't put a damper on the evening.

Sighing in relief, Teira pulled her car away from the parking lot. Then she glanced in the rearview mirror. Rolf stood outside watching her drive away.

Teira shivered.

She was exhausted. Having slept very little the night before, she just wanted to go home, get something to eat, and sleep.

* * *

When Teira arrived home that evening, she paid close attention to the bushes across the street and parked her car closer to the house. With key in hand, she walked to the door and entered swiftly, shutting the door behind her and locking it instantly.

There was no way she was taking any unnecessary chances.

Turning on several lights, she shut the blinds and drapes in all the rooms before changing from work clothes into sweats and a T-shirt. Pulling her hair into a ponytail, she went down to the kitchen to make herself an omelet for dinner.

Her cell phone rang. Checking her caller ID, she answered with a smile. "Hey, there. Is our corporate leader still TCB-ing?"

"What is TCB-ing?" Christian asked.

"Taking Care of Business!" She laughed.

"Nope. I'm all done and at home. What are you doing?"

In her best imitation of the Swedish chef from Jim Henson's Muppets, Teira described cooking her omelet. "Furst yuoo get yuoor iggs und yuoo vheep zeem reel guud. Edd zee feexings und cuuk it sloo. Toorn it in helff, und zeere-a yuoo gu! Bork! Bork! Bork!"

Christian burst out laughing. "You might convince me you're a pro except that I was there the day you made lemonade, remember?"

"How can I forget? So, did you bring me some fish?"

"What kind do you like?"

"Those Swedish fish."

"I brought you back something better," Christian said with a chuckle.

"Better than Svedeesh feesh? Is that possible?"

"Me!"

"How can I argue with that?" She giggled. "In all seriousness, I have a couple of confessions to make."

"That doesn't sound good."

"I talked to Adam today. Now, I know we decided not to talk about the problems with other people, but I swear I never said a word about Kort Madsen and I didn't go into detail about my problem either. I just briefly told him what was going on. I got to thinking that if anybody was going to get wind of who was angry, they weren't going to come to you or me. I thought maybe he'd heard something from the gossip mill."

"I trust you," Christian said. "How did he react?"

"Well, that's what I wanted to talk to you about. The funny thing is, at first he acted blasé, like I was getting myself worked up over nothing. But when I told him about the DVD, it was different."

"Whoa! What DVD?"

"That's my next confession. I didn't tell you about it this morning because I didn't want you to worry all day. Last night after I got home someone recorded me walking in from my car. They dropped it off at my doorstep during the night for me to find this morning. There was another message taped to it saying they were watching me and they want me gone—now."

"Is that everything recorded on the DVD?"

"That's it. As soon as they saw me close the blinds, they stopped taping. There's nothing obscene or inappropriate or even threatening. What's upsetting is the fact that I had no idea at all I was being watched."

"Teira, maybe we ought to contact the police with all of this."

"I would agree except that nothing has been done," she replied.

"I don't think we should wait until something has!"

Rather than making her feel better, Christian made her think about issues she'd pushed to the back of her mind. "I didn't want to bring this up," she said, "but Adam had a really strange reaction when I told him. And that new security guard is a real different character, too." She sighed. "Or maybe I'm imagining things and this whole situation has started to play games with my head."

That night as Teira pulled the covers back and climbed into bed, she thought over each letter carefully and wondered for the millionth time if she was imagining things or if they were as bad as they seemed.

She couldn't go to the police because there had been no actual threats made. No one had tried to cause her harm, and there was no single suspect to pursue. She wasn't even sure these actions fell under the category of stalking. Surely it was at least some sort of harassment. If only she knew who was behind it.

So what choices did she have? Until she knew what she was dealing with, they were very, very limited.

18

Teira tapped on Christian's door with her attaché case in hand. She had dressed to impress, and from the look in his eye she had succeeded.

Christian stuffed papers into his briefcase. He wore a black suit with a white shirt and red tie. Teira's heart flip-flopped. When he looked up and smiled, she felt decidedly weak in the knees. He was hers for the whole day!

"I'm ready whenever you are, Mr. Tanner," she said. "We have just enough time to get to the airport for our commuter flight."

"Good morning to you too, Miss Palmer." He laughed. "You seem to be in a hurry. Any particular reason?"

"You might say I am anxious to get this day rolling. I've been looking forward to spending some time in that part of the country."

"It's only the country you're looking forward to seeing?" he asked, feigning innocence.

"There's a lot of scenery to be seen." Teira smiled slyly.

"Well, let's get going. I'm in a hurry myself." Christian chuckled as he snapped his case closed and lifted it off his desk.

"Oh, really? Any particular reason, Mr. Tanner?"

"Yep. I've got a hot date as soon as I can spring loose from the meeting." Christian smiled and walked to the door, motioning for her to precede him. She laughed and obliged.

They took a taxi to the airport and boarded the plane for the forty-five-minute flight to Aalborg. Once they were seated, Teira asked Christian if he had flown there before.

"Several times, why?"

"I've never flown in a prop plane," Teira said. "Are you sure that little propeller will spin fast enough to keep us airborne?"

"Have no fear. The seat is used as a flotation device and we barely fly above the water. In fact, you can see the eels swimming from your window. But the water is too cold for sharks," Christian assured her.

Teira looked out the window and mumbled, "What a comforting thought." She clicked the seat belt fastened and settled into her seat.

During the short flight they talked, and Christian even reached over to hold her hand. They both looked at their interlocked fingers from time to time, Teira finding that she couldn't wipe the silly grin from her face.

It seemed like only minutes before the small commuter plane landed. They rented a car and were on their way to the Aalborg office.

"There's supposed to be a big store here that is famous for its trolls," Teira commented.

"I've heard Denmark is famous for trolls. Do you know where the store is?"

"I have the address," she confessed. "Could we stop there after our meeting?"

"We can go anywhere you like," Christian said. "Is there a special kind of troll you're looking for?"

"The original troll dolls were made by Thomas Dam and his family in the 1950s," she said. "At first they were made from wood, then soft rubber, and finally vinyl. A lot of other companies have replicated them, but the original Dam trolls were the ones I played with as a little girl. My grandma always sent me one for Christmas. I had quite a few until I became too old for dolls and she stopped sending them. I still have them, though, and each time my mother visited Denmark she bought me another. I'd like to add to my collection and send my mother one, too. They're supposed to bring good luck, you know."

"We'd better pick up several." Christian smiled. "I know a couple of girls who'll love them. Let's go there as soon as we end our meeting."

Although Teira nodded, she wasn't thrilled that Christian would be shopping for other girls while he was out with her. Did he realize what he'd said or was it a slip of the tongue? And was Sophie one of those girls? Teira tried to hold the green-eyed monster in check, but the comment didn't sit well with her.

Once the meeting began, Teira sat back and watched Christian with interest. He was focused and at his best, captivating the managers. After Christian presented a company plan and outlook for the future, he listened with interest as the managers voiced concerns. As he answered questions, Christian was able to maneuver the group into his way of thinking and inspire them with his vision.

It wasn't the way he spoke, Teira decided, but the way he interacted with people. Her grandmother had said he was a charmer, but the truth was that he had a knack for getting along with everybody. Christian was as much at home in a boardroom as he was with elderly women or young women. He was a people person. He knew how to carry himself whether he was in a dark business suit or jeans and a T-shirt. In short, he was a classy man. It was no wonder he attracted attention.

She had known him almost a month now. Teira gulped as she realized that she was falling for Christian fast and hard. While she sat there only half listening, she decided to give this relationship her all. The thought scared her, but what she felt for him was even stronger than her doubts and fears. There was a lot of competition, she knew—including his boss's daughter—but just looking at him told her he was worth the fight. Besides, hadn't her grandmother taught her that the only way to live life fully was to love deeply, completely, compassionately, and passionately? The reward of that kind of love returned was well worth any risk.

Teira continued to watch Christian and thought about how he made her laugh, made her ponder, and—in the way he looked at her when she caught his eye—even made her feel beautiful.

"Miss Palmer?"

Teira came back to the meeting with a jolt to meet Christian's quizzical gaze. "Are you ready?" he asked.

Teira looked around in panic, but everyone else was occupied with flipping through the next folder that had been placed before them.

"You were going to talk about training procedures," Christian prompted.

"Yes, of course," she said, quickly rising from her seat and battling to hide her embarrassment. She walked to the front, more confidently than she felt at that moment, and stood at the head of the boardroom while Christian took his seat. Daydreaming would have to wait until her part of this meeting was completed.

Once Teira's presentation got under way, she forgot her embarrassment. Happy to be back in her comfort zone, she sailed through the training procedures. All in all, Teira knew her part went very well despite the distraction of Christian never taking his eyes from her face.

As they left the offices a little later, Christian sidled up alongside Teira. "Excellent job in there," he whispered in her ear. "I knew I could count on you."

His breath against her ear sent a rippling through her heart. She beamed with pride and happiness.

After a brief lunch in an outdoor café, they headed for the troll shop. Located on a side street along a little cobbled path, it was one of many, Teira noted, that sold this particular brand of trolls. In fact, the Dam brand was everywhere.

Upon entering the shop, Teira looked in amazement and joy at the shelves lined with trolls of every shape, size, and description.

Finding it almost impossible to choose, Teira finally selected two Viking trolls. A boy and a girl for her parents and a Hans Christian Andersen one for herself. Surprisingly, Christian picked two identical ones for "his girls"—both ballerinas but in different colors. Finding them not very original, Teira kept her opinion to herself. When Christian insisted on paying for them all, she consoled herself that at least hers was different from the other girls', not only in color but in character as well.

The drive to Skagen was enthralling. Windmills unlike any she had seen before dotted the landscape. They were tall, white, modern-looking metal structures that generated power rather than pumped water.

Next they drove through an area of tall trees, thick with dark green foliage. While on the motorway, they talked about everything from growing up in California versus Utah to the similarities in their families. Both came from homes with loving parents who were very much on hand for them. However, there were differences too.

"I hated being an only child," Teira confessed. "But I do have one cousin on my dad's side that is like a sister to me. Her name is McKinley. She's my best friend. But boy, you have never met two people who were more opposite growing up!" Teira laughed.

"Opposite in what way?" Christian asked, grinning at the sparkle in Teira's eyes as she reminisced.

"She was kind of a tomboy at heart, and I was always a girlie girl. It was good for us though, you know. I think she taught me how to loosen up a bit and I kind of rubbed off on her too. I taught her that fingernail polish does not cause cancer and she taught me how to slam-dunk a ball." Teira winked.

"No way!" Christian exclaimed, clearly impressed.

"Well, it was a five-foot Nerf hoop. Anyway, one summer she got me in so much trouble, I will never forget! We went boating down in southern Utah at Lake Powell. McKinley caught this blue-bellied lizard and wanted to keep it at my house because she knew her parents would never approve. Like *my* mother would!" Teira shook her head in disgust.

"Okay hold it," Christian interrupted. "You are scared to death of mice, but lizards are acceptable?"

"Not even a little bit. That was the problem. She put it in my Barbie Dream House. I wasn't about to touch the thing! The plan was, the following weekend she would come to our house to get it and take it home with her."

"So how were you going to take care of it all week?"

"Umm, that was an oversight on our part. That first night at our house I heard it crashing around in the dream house looking for a way out. I thought it must be trying to find a way back home to its family. I was pretty upset by the banging around, not to mention the overwhelming guilt about removing it permanently from its environment. By morning I was bawling."

"So what did you do?"

"Like any brave little girl, I got up enough nerve to touch the creature and stuck it in the trunk of my Barbie remote control car."

"You what?!" he asked with a mixture of disbelief and confusion.

"I did! Then I attached a letter I had written explaining everything to my mom and maneuvered it down to the kitchen where she was cooking breakfast and stopped it by her feet. The letter was asking her to take it back to its parents. What I hadn't expected was for her to hear scratching noises coming from the trunk of the car. How was I supposed to know she'd open the trunk rather than the letter? She said all she saw were two beady eyes glaring at her before it jumped out at her. That's when all the mayhem broke loose. Mom started screaming and running around, the grease in the frying pan nearly caught fire, the house filled with smoke. It was a mess! For days the house smelled. Needless to say, the lizard got away. Mom swears to this day it's lurking somewhere down in the basement."

"I'm sorry you had so much trouble, but that would have been awesome to see!" Christian burst out in a full, hearty laugh. "If you want siblings, you can have a couple of mine," he offered with a smile once he composed himself.

Christian regaled Teira with stories of growing up with three brothers and the mischief they got into.

"Tell me another one," she implored.

"Well," he stalled. "I sort of went through this Rambo phase."

"This has got to be good," she said.

"You have no idea!" He laughed.

"What exactly is a Rambo phase?"

"When I was around twelve, I wore my combat fatigues, face paint smeared on my cheeks, and a bandanna tied around my forehead."

When Christian saw that Teira could barely contain her laughter, he defended himself with good humor. "You're a girl, and so I wouldn't expect you to understand. My brothers, Matt and Ryan, and I were out to conquer the enemy forces with our special ops missions. We even had our own weaponry. We had dirt bombs and grenades."

"Grenades?" Teira asked.

"They were Dad's old Christmas lights."

"I don't understand."

"They make a cool popping sound when they hit the ground. When Dad found out, he wasn't happy, to say the least. He put a quick end to our military careers."

"Is this special training mentioned anywhere on your résumé?" she asked with a grin.

"No, but you'd be surprised how useful it's been at corporate retreats. Those guys love to play paintball, and I'm the MVP third year running."

Christian continued to regale her with tales of secret missions and stories from his youth. He had her laughing so hard at times that tears sprang to her eyes. She confided that she'd like to have several children of her own one day, and Christian said he wanted a big family as well.

They reached Skagen just before two in the afternoon and stopped at a fishing port where large vessels were bringing in the catch of the day. They walked along the enormous docks, looking at the boats as the fishermen unloaded their bounty.

As Teira leaned over to peer into a bucket of flounder on ice, one flipped up in front of her face. Christian burst out laughing at her squeal.

"I wasn't expecting it to be quite that *fresh*!" she said. "Its gills were still moving!"

After a short stroll around the docks, they walked back to the car and drove to a small souvenir store a few miles away. When they walked in, Christian bought two tickets to ride a sand bus that would take them down the beach.

"You have to see this to believe it," he said enthusiastically. By now he had discarded his jacket and tie, rolled up his sleeves, and unbuttoned the first couple of buttons of his white shirt. A soft sprinkling of dark hair covered his forearms. His gold watch reminded Teira that the hours were swiftly ticking by.

Teira had taken off her sweater and was wearing dress slacks and a blouse.

"You may want to take off your shoes and socks," he suggested as he sat down to do the same before rolling up his pants into cuffs.

Teira sat next to him and followed suit.

They hopped aboard the sand bus for a bouncy ride down the shore. At last the driver let them off, telling them the bus ran every thirty minutes and they could return whenever they wished.

Christian took Teira's shoes along with his in one hand and held her hand with the other as he led her near the water. "See that disturbance of water that runs perpendicular to the beach as far out as you can see?" he asked. When she nodded, he continued, "If you look at one side of it, the water flows east. The water on the opposite side flows west. They come together and meet in the middle. That disturbance, then, is the waves crashing into each other and rippling out as far into the ocean as you can see."

"Oh, wow!" Teira said in awe. "What makes the water do that?"

"On the west side is the North Sea and on the east is the Baltic. This is where the two come together. It all has to do with the rotation of the currents. It's pretty amazing, isn't it? It seems to go on forever."

"That's incredible!" she said, watching the waves in wonder.

Both stood watching until Christian broke the silence. "What are you thinking?"

"I was thinking how overwhelming it is to stand beside two seas. One can feel amazingly small in the grandeur of God's creations."

"Yet, He's aware of even the tiniest of creations like this little guy here." Christian bent over and picked up a sand crab and showed it to Teira.

"It's pretty impressive, isn't it?" she said.

"The sand crab or the sea?"

"Both. All of it." She laughed.

"It absolutely is."

Christian sent the crab on its way, then took hold of Teira's hand. "What I find impressive is that you can find God's hand in everything and feel His spirit and influence in so many ways," Christian said thoughtfully. "For example, I've felt it in the majestic mountains back home, through certain kinds of music, in acts of kindness . . ."

"So, what brought you to the Church?" Teira asked as they walked along the beach.

"Back home I worked with a guy named Dallin Olaveson," Christian replied. "We hit it off quickly and got along great. Dallin was a member of the LDS Church. He and his wife, Jessica, have two daughters. The oldest is three—her name is Sidney—and the other is a year old. That's Carly. Sidney seemed to be pretty clumsy as a baby. She was always falling—getting bumps and bruises. Although at first they didn't think a lot about it, because she was learning to walk, they did ask the doctor if that was normal. He wasn't alarmed. He said children learning to walk do that and told them to keep the floor clear and cover the sharp corners of their furniture. He assured them she would 'grow into her feet,' if you can believe that."

Teira shook her head.

"Nothing changed, and they didn't feel good about what the doctor had said so they got a second opinion. This doctor said pretty much the same thing. She was eating and sleeping well. She was happy and healthy."

Teira looked at Christian. "So the biggest problem was her clumsiness?"

"Pretty much. One day, shortly before I was due to come here, Jessica took the girls to a park to play. Sidney was running toward her mother for a drink. Jessica said that midstride Sidney got this terrible look on her face, went pale, and collapsed. She went into a seizure. By the time the paramedics got there, Sidney had come out of the seizure but was delirious, so they took her to the hospital where Dallin met them."

"What was wrong with her?" Teira asked, afraid to hear the answer.

"They suspected a brain tumor. They ran a bunch of tests and scans. The preliminary results showed a mass. By nighttime, however, Sidney was back to her usual self, so they let her go back home the next day with the promise they would check with a specialist."

He looked out at the sea then back at Teira. "But there's another part to the story. I went to the hospital to see if there was anything I could do. I love those two little girls like nieces. Dallin had called his dad to help give Sidney a priesthood blessing. I have to be honest with you, Teira. I figured there was a god, but I could count on one hand the hours in my life I'd spent praying to Him. But I knew Dallin was faithful and had a good family. I figured their prayers deserved to reach God's ears. I didn't know if it was fair for me to all of a sudden ask for something, but I was willing to give it a shot. I made a few promises that day. For one thing, I promised God I would pray more often if He would bless Sidney."

Christian grinned and squeezed Teira's hand. "During Sidney's blessing I was overcome by a powerful feeling I didn't recognize. I knew I needed to find out what it was. When I got to Denmark, I took a walk one day and found myself in front of the LDS temple. Elder

Wolff and Elder Olson were there. They later told me they'd prayed for someone who needed to hear their message and had felt inspired to go there that day. Anyway, when they introduced themselves and I learned that their religion was the same as Dallin's, I knew they had what I needed. I will never forget what they have done for me."

Teira's eyes filled with tears. "What about Sidney?" she asked quietly. "How is she?"

"Further tests showed that the mass was gone. Dallin's last e-mail says she's as graceful as a ballerina now."

That was when Teira's tears spilled over.

"I can't help but think how much my life has changed by witnessing that miracle," Christian said.

"Our Heavenly Father is aware of our needs, and oftentimes people are instruments in His hands to meet them," Teira said.

"I seem to keep meeting people who make a big impression in my life."

The two troll ballerina dolls are for Sidney and Carly, Teira concluded happily. She felt bad for misjudging him, especially now that his story had touched her so deeply.

They walked along the shore toward a lighthouse that rose from the sand to give guidance to seafarers on their journeys. It was an impressive site. Then they turned and walked back to catch the bus to the souvenir shop. Afterward they drove to the Skagen Art Museum.

From the 1870s to the turn of the twentieth century, Skagen was an international venue for young artists. Paintings of magnificent landscapes, beaches, fishing villages, and local people still hang there and are among the most admired and beloved Scandinavian art. Christian and Teira walked through the museum admiring the artists' favorite motifs.

Next they crossed the road to Brondums Hotel for a dinner of fresh fish. Teira had never tasted anything as wonderful as the flounder.

"It's not Sveedesh feesh," Christian teased.

Teira sputtered with laughter. "It's better! You can poot dat in der Sveedesh kookin bookin!"

After they had finished dinner, it was time to start the hour-long drive back to Aalborg.

They entered the city, both silently regretting that the day was ending. It seemed that before Teira could blink, they were seated in the plane. She looked out at the city lights and then back at Christian as the pilot waited for clearance from ground control to take off. "I hate to see this day end," she said. "It's been wonderful. Thank you so much."

"We can do it again. There's still a lot of Denmark to see before our time here is up."

"That sounds good," Teira said, but thought that the "before our time here is up" part sounded too final. She refused to dwell on it. Nothing, she determined, would mar her perfect day.

"In fact," Christian continued, "I have to go to a party two weeks from Friday. It's for a bunch of bigwigs. To be honest, I hate these kinds of things, but since the company is receiving an award, it's a must-go. Can I talk you into suffering with me?"

"ComTech is already getting an award?"

"Well, the company we're merging with is, so its owner wants me to tag along. It's a formal affair. Want to party hardy?"

Teira laughed. "You bet. Count me in."

* * *

By the time they reached ComTech, Teira barely had time to walk in and begin her training class. Christian went to his office and later slipped into the back to observe the class.

He noticed Rolf watching Teira so intently that he hadn't realized Christian was in the room. Not that his presence commanded recognition, but Christian was surprised the man would be caught shirking his responsibilities. More disconcerting was the way he looked at Teira. He was practically staring her down. It made Christian's defenses rise.

At the end of class, Teira stood at the door and thanked everyone for coming and reminded them that the next night would be the last. Then she walked with them to the lobby of ComTech where Rolf stood by his security desk. It was at that point Rolf noticed Christian and sprang forward with a greeting and a handshake.

This wasn't the time to talk frankly to the man, Christian knew, but he'd do it soon. "Please see everyone out," he said. "I'll help Miss

Palmer clean up the room and get ready to leave. I have a few things I'd like to discuss with her." Christian didn't wait for a reply. "Does Rolf always watch you like that?" he asked when they were out of earshot.

"Kind of creepy, isn't it?" Teira grinned. Christian didn't.

"Teira, why didn't you tell me?"

"Tell you what? That the security guard looks at me funny? While I'm at it, I might as well tell you he talks funny too."

Christian stopped in his tracks. "What do you mean by that?"

"I don't know how to explain it. He says things that might have a double meaning, I guess. Maybe it's the language barrier."

"Can you give me an example?"

Teira thought over the past week and gave him a couple of examples. Christian listened quietly. By this time, they were back in the classroom and sitting at a table with the door closed.

"That's what you meant the other night went you said he was a different kind of character?" Christian asked.

"Yes."

"I'm with you. I don't like the way he watches you, either. Come on, I'll walk you to your car. It is, after all, the end of our first date." Once they got there, Christian took the keys from Teira's hand and unlocked her door for her. "One of these dates, I'll walk you to your door instead of to your car."

"I look forward to that. But," she said, "I have to warn you, I have nosy neighbors."

"Isn't your nearest neighbor a mile away?"

"Mrs. Swensen lives a boring life. I happen to know she has binoculars and keeps everyone informed of all the latest gossip."

Christian laughed and held Teira's hand up to his lips, kissing it gently before helping her into the car. "I plan to give her plenty to talk about soon." Christian winked. "I'll give you time to get home before I call."

"Thank you for everything today," she added with a smile. "I had a wonderful time."

"I should thank you. You had the management in the palm of your hand in the meeting, and you had me there the rest of the day. I'll call you," he promised as he shut her car door.

19

Teira awoke Friday morning feeling refreshed. It was the last day of her evening classes and it was a relief to know she would no longer have to endure Rolf's strange looks or tendency to talk in riddles.

With a light heart she was driving down the motorway toward Copenhagen when she decided that today would be the perfect day to see her grandmother. It was payday and she could celebrate by taking her grandmother shopping. She'd buy a new dress for each of them, and then she and Grethe could stop for lunch afterward. She didn't feel guilty about missing work; she'd certainly put in enough overtime. So Teira called the office and left a message that she'd be in after lunch. In an emergency, they could reach her on her cell.

Grethe was thrilled by the unexpected surprise. Although she was reluctant at first to accept an expensive gift, Teira finally convinced her to pick out not only a pretty skirt but a silky flowered blouse and matching sweater too. As a final splurge, Teira added a new handkerchief, which she used to dab her grandmother's eyes when the older woman cried over having such a thoughtful, generous granddaughter.

With her thoughts on the upcoming party, Teira tried on several different gowns and finally settled on a dark green dress that was her grandmother's favorite.

With purchases in hand, they walked to a nearby sandwich shop called Ida Davidsen's for a lunch of Denmark's famous *smorrebrod*—open-faced sandwiches. The shop offered over 270 different kinds of sandwiches and had been a family-owned business since 1888. There, Teira and Grethe laughed and giggled like schoolgirls. Grethe said Zella came to the senior center periodically to visit with her and had been such a sweet friend to her.

Too soon it was time for Teira to take her grandmother back to the center and go to work.

At ComTech she learned that Christian was out. He had gone to one of the other offices.

He still hadn't returned by the time her evening class ended. After she wished her class good luck and bid them good-bye, Rolf saw them to the van while she went back to the classroom to clean up and prepare to leave for the night.

Teira picked up stray papers, threw them in the trash, and bent to pick up a bottle of soda pop that someone had brought in. It slipped from her fingers and spilled. She hurried to the janitor's closet down the hall for a wet sponge and paper towels to clean up the sticky liquid.

Luckily, it came out of the carpet fairly easily, so it wasn't long before she was able to gather her things and head for home. When she reached the front of the building, Rolf was nowhere to be seen. She wondered whether she should wait a few minutes to let him know she was leaving, or go ahead and slip out the door and call it a day. Surely he would note her absence as he made his rounds.

She finally let herself out into the parking lot and walked toward her car, wishing her eyes would adjust more quickly to the dark. With keys in hand, Teira reached her car and pressed the security release. Nothing happened. Her brows creased in confusion. Usually there were two quick beeps to let her know the alarm had been deactivated.

Teira slipped the key in the lock and found that the car had already been unlocked and the alarm turned off. She must have forgotten to lock it earlier. Berating herself for such carelessness, especially in light of the letters and DVD, Teira looked around nervously. Because of the darkness, her vision was obscured. She could see even less as she tried to peer through the tinted windows into the interior of her car.

Then she noticed that the vehicle had an awkward tilt to it. Looking at the back tire, her suspicions were confirmed. The tire was flat. Groaning in dismay, Teira opened the back door, tossed her attaché case in the car along with her jacket, and slammed the door. Then she noticed her front tire was flat as well.

A prickling sensation ran up her neck. Two flat tires at the same time? That was a little too coincidental, wasn't it?

Teira walked around to the other side of the car. Only one flat there.

Teira's head jerked up as her eyes darted all around. As dark as it was, she could see very little, but the shadows of the night formed ominous shapes. The shrubbery could easily conceal the perpetrator who had vandalized her car.

Frightened, Teira walked quickly back to the building for help, only to find the doors already locked. She pounded on the glass, but Rolf was nowhere to be seen. Fear overtook her and her heart began to race. She was outside in the dark, alone, with no way to escape except on foot. What if the person who had sabotaged her car was still out there . . . waiting? Was he watching her now?

Teira pounded harder on the door and called out for Rolf to open up. There was no response.

She willed herself not to panic. Rolf would see her car and come looking for her. Wouldn't he?

Fearing it was futile, but without a better plan, Teira was still pounding on the door and trying to peer through the tinted glass when a hand reached out of the darkness and grabbed her shoulder.

Teira screamed. Then she whipped around, ready to swing or kick out in self-defense.

There stood Christian.

Teira fell into his arms, and he held her tightly to try to quiet her trembling body. "What's going on?"

Before she could reply, Rolf appeared at the door and unlocked it from the inside. "Good evening, Mr. Tanner," he said. "Miss Palmer? What happened here?" He opened the door and stepped back to allow Teira and Christian to enter.

"I was locked out," Teira said, not altogether convinced that Rolf didn't know that already.

"I always meet you here," he said. "When you didn't come, I went looking for you, but you were nowhere to be found."

"I decided to leave," Teira said. "But when I got out to my car, I had three flat tires so I came back for help. The doors were locked." Her cheeks burned in embarrassment. Now that she'd said it aloud, her former panic seemed overblown. But that hadn't been all that frightened her. She could have sworn she was not out there alone.

Tears of confusion and frustration, mingled with embarrassment, welled up in Teira's eyes, but she refused to cry and add to her humiliation.

"What do you mean *tires*?" Christian asked. "More than one?"

"Three of four," she muttered. "I guess that either makes me extremely unlucky or proves someone truly dislikes me."

Christian's expression darkened. "Rolf, let me use your flashlight, will you?"

"Sure," the guard said. "I'll go with you."

"Me too!" Teira said. There was no way she was waiting in there alone.

Back at her car and with more light now, Teira's fears were confirmed. All three tires had a deep puncture about an inch wide—as if someone had quickly walked around and stabbed them with a knife. It had been fast, clean, easy.

"I'll call the fleet manager and see what he wants us to do with the car," Christian said. "Most likely he has a garage he'll want it towed to, but I don't think we should leave it in a dark parking lot overnight."

"I'm sorry," Teira murmured.

"You have nothing to apologize for," he said quickly. "What I want to know is why you were out here alone in the first place." Christian's eyes narrowed as he turned them on Rolf.

"That would be my fault," Teira said. "I should have waited for Rolf, but I was impatient to get home."

The guard shrugged nonchalantly. "I can't help it if female employees won't wait for an escort."

Christian was clearly unhappy with the response. The worry that had shone in his eyes was now replaced by a flash of anger. Rolf glared back for a moment, but when Christian's eyebrow shot up, he backed down and looked away. He got the message.

"I'll take Miss Palmer home," Christian told the guard. "Rather than keep her waiting while we talk this over, I will see you first thing Monday morning." His voice lowered for emphasis. "And I do mean first thing. Be in my office the minute your shift ends."

"Very good, sir," Rolf said.

The tone of Rolf's voice told Teira he thought the idea of meeting with Christian was anything but good.

* * *

After being assured by the fleet manager that the tow truck was on its way, Christian drove Teira home. On the way he said, "I don't like this."

"I was frightened to death," Teira confessed. "I guess my imagination got the better of me, but I kept thinking 'what if they're still out there?'"

"They could have been."

"How did you know to come?" she asked.

"I'd been trying to reach you on your cell, but there was no answer. I was nearby so I thought I'd stop in to see if you'd left. I saw your car in the lot and went looking for you."

"I left my cell in my purse when I threw my things in the car," Teira said. "The car being unlocked should have warned me that something was amiss." She considered. "I should have known I'd locked it. Do you suppose it's some kind of warning that they could mess with my car like they did Kort's?"

Teira had voiced what Christian had foremost in his mind. He looked over at her and then back at the road, his insides churning. "I honestly don't know, but I have to assume that if they wanted to sabotage your car, they would have. They wouldn't warn you first. They'd just do it."

Despite what he'd told Teira, Christian had his doubts—doubts which led him to give explicit instructions to the garage to thoroughly inspect the car, top to bottom, before returning it the following week.

* * *

On a beautiful, sunny Saturday afternoon, Teira sat beside her grandmother and watched Christian enter the waters of baptism. The Spirit was so strong it was felt by everyone in the room.

Elder Wolff performed the baptism. Afterward, Elder Olson confirmed Christian a member of the Church and gave him the gift of the Holy Ghost. Each of the missionaries spoke for a few minutes and then Christian's bishop spoke. Then Christian stood to bear his testimony.

"Every day I see what a fast-paced, technological world we live in," he said. "The world has become so advanced that it tries to rationalize and explain everything. Even when we experience a spiritual event in our life, the world finds it far too easy to reason it away rather than see it as the spiritual manifestation it really is. We rely too much on our own intelligence and not enough on our Father in Heaven. I was that way. But I have been lucky enough to have had a life-changing experience as well as good examples of members of the Church to spark my interest in the gospel, but it wasn't enough to sustain me. I had to find out for myself what was missing in my life. The answer came when I met these two missionaries you heard from today . . ."

Teira listened intently as Christian bore his testimony. He closed by saying, "I hope that I will always remember how right this day feels and build on the testimony that burns within me now. I want you to know that I *know* my Savior lives."

Teira was touched beyond words. Seeing someone discover and accept the gospel renewed and strengthened her own testimony. It reaffirmed what was so exciting and unique about the Church. Teira looked at her grandmother and knew Grethe had been touched by the Spirit as well.

After the baptism, the bishop's wife served dessert in the cultural hall. Teira talked with the missionaries and learned that Elder Wolff was from Idaho and Elder Olson from Washington state. As she sat listening to them visit with Christian, she noted the camaraderie between them and suspected that Christian would keep in contact. They were impressive young men.

After everyone left the stake center, Christian and Teira drove Grethe home. Then Christian surprised Teira with an invitation to Tivoli Gardens. It was dusk as they arrived at the historic main entrance and walked past the famous Pantomime Theatre and the Concert Hall. The garden was filled with places to eat, games to play, and rides to enjoy. They walked around Tivoli's lakeside, which was once part of the old city moat. Ducks darted beneath the water while swans glided back and forth in search of bread crumbs guests tossed to them. All around were the most colorful varieties of tulips Teira had ever seen. The beautiful tulips, roses, chrysanthemums, and other flowers grew in beautiful wooden baskets. The fragrance was as aromatic as perfume.

"It's beautiful here," Teira said.

"It sure is," Christian agreed. "It's quite a place. It's been quite a day." They strolled, holding hands, beneath millions of tiny bright lights that were sprinkled amid the trees and flowers to create a fairyland as the sky darkened.

"How do you feel about it all?" Teira asked.

Christian took a deep breath. "Wow. How can I put it into words? Exhilarated. Clean. Excited. I have been very fortunate in my life. I've been given some good opportunities that have enabled me to achieve, but nothing compares to this feeling inside. I'm humbled by what I have received and by what is now required of me."

Teira walked with Christian in silence for a few steps before she spoke. "There are times when life seems overwhelming, but there's a scripture that helps me keep things in perspective. It's in Doctrine and Covenants 20:14. 'And those who receive it in faith, and work righteousness, shall receive a crown of eternal life.' With your faith and good works, you'll be able to accomplish all that is required. We're all here learning, growing, progressing—increasing our faith and understanding. It's a lifetime journey."

Christian reached over, put his arm around Teira, and drew her closer to him. He leaned over and kissed her lightly on the temple. "Thank you for sharing this day with me," he whispered.

"I wouldn't have missed it for the world."

Off in the distance the Tivoli fireworks showcase began its remarkable display.

It was the only chance Christian would have to see the security tapes before Rolf came back on shift, so Sunday morning he was at the front doors of ComTech. He had called ahead to let Henrik Klemensen, the security guard on duty, know he was stopping by.

When Christian entered the security office, Henrik stood and shook his hand. "Good to see you again. It's been awhile since you've been down here."

"How are your wife and children?" Christian asked.

"They're fine. What is this about the tape you mentioned on the phone?"

"I hoped you could show me the surveillance tape from Friday night," Christian said. "An employee had a problem in the parking lot around eight or shortly thereafter. Can we look at that?"

"Sure can. It will take me a minute. Have a seat and make yourself comfortable." He took in Christian's attire. "I thought you decided to take Sundays off."

"Actually, I'm going to church," Christian said as he loosened his tie and sat down next to Henrik before the double rows of security monitors. Every few seconds one screen or another switched to a new scene of various areas throughout and around the ComTech building.

"Is that why you quit coming in on Sundays?" Henrik asked.

"Yes."

Henrik turned to the screen and fast-forwarded the tape. "This is the one you want. The numbers in the corner show the time . . . and here we go."

Christian and Henrik watched a tape of shots of each area compiled into one smooth-running film. At eight fifteen they watched Teira walk down the hall and into the closet carrying a sponge. The next frame showed the closed door and Teira walking back toward the training room. A few seconds later, her briefcase in hand and her coat thrown over her arm, she shut the door to the classroom and walked to the front lobby. She paced back and forth for a few moments before walking out into the night. Another frame showed Rolf at the front, sitting with his feet up on the desk. Henrik cleared his throat. In the next frame Rolf was gone from the screen.

"Stop the tape," Christian said. "Could you rewind and show me that again?" This time he looked more closely. "Why is he there one second and gone the next?"

"It's just the camera switching angles." Henrik played the tape further to show that Rolf was wandering through the empty halls. "There he is now," Henrik pointed out.

Teira didn't come back into view until Rolf opened the doors for her and Christian.

There were no shots of the parking lot.

Christian pointed that out and asked Henrik about it.

"We have cameras set up," he explained, "but it's too dark at night to pick up much so we don't record. We need better lighting out there if we want to film it."

"Do you know if the guard sitting here saw anything unusual on the monitors?" Christian asked.

"I was on the cameras that night," Henrik said. "And I didn't see anything. What happened?"

"One of our employee's cars was vandalized."

"I assure you, I keep a close watch on these cameras. Still, it might have happened after dark. We sure could use some lights out there," Henrik remarked.

"I'll check into it. It's a safety issue that can't be overlooked." Christian stood to leave and ejected the tape. "I'd like to keep this if you don't mind."

"Sure thing," Henrik replied. "I hope everything's okay."

"Oh, yeah. Fine. I'm only wondering what happened."

"I'm sorry the tape was of no help. Have you talked to Rolf? He may have heard or seen something."

Christian shook his head. But he *would* talk to Rolf. It was the first thing on his agenda Monday morning, and he was looking forward to it.

* * *

Teira and Grethe prepared an authentic Danish dinner for Christian on Sunday afternoon—*frikadeller,* or Danish meatballs. As they worked together in the kitchen, anticipating his arrival, wonderful aromas filled the air. Teira's mouth watered.

Together they sang Danish songs Teira had learned in childhood and laughed when they discovered she had not remembered them correctly.

Her favorites songs, "Se den lille Kattekilling" and "Tinge—linge—later" were about a kitten wanting to play with a mouse and a little tin soldier. These brought back the sweetest memories. They giggled as they sang together and laughed at the silliness of Teira's mistakes. Half the time, her incorrect version didn't make sense.

"Well, no wonder! I thought whoever made up the words to these songs was crazy!" Teira laughed. "I figured the Danes needed English lessons!"

"My granddaughter needs Danish lessons," Grethe said, laughing so hard that tears ran down her cheeks. "And a few singing lessons wouldn't hurt, either!" Although the implication was that Teira was off-key, it was more likely she had learned the wrong tune in various places.

Teira and her grandmother decided Grethe would stay the night and return to the senior center on Monday morning. As they stirred pots and mixed dough together, the doorbell rang. Teira dropped the spoon on the counter when it rang again. Looking at her grandmother in surprise she said, "Looks like we have an impatient caller!"

The bell rang again.

"Ya!" her grandmother said, giggling.

"I'm coming!" Teira called out as she went to answer. Her grandmother followed, thinking it might be Christian surprising them with an early visit.

Teira opened the door to Adam. The man was unshaven and his clothes were wrinkled.

"Adam? This is a surprise," she said, not mentioning how unpleasant the surprise was. "I didn't know you knew where I lived." The idea made her uncomfortable. Feeling her grandmother's eyes on her, she at last stepped back and said hesitantly, "Come in."

"I didn't realize you had company," he said.

"Hardly company, this is my grandmother. It's her home. Grandma, this is Adam Carson. I work with him. Adam, I'd like you to meet my grandmother, Grethe Pedersen."

Adam shook her grandmother's hand. "Pleased to meet you," he said, though not warmly.

"Do you want to come in and sit down?" Teira offered, along with a silent prayer that he'd refuse.

"No, I can see you're busy. I was in the area and thought I'd stop by."

Teira wasn't convinced. Adam obviously had something on his mind. His eyes darted about nervously. He had come for a specific reason. Finding out that she wasn't alone had changed his plans. She wondered how he'd found out where she was staying. She'd kept the information very private on purpose.

Thinking she was doing her granddaughter a kindness, Grethe quickly excused herself and left the room before Teira could finish objecting.

"Are you sure you didn't want to have a seat?" she asked, backing away a little instinctively.

"Maybe for a minute," he conceded.

She thought so. "So what are you doing out this way?"

"Teira, I need to tell you something and I don't know how." He sank onto a chair, careful to keep his distance.

"Just say it. It's usually easier that way." Teira was apprehensive. She wasn't at all sure she wanted to hear what Adam had come to say. By the look on his face, it couldn't be good.

Adam leaned forward and put his hands over his face. At last he looked up with pain-filled eyes. "I love you."

Teira sat silently, wondering what to say. She hadn't missed Adam's growing infatuation with her—nobody in the office had—but *love?*

This confession was different and caused her heart to soften. She didn't want to hurt him.

She was still wondering what to say when he interrupted her thoughts. "No comment? I didn't think there would be. There's somebody else, isn't there?"

She nodded.

"I thought as much. Would you say we're friends?"

Probably not, she thought. But she said, "Of course."

"Then I'm going to ask the biggest favor of my life. Promise me you'll hear me out."

"Is that the favor?"

"Yes."

"You're not asking for the world, are you?" she said, trying to make her tone light—and failing.

"Teira, you have the power to destroy my world," he said.

The anguish that was so evident on his face got her attention. She felt the worry lines between her brows deepen as she listened intently.

"When I first came to Denmark," Adam began, "Sophie Blackman and I were introduced to each other by Christian. In one of our conversations, I mentioned my interest in you. After the company party she acted as though we were friends. You know she's planning to marry Christian. She even said as much that following Monday after the company party in your office. Remember?"

"But—" she started to interrupt.

Adam looked at Teira and she said, "Go on."

"I know he doesn't feel the same," Adam said bitterly. "Any idiot who's seen him look at you knows that." He leaned forward. "The point is that Sophie is obsessed with Christian. She insists they were meant for each other, but she believes he's had a thing for you since he met you and that he's been pursuing you." He steepled his fingers and wouldn't meet Teira's eye. "So Sophie came to me with a plan. That friendship she offered? It was just a way to use me to get what she wanted. She said Christian hates incompetence, so we decided to do little things to make you look bad and hopefully turn him off that way. Not enough to get you fired, of course, because that wouldn't achieve my purposes."

"And what were *your* purposes?" Teira asked, knowing the answer even as she asked the question.

"To keep you here with me, but away from Christian."

"So *you* sabotaged me."

"Yes and no. That's why I'm here. Teira, I only messed up the meeting I knew Christian would be there to see. I sent the one letter that was on your desk, and the e-mail." He looked defensive. "And if you read through them again, you'll see that you might have misinterpreted them."

Teira's jaw dropped. "You tried to ruin me in front of my boss, sent anonymous letters with cryptic messages, and now you have the nerve to sit there and fault me for not interpreting your games correctly?" She was astounded at his gall.

"That's not what I meant!" he said quickly. "I wrote them. I know what they said. The first one said you found success coming here, but your days could be numbered so watch yourself. The second was about playing games. I felt you were playing games with my feelings because by then I felt sure you knew how I felt about you. The thing about your days being numbered was a warning about Sophie doing anything she could think of to get you out of the way."

Teira sat dumbfounded. It was twisted logic, especially for a guy who was supposed to be so brilliant. It made her want to scream.

"I wanted to warn you," he repeated. "It's all I could say considering that the owner's daughter put me up to it."

"Don't you get it, Adam?" Teira said, trying to remain calm while feeling outraged for what he had put her through. "Even if Sophie was the mastermind, you did the deed."

"I know," he said, looking more contrite than Teira would have believed if she hadn't seen it. "And I *am* sorry. That's why I'm here. I came to tell you what I did. Teira, I never meant to hurt you. I didn't even want to embarrass you. I just wanted you to notice me." He threw up his hands. "Everything backfired and now the whole thing is out of control. I'm sorry."

Before she could respond he continued, "But that's not the most important thing you need to know." Now his face was grave. "I couldn't stop thinking about the other threats you told me about—the DVD and the letter that came with it. You have to know Sophie and I had nothing to do with that." He leaned forward. "Teira, you have a much bigger problem than anything we created."

21

In a word, Christian was furious. His dark eyes shadowed and his lips turned downward as he struggled to keep his anger in check.

Grethe had stayed at home while Teira and Christian went for a barefoot walk on the beach after dinner. He had noticed Teira's subdued mood and now she had finally confessed what caused it.

He couldn't believe Adam's nerve. "He actually asked *you* to go to bat for him to keep his job?"

"Not really," Teira said. "He knew when he came to me there was a good chance he'd be fired." She sighed and took the plunge. "But you need him, Christian. He's been in on this merger since the beginning. Changing hands now would seriously affect the transition. He's a department head. You can't get anybody else up to speed fast enough."

Christian's frown deepened. "Keeping him on goes against everything I believe in. Regardless of his motivation and last-minute confession, what he did was totally unacceptable!"

"I know," Teira said quietly.

They walked farther along the beach, both lost in thought. Teira broke the silence. "Christian, looking at it from another perspective, his part was rather harmless. The letters *could* have been interpreted as a warning. And the workbooks, well, that project was funded by Sophie, after all. She put him up to everything. I know he needs to take responsibility, but I hate to see everybody at ComTech suffer because of his mistakes. And what about Sophie? She gets off scot-free because she's the owner's daughter? That hardly seems fair."

Christian's eyebrow rose. "Anything else?"

"Just a closing argument. I have bigger worries than the Adam thing—and it's thanks to him I know that I do." She smiled up at him. "Okay, I'm done. Just know I'll respect and support any decision you make."

"Thank you. You made some good points, counselor, but the jury is still out. One thing is assured though. The owner's daughter is on trial as well."

They paused to look out over the ocean. Christian held Teira's hand and gently rubbed the back of it with his thumb. They watched the waves crash into the shore. After a minute or more Teira said quietly, "Penny for them."

"I was thinking about Grethe trying so hard to push us together," Christian said. "And about her telling us about the magic of a first kiss." Grinning, he turned and cupped her cheek in his palm.

Teira giggled. "It was the most singularly mortifying day of my life to date."

Their noses touched as Christian looked deep into her eyes. Teira felt the warmth of his breath against her lips as he spoke. "I have a lot to thank her for," he said. By now his lips were barely brushing hers. It would be only a moment before he indulged.

"So do I," Teira whispered as she closed her eyes.

He kissed her so lightly that Teira wondered if she'd dreamt it.

That was all it took for the glowing embers to flare to life. Immediately they came together for the long-awaited kiss. Christian's arms encircled Teira's waist and gently he pulled her closer. Teira's arms slowly went up around his neck.

After the kiss, Christian leaned his forehead against hers. Teira wound her fingers into the silky strands of hair at the nape of his neck while he lightly kissed her cheek. The kiss had been everything she dreamed it would be—and so much more.

* * *

After Christian left, Teira and Grethe settled down on the couch in the living room to talk. Spurred by her earlier discovery of the uniform, Teira steered the conversation to the days just after the war and Soren's death.

"Everybody knew that King Christian was never without his ring," Grethe said. "So, of course everyone noticed when all of a sudden he stopped wearing it."

"Why did the Royal Guard come to see you?" Teira asked. "Was it awful?"

"I suspect they went to everybody with any connection to the king. As I said, your grandfather and King Christian had been friends. When the men asked me about the ring, I was treated very kindly. I didn't know anything, of course."

"It seems to me," Teira said, "that the fact they were looking at all gives credence to the theory that the ring was stolen, or that the king gave it to someone rather than lost it. Don't you think?"

"Of course it does," Grethe replied. "But I never saw it. I'm afraid I was no help to them at all."

"They must have believed you if they never asked again."

"The Royal Guard didn't return, but one of their own did."

Teira was intrigued. "Who?"

"The man I'd met the day Soren died. The one I told you about."

"The one who was supposed to deliver the message?"

"Yes, he's the one. He came here asking after the ring. I told him the Royal Guard had already inquired and I was afraid I could be of no help to either of them. I knew nothing."

"Grandma," Teira said, "there has to be a way to find out who he is. If we can track him down, I think he could answer a lot of questions. Was he part of the Freedom Council?"

"My first instinct would be to say yes, but I can't be certain of it. I just don't know, Teira. I wasn't supposed to know anything. It was the only way I could be protected—the only way we could protect our daughter. I don't know who he was, but I can't imagine that Soren would have asked anybody else for help."

Teira pondered. "Maybe he was part of the council, but maybe he was also working with the German soldiers and Grandpa didn't know it."

"Oh, Teira, do not misunderstand. It was the gestapo, not the soldiers, whom I feared. I met many German soldiers who were nice to me. I also feared and resented the Danish Nazi party. War has a way of bringing out the very best and the very worst of human nature regardless of which side you are on, and it had very unfortunate consequences. In the end, far too many innocent people died."

Teira thought of the people who were in the train car the day of the explosion. Tears sprang to her eyes. Then her thoughts turned to her grandfather's injuries. "I can't begin to imagine what it must have been like for you that day," Teira said, her voice barely above a whisper.

Grethe tearfully recalled the knock on the door that had come shortly after sundown on that fateful day. A stranger, a doctor, had come to tell her that Soren had been seriously burned and injured. He said he didn't know the details, only that it was dangerous for her husband to be taken to a hospital because a man so badly wounded after an explosion at the train station would be sure to attract attention from the gestapo. Grethe knew they couldn't take any chances. If a member of the Resistance was captured, he risked torture and deportation to a prison camp or possibly execution.

The doctor said that in addition to the severe burns there was a bullet wound to his side and lacerations from the explosion. He assured Grethe that he had done the best he could for Soren, but she would need to tend him through the night. He promised to return in the early morning. Perhaps by then it would be safe to take him to a hospital. A few minutes later, another car pulled up and an unconscious Soren was brought into the house on a makeshift stretcher. Tears streamed down Grethe's face as she told Teira how merciful it was that he'd never regained consciousness during those long hours before he passed away. The agony would have been unbearable.

Grethe recalled falling to her knees in anguish at the sight of her husband's injuries, despite the doctor's warning. The look and smell of his charred flesh caused her stomach to roil and her head to spin. She never knew where she found the inner strength to follow the doctor's orders in tending him.

Thankfully, a neighbor came for Hanne and took her away for the night so that she was spared her parents' anguish. Tears rolled down Teira's cheeks as her grandmother concluded. "He never opened his eyes or said a word to me. He lay there, each breath more painful than the one before. His wounds were so severe that although I wanted to beg him not to leave me, I knew I couldn't. Instead I sang to him and told him how proud I was of him. He was such a good man. After I said I loved him, he died in my arms. A part of me died with him that night."

Teira held her grandmother in her arms while she sobbed. When Grethe recovered she said, "I only carried on because my daughter gave me something to live for. I knew she had her life to live too." She looked into her granddaughter's face. "Having you come home to me has given me new purpose once again." She managed a wan smile and changed the subject.

The two women stayed up late, chatting of happier times. But even after Grethe had finally grown tired and gone to bed, Teira couldn't sleep. She lay on her bed, watching the glowing red numbers on the digital clock change from one hour to the next. Her grandmother's words weighed heavily on her mind and her thoughts raced forward like a train plunging down a steep grade totally out of control.

At last Teira shifted positions, turned toward the window, and stared outside. She had to get some sleep before work in the morning. With effort, she forced her thoughts elsewhere. There was only one other place for them to go.

Kissing Christian had been incredible. Possibly too incredible. She wanted to do it again and again. Not that that was a bad thing, but was she kidding herself? One kiss on the beach didn't guarantee happily-ever-after. What happened when the merger was complete and they both left Denmark? Worse, what would happen if they broke up before that? Could she still work for him?

She was relieved when her heart told her that she could. She was a professional. Besides, she'd had more reasons for coming to Denmark than to work for ComTech. She'd wanted to be here for her grandmother. No matter what else happened, this opportunity to better know and love Grethe was one of the greatest blessings in her life.

She wouldn't worry about her relationship with Christian, then. A few dates and one kiss made it a little early for that. She would hope and pray for the best and accept what came.

But she *did* have something to worry about.

Adam's words echoed in her mind. If he hadn't made the DVD or written the truly threatening letter, who had?

She rolled to her side in a fetal position and wrapped her arms around her knees. She had no idea what was going on or why. The letter said they wanted her gone. How *gone* did they mean, exactly? Back to the States gone—or *gone* gone?

With those depressing thoughts rolling around in her mind, Teira finally drifted into a restless sleep.

* * *

When Teira arrived at work on Monday morning, she noticed immediately that the door to Christian's office was closed. By the time she'd finished the morning training and most of the office had gone to lunch, the door was still shut.

Christian's secretary caught her checking once again and said, "He's been in there most of the day. Would you like me to see if he is available for you?"

"Oh, no. That's okay, but thank you." Teira walked back to her office, hating that she'd been caught pining away at Christian's door like a lonely puppy.

So much for her professionalism.

At her desk Teira reached for her purse and pulled out the brochure the receptionist at Christiansborg Palace had given her. Minutes later she walked out the doors of ComTech.

Teira parked her car at the museum and was walking toward it when her cell phone indicated that she had a text message from Christian. Teira couldn't help smiling.

> HI THERE, the message began.
> HI 2 U 2, she replied
> His message came back:
> CAN I C U 2NITE?
> Teira quickly punched the answer into her cell:
> OK WHAT TIME?
> His then wrote: 6 WEAR DARK CAS CLOTHES
> SOUNDS MYSTERIOUS, wrote Teira.
> ENCHANTING
> He signed off.

Hmm, very intriguing! Teira looked at her watch. She had plenty of time to go to the museum and then drive home to shower and change for her date.

* * *

As Teira walked through the museum, her heart pounded wildly in her chest. Her initial reason for coming was to find out if there were prominent members of the Danish Resistance still living, or at the very least to discover what had become of the leaders of the Freedom Council. She wanted to find others who may have known and worked with her grandfather. However, once she stepped inside the museum, she was moved in a totally unexpected way.

Teira knew the Danish Resistance was an underground movement formed to oppose the occupation of the Germans. Denmark had changed during the occupation. There was censorship and intolerance. German troops were stationed throughout the country.

Teira looked at the pictures and read the illustrations that told the story. As German demands increased, so did the acts of sabotage. In August of 1943 the Germans took full authority over the administration of Denmark. This, they felt, gave them the right to deal with the population as they saw fit. They introduced martial law. More photos depicted retaliation killings, burning buildings, and an array of armored tanks and guns unlike any she had ever seen.

She sat and listened to recorded testimonies of those who lived through it and then watched videos of the stark images of war. All gave her a somber appreciation for the hardships the Danes had endured.

But there were triumphs as well. The biggest success of the movement was the relocation of thousands of Danish Jews. Another was the disruption of the railway network.

A lump formed in Teira's throat as she read how after D-day the German troops' arrival from Denmark into France was delayed because of the sabotaged railway. Britain's field marshal called the Danish Resistance movement "second to none."

Her grandfather had contributed to the success, and he had done it because he loved his country. By the end of the war more than 850 members of the Resistance movement had been killed in action, jailed, or sent to concentration camps. Teira looked at the number until it became blurry through the tears. Her grandfather had been one of them.

Why all these people had fought for freedom wasn't a hard concept to grasp. What was difficult to understand was why her grandfather would ever consider turning against his fellow countrymen. But at that moment Teira knew, as indisputably as she knew she was standing there, that he hadn't. She might never be able to prove it, but she would forever believe that something had gone very wrong that day and that her grandfather had paid for the mistake with his life.

Upon leaving the museum, Teira walked past a military base parking lot toward her car. There she ran into the receptionist from Christiansborg Palace—the one who had given her the information about the museum. "You probably don't remember me," she said, "but you gave me a brochure on the Danish Resistance Museum. I've just come from there. It was so interesting!"

The woman smiled. "Did you find the information you were searching for?"

Before Teira had a chance to respond, they were interrupted by someone who approached them from behind Teira. When she turned, her breath caught in her throat. It was the chief of security from the Rosenborg Treasury. Teira could only assume his being near the military base had something to do with the soldiers he supervised at the castle.

"Ah, this is my boyfriend, Olaf," the woman said.

"I believe we've met," Olaf said, his eyes narrowing as if trying to place Teira's face.

"I believe you work security at the Rosenborg Treasury," she said. "I toured the castle a few weeks ago. We talked then."

"And how have you two come to meet?" he asked Eva.

"She was looking for information about the Freedom Council," Eva explained. "I told her she would find the museum helpful."

Olaf looked pointedly at Teira but made no reply. When the silence dragged on too long and became awkward, Teira tried to force a smile. "I'm a history buff, remember?"

Olaf took Eva by the arm. “There are some things one never forgets.”

22

The man could wear anything and look good enough to melt her heart. Tonight Christian came to her door in black jeans and a black sweater with only the band of a T-shirt showing beneath it. With his short, dark hair, he was the epitome of a handsome spy.

"Are we going on a reconnaissance mission?" she asked.

"No, my lady." With a grin, Christian bowed, took her hand, and kissed it. "Allow me?"

Teira laughed as he led her to the driveway and a gleaming silver BMW motorcycle. "What's this?" she asked.

"Besides being one of my fantasies, it's our ticket to another kingdom. Didn't you say you wanted a knight on a fast steed to sweep you off your feet?" His eyes twinkled. "Believe me, this baby has some serious horsepower!"

Teira was thrilled and more than a little touched. "And the dark clothes?"

"So we don't get caught," he said sheepishly. "It's after hours and the magical kingdom closes at dark." He handed her a helmet and put on one of his own. "Ready?"

Teira knew she was grinning from ear to ear but couldn't help herself. Grabbing hold of Christian's shoulder with one hand, she stepped onto the footrest and swung her other leg up and over until she was seated behind him.

Christian felt Teira wiggle onto the bike and settle snugly behind him. A warmness filled him—the one he felt each time he was with her. This feeling was as invigorating as it was calming, and it grew in intensity the more he got to know her.

"Okay, I'm all set to go," she said.

"Hold on tight."

She wrapped her arms around his waist and Christian started the engine. Teira squealed with delight. "This is so cool!"

The evening air blew against their skin as they rode past farmland and stables. Cows dozed in the fields as the first stars of the night glistened in the sky. As they rounded the bend, Christian shifted gears and gunned the throttle. They zoomed down the motorway.

Teira pressed her cheek against Christian's back to keep the wind from blowing her hair in her face. She could feel his warmth and smell the fresh scent of soap mingled with cologne. She closed her eyes, loving every minute that passed. How many more minutes like this would they share? She didn't want her time with him to end.

"Are you okay?" Christian yelled over his shoulder.

"This is great! I feel like I'm flying!" she yelled back.

Teira sighed and held on a little tighter, physically and emotionally. She was thrilled he had been so thoughtful to go to such lengths to fulfill her fairy tale.

Christian pulled the bike off to the side of the road at a town called Klampenborg. They were about twenty minutes from Copenhagen in Zealand.

"What is this place?" Teira asked Christian as she got off the bike.

"Three hundred years ago this area was set aside as a royal hunting ground, but now it's used as a picnic spot. There are herds of deer that roam the park, including species almost extinct in other parts of the world. See those trees over there?" Christian pointed to a grove just past the gated area. "That's the enchanted forest. Care to survey your domain, my lady?"

"Are you sure there are no gangs afoot?" Teira asked, looking around for any sign of security.

"Don't worry, I'll rescue you should the need arise. You're perfectly safe with me."

Somehow she truly felt she was.

Christian parked the bike behind some trees and pulled a bag from each of the two luggage compartments draped over each side of the bike. Then he took Teira's hand and led her to the fence. After helping her over, he followed. Moonlight showed them the path to the picnic area beneath a star-studded sky.

"I came prepared," he said as he spread out a tablecloth. In the center he placed a fruit jar, lit a candle, and dropped it inside so the night breeze wouldn't blow out the flame.

After all this, was she still prepared to let him go if she had to?

"You're quiet tonight," he said, standing in front of her. "Look up there." He pointed to the darkened sky filled with millions of magnificent little lights.

"It's magical," she breathed.

"It sure is. Perfect for our enchanted evening."

Teira smiled.

Christian led her to the "table."

"Care to dine with me, my lady?" he said, pulling deli items from the bags—meat, cheese, bread, and several kinds of fresh fruit. Best of all, he brought out sliced *smorkrger* and held it up with a smile. "I didn't forget."

"You really are my knight in shining armor!"

"I hope so."

They ate, drank fruit juice, laughed, and talked. Hope filled Teira's heart while she stuffed herself silly on the delicious delicacies Christian had brought.

"That was wonderful, but I think I ate too much," Teira said with a groan.

"After the day I had today, I'm afraid I worked up quite an appetite."

"Long day?" she asked.

"Well, I didn't let Adam go," Christian said quietly. "Though I still don't feel good about my decision." When Teira didn't reply, he continued. "He came to me this morning and told me pretty much the same thing he told you. I made sure he knew the only reason he was staying was because you went to bat for him. I would have brought in someone new and trained him myself if I had to. As it was, I told him not to look for a project bonus at the end and told him he was on probation. One more move in the wrong direction and he's gone."

"It's more than Adam deserves," Teira said, "but I don't think you'll regret your decision."

"Speaking of something I won't regret," he continued, "Sophie is catching a flight to L.A.—tonight, if possible."

"She's leaving?"

"She's been . . . persuaded to go after bigger game," he said ruefully.

"Really? It couldn't have been easy to get her off your trail."

"Actually, it wasn't that hard. But, I had reinforcements."

"Meaning her father?" Teira asked incredulously.

Christian nodded. "And I didn't have to go to Blackman myself." He grinned. "He and I were on a conference call when Sophie ignored my secretary and burst into my office. Before I could say anything, she started defending her part in the scheme she and Adam initiated. She was saying how she'd done it all for me when she realized her father was listening in on the speaker phone."

Teira tried to suppress a smile.

"Understandably," Christian continued, "the idea that his own daughter had threatened and sabotaged a key employee to get to me didn't sit well with Mr. Blackman." He leaned back. "Frankly, I was impressed with him—as a CEO and as a father. He handled it beautifully."

By now Teira's smile was full blown.

"Now that that's settled, why do I get the feeling there's something on your mind?" he asked.

Teira looked up at Christian in surprise.

"Come on, you're usually quick to laugh, easy to smile, but tonight you seem melancholy. It's in your eyes."

Teira took a deep breath and looked away.

Christian moved her face back toward his. "You can tell me."

"I suppose I can't help but be worried about everything that's happening."

"Did something else come up that you haven't told me about?" Christian asked.

"No, it's not that. I just keep wondering what it all means. I feel like I could go crazy with worry. I wonder who it could be, what it means, what it's connected to, if anybody else I know is in danger. Now that I know Sophie and Adam are only partially responsible, it leaves the field wide open. It's frustrating. And a little creepy."

"You're not in this alone," Christian said, looking into her eyes. "I'm here to help slay the dragons, you know."

"Thank you," Teira said as she leaned over and hugged Christian.

"It's what knights are supposed to do," he said with a wink.

Wrapped in his arms, Teira gave a contented sigh.

Christian pulled back. "Let's walk."

Teira nodded and took Christian's hand as he led her along the darkened path between tree branches. As they walked along, Christian let go of Teira's hand long enough to pull a few short pine sprigs from their boughs. After some twisting, he showed her how he had managed to manipulate them into a circle.

He placed it on her head. "A crown of emerald green for the fairest princess in all the land."

Teira sighed with pleasure. "I don't think anybody could ever top this date!"

"Nobody had better even try," Christian said.

* * *

Christian took Teira home. "So I finally get to walk you to your door," he said. "Do you suppose Mrs. Swensen is watching?" Christian asked, clasping his fingers around Teira's waist.

"Do you want her to?" Teira asked. She brought her hands up to his shoulders.

Christian shook his head. "I'd rather have the privacy. But if she is, she's in for a real treat."

Teira, mesmerized by his dark eyes, smiled softly when she saw the slight grin playing on his lips. When Christian leaned forward, she was barely aware of her eyes closing or the sigh that escaped before he kissed her.

"Mm, that was nice," she said.

"*Nice*? Only nice?"

"There's a lot to be said for nice."

"Clearly I'll have to try harder." He kissed her again, this time more thoroughly, and left her speechless.

* * *

During the next week, daily visits and calls to her grandmother assured Teira that Grethe was fine. Her home remained undisturbed and no more unexpected deliveries came her way. The previous mountains and valleys of her life had smoothed out.

It was nearly noon on Wednesday a week later when Christian stepped into Teira's office. "Hey there. Are you hungry?"

She turned away from her computer. "I sure am."

"I thought we could rent a couple of bikes and ride over to Stroget for a bite to eat. There's a hot dog stand that I've become addicted to."

Teira had been to Strøget. It was the longest pedestrian boulevard in Europe, connecting five streets and running through Copenhagen from Rådhuspladsen (City Hall Square) to Kongens Nytorv. It was filled with shops, cafés, and street performers.

"I guess there are worse addictions in the world," she said. "Although I can think of better ones, too." She scrunched up her nose.

"You obviously haven't tried one of these hot dogs. Picture this—a long, thin, red hot dog like nothing you have ever tasted in your life, wrapped in bacon, and put inside a baguette-style roll. Doesn't that make your mouth water?"

"As long as we can wash it down with a large helping of *smorkrger*."

"You can't wash down a hot dog with cake."

"*Smorkrger* goes with anything."

"You're on. You try my hot dogs, I'll find you a bakery."

"That sounds like fun. I'll be ready when you are."

Once the lunch hour came, Christian and Teira got two bikes. Free use of them was available all over the city. By placing a token in the slot, a bike could be taken from the rack. When the person returned the bike, the coin was released and the lock snapped back into place. All around her, people zoomed past effortlessly on bicycles. Teira, on the other hand, felt as though her brains were being jiggled right out of her head as the wheels bounced over the rough cobblestone walks. It took all her strength and balance to follow Christian toward their destination.

Teira was keeping a close watch on the cobblestones, glancing up occasionally to avoid hitting oncoming traffic, when disaster struck. It wasn't hard to guess how it had happened with all the jiggles, wiggles, bumps, and ruts. Near Strøget the chain came off her bike. Realizing in horror what had happened, she rang the bell on the handlebars over and over and screamed for everyone to get out of the way. With no chain, she had no brakes. Teira didn't know whether to laugh or cry as the scene played out before her.

The slight downhill slope of the road caused her to gain momentum, and dragging her feet on the cobblestones did little to slow her down. People yelled and waved their arms to avoid being hit by the oncoming maniac, but many shoppers and shopping bags went flying as people scrambled to get out of her way. Children chased after her, laughing and enjoying the spectacle.

Christian turned his head to look over his shoulder when he heard Teira scream his name. Shock registered on his face. He stopped his bike immediately as Teira zoomed past.

Her backside banged against the hard bicycle seat as her feet continued to drag uselessly along. Teira's head bobbed up and down with each cobblestone her heels hit. Her eyes grew wider as the bike went faster.

Christian flung his bike down and chased after her, trying to catch her in motion.

An elderly woman, apparently hard of hearing and oblivious to the commotion, stepped from a store as Teira approached it. Teira yelled at the top of her lungs for the woman to move, then swerved to avoid a collision. The bike tire hit the edge of a cobblestone and swung out of control. With one last ring of the bell, the runaway bike headed straight for the fountain that stood in front of the Royal Copenhagen china store. Teira closed her eyes and screamed as the tire hit the lip of the fountain. The bike ricocheted back and away, but Teira's forward momentum sent her somersaulting over the handlebars and landed her smack-dab in the middle of the ice-cold fountain.

Christian caught up with her just as Teira came up, gasping for breath. He looked almost as frightened as she had felt. "Are you all right?" he asked, reaching out to try to help her.

"I think I swallowed something. Are there any tadpoles in this giant fishbowl?" She shook the water from her face. Clearly, the only thing injured in the near-disaster had been her pride.

Before she could recover, let alone stand up and wade out of the water, people nearby saw that she was unhurt and started to laugh.

Then a few people reached for their cameras. Christian was one of them.

"Smile," he said, using the camera on his phone for want of a Nikon. "You're on *Candid Camera*!"

"If you don't want an office memo being sent about some girlie fear of a little gray mouse, I wouldn't show that to anybody if I were you," Teira said, determined to be a good sport, despite everything, and thus hopefully lessen the damage to her reputation. "Now get me out of here." She burst out laughing.

"Trust me," he said, extending a hand, "this is way better blackmail material."

In the next moment a police officer arrived. When he ascertained that nobody was hurt but that Teira was still sitting in the middle of the fountain laughing while Christian took pictures with his cell phone, he demanded they leave the premises.

"So much for my hot dog," Christian chuckled as he helped a soaking wet Teira out of the fountain. Some people in the crowd cheered, others laughed, some were disgusted, but all were astonished by the American.

"I still want my *smorkrger*," Teira insisted, teeth chattering.

* * *

Much later that night, nursing a steaming cup of soup and still fighting off a chill, Teira snuggled onto the couch. When her phone rang, she set aside the soup and laid down her book. It was Christian.

"Hurry and turn on the television to DR2," he said, indicating a local channel.

"Okay, I'm doing it, but why?" Teira flipped on the television before Christian could answer. A local reporter was just finishing up a comical story about an American who didn't know how to ride a bike and had landed in the middle of one of the Strøget fountains. There was even a film clip, courtesy of some too-well-prepared tourist, of Teira's bike ricocheting off the edge and her somersaulting into the water.

"Well, isn't that a grand two minutes of fame?"

"This is so much better than the picture on my camera phone," Christian said, laughing.

"You know this is going to end up as one of those rotten little video clips forwarded around the world by e-mail." She groaned.

"I'm sure of it. I already sent it to my family. They can hardly wait to meet you."

"Tell me you didn't!"

"Not yet, but I do have it on my DVR. I plan to send it to everybody."

* * *

The news broadcast ended abruptly when a remote control, flung from across the room, impacted with the expensive plasma screen. The picture blurred and the controller broke into several pieces.

"Get rid of her!" the man yelled. "Do whatever it takes—"

The younger man's eyes darted toward his companion and away. He held his tongue. He owed this man his loyalty after all he had received.

Still, was his mentor losing touch with reality? His outbursts were becoming more frequent—and more violent in nature.

It was the girl. She was the cause of this. She made them all nervous.

But this instruction was too much. If she died now, how could they get what only she could give them?

"See to it!" the older man commanded.

The younger man sighed. "Done."

23

The morning training went well and lunch with Grethe had been very pleasant. With Christian in Sweden for the day, Teira finished up her work early and decided to call it a day. Within a half hour she was parked at the side of a sandy road that turned off the main motorway. She loved this stretch of beach. She slipped off her shoes and let her toes sink into the soft, warm sand.

Walking down to the shore, she spread out the blanket she'd brought from the trunk, sat down, and watched the waves roll in and out. She was alone on this area of the beach. She hadn't expected that, but after all it *was* a workday afternoon, this wasn't a vacation spot, and the water was far too cold for a swim. She assured herself that she would stay only a few minutes—just long enough to gather her thoughts and gain the strength and serenity she always found at the seashore.

The waves exercised their calming effect almost immediately. Overhead, puffy white clouds floated amidst a pale blue sky that seemed to merge with the dark blue waters of the Baltic Sea. A light breeze made the tall grasses sway, and birds dotted the sky, swooping down occasionally to land on the abandoned beach.

From here Teira could see Sweden. Briefly, she wondered what Christian was doing at that moment. Was he thinking of her like she was of him? The thought brought warmth to her soul.

But slowly Teira's thoughts turned to her grandfather and the truths she had learned. She now believed that Soren Pedersen had given all he had to fight for what he believed in. He'd risked his life many times over to safeguard his country and had saved lives in the process. If there was one thing she had learned since coming to Denmark, it was that he was not the kind of man to sit around and discuss what ought to be done. He was the kind of man who rose up and did it.

Grethe was right. There was good and bad on both sides of war. Boys who were barely men were drafted or had enlisted to fight for their beliefs and to serve their country. Patriotism. Freedom. Liberty. Some things are worth fighting for. And yet there was horror on all sides. Though many were protected, nobody was spared. Many people lived through terrible, unspeakable things.

Teira's chest burned with emotion as she recalled the heart-wrenching story her grandmother had told of her charred husband being brought home after the explosion, burned almost beyond recognition and with a gunshot wound in his chest. What a horrible way to die. There may or may not have been an error with the mission that day, but Soren's war record spoke for itself. In her heart Teira knew he was doing what he thought was right. Maybe it was time to let it rest. What good he had done was enough for her. She might not understand what had happened, and maybe she never would, but she could now believe that he was a good man.

Still, her heart ached for what never was. Grethe had lived most of her life without the only man she could ever love. Hanne had grown up without a father, and Teira had never met her grandfather, a wartime hero.

Caught up in a myriad of emotions, Teira decided to chase her thoughts away by sinking her feet in the cold ocean water. Looking around to be sure no one could see, she removed her nylons, hiked up her skirt, and made her way to the water's edge. There she let the incoming tide shift the sand around her feet and between her toes.

The breeze had picked up and with it the swell of the water. But the warm sand all around her had cast a peaceful spell. Teira stepped farther out into the tide until the water came just below her knees. The water was getting rougher, and it would be crazy to go much farther. Reluctantly, she stopped. Taking deep breaths, she took in the smell of the seawater and watched as the water swirled in and out in one eternal round. The sun shone brightly and the water sparkled, but it was so cold that Teira's feet were starting to go numb. She knew it was time to head back to the shore. Perhaps because she was lost in thought, the next wave that crashed in almost toppled Teira. She hurried now toward the blanket she had left on the beach.

Focused on warming her cold feet, she neither heard nor sensed the person come up behind her. It wasn't until someone roughly grabbed her that she realized she was not alone. Teira felt herself being dragged back into the water. The element of surprise, combined with the greater strength of her assailant, made it impossible for her to pull herself away from his tight grasp.

The cold water was now up to her shoulders. Shock raced through her as she tried to suck in a breath before losing her footing and being thrust head first into the freezing surf.

Instinctively, she gasped for air, filling her mouth and nose with salty water. Desperately trying to expel it, she swallowed even more. The frigid water burned her face and stung her eyes. She fought with all her might, kicking out to escape so she could get to the surface. She finally succeeded in surfacing to inhale a lungful of air, but then the person grabbed her once again and shoved her into deeper water.

Panicked, Teira fought for air. The cold temperature caused her to lose her oxygen supply even quicker. She couldn't hold on much longer. Adrenaline made her fight, but she feared it was a losing battle.

Suddenly the pressure against her body gave way and she swam frantically for the surface, gulping for air. Her muscles quivered from exertion, but she came up ready to fight with all she had left in her. However, her attacker had fled. Teira frantically looked around and saw someone in a wet suit swimming, then running for the shore as a small fishing boat trawled toward her. Whoever had tried to drown her was far ahead and now disappearing into the tall grasses.

Limp from exhaustion, Teira tried to swim toward the boat. She barely made it.

A man called out in Danish, "There now, we've got you!" Two sets of hands grabbed her by the wrists and pulled her awkwardly into the small boat. Spitting and sputtering the freezing cold water from her face, she gratefully accepted a warm, thick blanket and wrapped it around her shoulders. She choked and spewed out a mouthful of water over the edge of the boat.

"That's very good. It will clear your lungs," the younger of two men assured her. She spit up some more water and felt dizzy as the boat slowed, making sweeping motions against the waves.

"Th-thank you for your help," she said hoarsely.

"We didn't do much," the older man replied. "We saw a struggle, but could only get here in time to help you out of the water."

"Did you see who attacked me?" she asked, shivering.

"We were too far away. Sorry."

With each rock of the boat, Teira's nausea grew. She again dived for the edge and lost more water and her lunch. Miserable, cold, humiliated, and terrified, she was immeasurably grateful when they finally reached shore and the men walked her to her blanket.

The men offered to take her home or at least call for help, but Teira declined. "I'll be fine, really," she assured them. The fishermen looked at each other then back at her. She promised the men she would be okay and that she'd go directly to the police to file a report.

They stayed with her until she was stronger, then saw her to her car where she wrote down their names, addresses, and phone numbers should the police need to question them.

"Thank you again," Teira said in farewell. "If it weren't for you, I would have been fish food." The thought of how true that statement was caused goose bumps on her arms.

Teira did as she'd promised the fishermen. After receiving directions to the nearest police station by phone, she drove the fifteen minutes to it, checking her rearview mirror every couple of seconds along the way. She wasn't being followed. Or, if she was, whoever did it was a pro.

Despite the fact that she was probably safe now, Teira stepped cautiously from the car and practically ran for the front door.

* * *

The visit to the police station proved to be a waste of time. Worse, it had been humiliating. As she drove home, still checking the rearview mirror apprehensively, Teira berated herself for not being more forceful in her claims. Instead of being convincing, her chattering teeth had likely made her sound hysterical, if not hallucinatory. Teira's story hadn't sounded completely credible, even to her own ears. The officer had taken a few notes and promised to look into it, but Teira knew by the look he exchanged with an associate that he had no real intention of keeping that promise.

Pulling into the driveway of her grandmother's house, Teira climbed from the car, looked quickly around, and once again darted for the door. Once inside she locked and bolted it behind her. She couldn't be too careful. Despite what the policeman believed, the note hadn't been a prank or a vague threat. Somebody wanted her dead.

Teira's heart slammed in her chest a moment later when her cell phone alerted her that she had received a text message. With cold, trembling fingers, she reached for her phone and read the message from Christian.

> STUCK IN LONG MTG.
> B BACK L8R
> SO SORRY
> WILL CALL SOON
> THINKING OF U
> C

Teira's heart sank. Now what should she do? She was terrified and wanted to call Christian, but not if it meant interrupting his meeting. Besides, he was in Sweden. There was nothing he could do from there but worry.

She could try a different police station, perhaps—or even the American embassy—but the result would probably be the same. She'd been scared and humiliated enough for one day. Besides, there was the almost subconscious fear she couldn't shake that going to the authorities might be walking into greater danger. After all, Ulrike Spelman *was* an authority. What if he was behind all of this? And what of Kort Madsen's "accident"? He worked for the city. Was it his association there, rather than with ComTech, that had made him a target?

At this point, Teira didn't know who in the whole country she could trust besides Christian, and he wasn't there. Confused and alone, she did the one thing that had always brought her comfort and strength in the past. She knelt in prayer.

Afterward she took a quick shower and packed an overnight bag, which included an outfit for work the next day. By the time she finished packing, she'd decided that until she knew who was after her and why, the fewer people she told about it, the better.

Teira looked out her window before closing the blinds and drapes. Then she walked out the door, locked it, and ran to her car. Heading down the motorway toward Copenhagen, Teira let her thoughts run rampant. She drove, trying desperately to calm her emotions and make some kind of sense out of her experience.

She did know one thing. She'd accepted this job to get to know her grandmother better. Since she arrived nearly two months ago, Teira had grown to love and admire Grethe even more dearly. This was her chance to be with her and she didn't want to lose that. Not yet.

And she had another meaningful reason to stay. Christian.

But what of all this? Wouldn't he want her to leave if he thought she'd be safer? Could she bear to leave him at this point? She could, she decided, but only if it meant keeping him from danger.

If she did go back home, would the trouble follow her there? How could she answer that when she didn't know what the trouble was? The only thing Teira knew for sure was that the attempt on her life today proved that whoever was after her meant business. She was scared—scared enough to run and hide if she only knew where to go. But that wasn't an option if she wanted her life back. For that, she would have to stay and face this thing head on.

* * *

Christian looked at his Rolex and noted the time. It was a few minutes after nine. He'd thought for sure Teira would be home, but by the looks of things she wasn't. He sat in the driveway of her grandmother's home and considered the dark house. Not even a porch light burned in anticipation of her return.

This is what he deserved for trying to surprise her, he told himself. He'd wanted to see her face light up when he told her his news in person, so he hadn't called ahead and spoiled it. Instead he'd stopped by on his way home.

It had been a long, meeting-filled day in Sweden. He'd had a hard time concentrating on anything but Teira and everything he had learned about her family. It had been impossible to focus on facts and figures when the pressing issue was who was trying to scare her, and whether that person had any connection with Kort Madsen. Fear for her was always at the back of his mind.

Even if he didn't know how to get to the bottom of what was going on, at least after his dinner meeting tonight he knew a way to bring a smile to Teira's face.

Rather, he could make her smile if he could find her. He picked up his cell. Teira answered her phone on the second ring. "Hi there," Christian said.

"Hi. How were your meetings today?"

"Long. Boring. How about you? Did you have a good day?"

Teira hesitated.

"Teira?"

"I need to talk to you."

"Is everything all right? Where are you?"

Teira looked around. She was sitting in a hotel room with the door locked, scared to be alone and angry with herself for not staying at home.

"I'm sitting in bed reading," she said. "Well, really I was waiting for you to call. At least, I was hoping you would."

Christian looked at the house. No lights were on. "I'm in front of your house," he said, more calmly than he felt.

"I'm in a hotel in Copenhagen," she said quietly.

"What happened today?"

"I don't quite know how to say it. It still doesn't seem real."

"Just say it," Christian prompted. "Tell me what happened."

"Someone tried to kill me."

24

Christian clutched the cell phone to his ear. "What? How? Are you okay? Have you seen a doctor? Where are you now?"

"I'm fine," Teira said. "I didn't need to see a doctor, and I'm staying at a hotel in Copenhagen not far from ComTech. I couldn't stand the thought of being alone tonight—and I didn't know where else to go, so here I am."

"You did the right thing." Christian felt beads of sweat forming across his forehead. He brushed them away with a shaky hand. "I'm pulling out of the driveway and joining you right now. You can tell me the details when I get there, but why didn't you call me sooner? I would have come back!"

"I didn't want to interrupt you when there was nothing you could do," she said.

"Did you call the police?" Christian kept the phone to his ear and his eyes on the road as he sped toward Copenhagen.

"Yes," Teira said. "I went in and gave a statement. I don't think they believed me."

Christian slammed his hand on the steering wheel.

"Are you still there?" Teira asked.

"I'm here."

"Can I ask you something?"

"Anything."

"Do you think Kort's accident and what happened to me are connected? I mean, I know you don't know for sure, but what do you think? Be straight with me."

Christian paused, torn between wanting to reassure Teira that everything would be fine and telling the truth. The truth was that someone had tried to kill her and he had no idea who. He knew that Teira wanted his honesty and wanted to know she could trust him.

"I think they are related somehow," he said at last. "I'll do everything in my power to find out who is doing this and put an end to it."

"That's the same conclusion I came up with," she said. "Christian, I have to tell you, I'm scared—not only for me, but for you and my grandma. I don't want either of you to get hurt."

Christian heard the emotion in her throat and felt his gut clench. He grasped the steering wheel so tightly his knuckles turned white. "It's okay," he said. "Nobody else has been threatened. Let's stay calm and figure this out together, okay?" Up ahead was the turnoff that led to Copenhagen. "Teira, which hotel are you staying at?"

"I'm at the Palace Hotel near the waterfront."

"I know where it is. I'll be there in about ten minutes, but don't go down to the lobby until I call and tell you I'm there. We'll talk this through and decide what to do."

Teira agreed and dressed quickly. She was ready when Christian called and found him standing outside the elevator doors when they opened. He grabbed her and held her tight in a brief embrace. Tears sprang to her eyes.

"Are you all right?" he asked, looking her over to see for himself that she was unharmed, at least physically.

"I am now." She smiled weakly.

"Let's go sit down. Have you eaten?"

"I wasn't hungry."

"You should eat something," he said. "Let's see if the restaurant is still open." He took her hand and led her to the hotel restaurant where they ordered soup and sandwiches. Once the waiter walked away, Christian took her hand again and said, "So tell me what happened."

Teira related it all as quickly as she could. Christian asked a question or two, but mostly he listened intently, his mind reeling. By the time she had told him the last detail, he felt as though he'd lost the ability to speak and think. He had to get her somewhere safe, but where? What safety was there from a lunatic?

At the end, Christian asked the question Teira feared the most. "Do you think you should go home? It certainly seems like the safest option."

Teira hesitated. "Someone wants me to leave Denmark. It has to be one of two things. Either they want me away from ComTech—which I think we've ruled out—or my grandfather started something he didn't finish. Although I have no idea how I might play into it, maybe I'm a threat to someone . . . someone who thinks I know more than I do." When Christian didn't immediately respond, she added, "Of course, that doesn't explain Kort Madsen's accident."

Christian snapped his fingers. "What if someone needed to get rid of Kort to plant someone else in his place?" He sat up straighter. "Wouldn't that explain Rolf Tycksen's strange comments to you, his incompetence on the job, why he was nowhere in sight when he should have escorted you out to your car the night your tires were slashed? Someone from the city hired him to take Kort's place after the accident."

"It would be hard to prove," she said, "but it makes sense. It also explains why nobody else at ComTech has had any problem."

"They damaged Kort's car. It's almost like yours was more of a warning."

"But it's like you said, why only mess with mine when they could have followed through and done away with me like they tried with Kort? It doesn't make sense."

"I don't know why," he conceded. "Unless at the time they were only trying to scare you, not kill you."

"Why did they change their minds today?"

Christian couldn't answer that question. Instead he said, "I've watched the surveillance tapes. The tape shows footage of Rolf at the front desk, lounging around, inattentive. The following frame shows him walking the halls. Next thing you know, he's letting us into the building. It doesn't show anything that takes place in the parking lot. It's useless as evidence as to who might have vandalized your car. There's not enough lighting outside so nothing is even recorded. However, Rolf would have known that."

"But if he's on the tape, doesn't that clear him as a suspect?" Teira asked.

Christian shrugged. "Unless he's turning a blind eye to someone else's deeds. That makes him an accomplice. And, for the record, I don't like the way he was watching you every night."

Teira's face fell. "So you think he's in on it? I feel awful to think Kort could have been killed because of me!"

"It's not your fault," Christian said quickly. "And we might be wrong about all of this."

Teira sat in silence, pondering. Then she said, "If these people really mean business, my leaving Denmark won't do any good. They could follow me anywhere."

"Then stay," Christian said. "I honestly don't believe anybody else is in danger. Besides, I'd like to bring them out in the open and catch them in their own game." He frowned. "But how about we find you an apartment in the city?"

Teira hesitated. It was probably wise, but she was drawn to her grandmother's home and hated to be forced out of it. Couldn't she make herself just as safe there if she tried harder? "I've been thinking about this ever since I came here tonight," she said, "and I want to go back home tomorrow. I'll be more careful. I'll make sure the house is securely locked at all times and if I ever feel the least bit uneasy—like I did tonight—I'll go someplace public." When Christian frowned, she added, "What about you? If they're watching me as closely as I think they are, they have to know you have as much information as I do."

"Teira, look, I want you to know how much it means to me that you're trying to look out for me, but I don't think I'm in danger."

"Yet! We have no way of knowing who or what we're dealing with. I don't want them to come after you to get to me."

"I'm just as worried about you as you are about me," Christian reminded her. "I don't want to lose you for *any* reason. The way I see it, we have two choices. We can either put you on the next plane home with bodyguards to deliver you safe and sound and alert the authorities there, or you can stay here with me and we'll resolve this thing together. But that means we are in it *together*. No protecting me, because I warn you now, sweetheart, I am going after this full force. They are not, I repeat *not,* coming near you again if I can help it. Now, take your pick."

Teira hesitated. "I want what's best for you. I want you to be safe."

"You're what's best for me and I want *you* safe," he reiterated.

Teira looked at him a long time. The man was totally amazing. Her appreciation for him deepened. "Christian," she said, laying a hand on his arm, "I have to be honest and admit I'm afraid. But if there's anything I've learned since coming to Denmark, it's that good people can't stand by and expect others to take care of things. They need to get involved and get the job done. I don't want to be a victim and I don't want to leave Denmark without you."

"Good, because I plan to take you home as my souvenir." They both smiled, remembering Paul from Kronborg Castle.

It was hard for Teira to imagine her world so perfectly right in one aspect, yet so devastatingly wrong in another.

"So we're in this together?" Christian asked.

"Together," Teira confirmed.

* * *

They met at the office the next morning, acting as if nothing out of the ordinary had happened the day before. They would carry on as usual at work, they'd decided, but in their free time they would conduct an investigation of their own.

After late-night brainstorming, they had a plan to set in motion. They'd agreed that Teira would be more aware of her surroundings, watching for familiar faces. Next they would contact as many people as they could from the former Freedom Council to see if there was anything more they could learn that way. At the top of their list was Magnus Spelman, but this time Christian would go with Teira. It was one of many things Christian planned to do.

For another, he didn't intend to let Teira out of his sight except when he had to. He'd programmed the number for the police into their phones and into their heads in case of need. The most difficult thing for him to do, however, was to conceal from Teira how uneasy he felt despite his best efforts to protect her.

* * *

On Friday evening, rather than meet in Copenhagen, Christian had insisted he would pick Teira up at home at 6:30 so they could be at the awards dinner and ball promptly at 7:00. When she opened the door and he saw her standing there, he suppressed a groan. She was so many things. She loved and lived her religion, she had a great sense of humor, she wanted to achieve her dreams, she valued honor and integrity, she made terrible lemonade, and was stubborn to a fault. He'd seen her drenched by rain, swimming in fountains, caring for her grandmother, addressing a boardroom, frightened half out of her wits, and chasing mice with rocks, but she was always a lady—a stunning and absolutely beautiful lady. There was no doubt he was in love with her.

Tonight Teira's hair was swept up into a clip at the crown with curls cascading down the back. She wore a small diamond pendant and matching earrings with an elegant green dress that shimmered near-black in certain light.

Christian whistled his approval. Then he managed, "Wow. You look breathtaking."

"Thank you. May I say you look quite handsome yourself?"

"I'll be the envy of every man there," he said. "Shall we go?"

* * *

A slight smile parted Teira's lips as she took in the magnificent sight of the enormous banquet hall. Chandeliers hung from vaulted, ornately carved ceilings, their multifaceted crystal teardrops shimmering from each tier. Walls of gold-framed mirrors reflected elegantly dressed guests, and waiters dressed in black tails and bow ties carried silver trays of crystal flutes that resembled spun glass.

Teira caught their reflection in a mirror and her heart leapt. She was excited to be there beside Christian. He looked better in his tux than she'd ever seen him. He kept her close with his hand at the small of her back or cradling her elbow. She felt like Cinderella going to the ball.

"What is that grin on your face?" Christian asked.

"I was thinking how happy I am to be here with you tonight. It's beautiful, isn't it?"

Christian, who had hardly taken his eyes off her, agreed. "It's very nice," he said. "Did you get my gift today?"

"I didn't know whether to be pleased or mortified," she said with a laugh. "Who knew that Royal Copenhagen China has made a plate with a picture of the Strøget fountain?"

"It will always be among my favorite memories of Denmark," Christian said, chuckling.

"I'm glad I could oblige you." They both grinned and Christian placed his arm around her shoulders and squeezed.

"There's quite a crowd here tonight," he observed. "Anybody who's anyone was invited. I understand that besides business and political leaders even some aristocracy is expected."

"That's a pretty impressive guest list. How did you score an invitation?"

"Not me," Christian reminded her. "The previous owner. I'm only here as the new leader from the acquisition. I think people have high hopes for the coming fiscal year."

Teira nodded her understanding.

A few minutes later they were seated. During dinner they visited with the previous owner of the phone company and his wife. After dessert, the awards program began. Committee members were introduced, achievements noted, and awards bestowed—all between segments of entertainment. It was when a certain company was receiving an award for innovation in their business practices that Teira first saw Ulrike Spelman. He was seated across the room next to his father.

She knew he had to have noticed her. When Christian and the previous owner stood for recognition, there had been no way of avoiding the bright spotlight that lit their table. A vague prickling sensation crawled up her neck. Teira tilted her head to ease the tension. Looking over her shoulder, she saw the man from the treasury at Rosenborg Castle. Olaf Jorgensen and Eva sat almost directly behind their table.

Seeing Teira look back, Eva smiled warmly and waved. Teira returned the gesture. Olaf maintained the harsh look that seemed to be permanently etched into his face. At least his expression didn't change when his gaze moved toward another table. Why she found comfort in that, she didn't know, other than perhaps it was an assurance that his animosity wasn't directed solely at her. He appeared to be a man who was angry with the world.

Another man seated at the same table caught her attention. Teira was pretty certain she had seen him before, though it took her a moment to recall exactly when and where. It was the same man who had dined with Magnus a couple of months back and with whom she saw Olaf Jorgensen at Christiansborg Palace the morning she went to inquire about the Resistance Museum. She acted as if she didn't notice his piercing stare, but even when she'd turned around, she felt his eyes still on her back.

Teira spent the next several minutes trying to convince herself that she had an overactive imagination, supposing conspiracy and animosity where none existed. But at last she turned to Christian. "There's a strange man here," she whispered.

He put an arm around her shoulder and bent close as if to whisper sweet nothings in her ear. "Where? Who?"

Following his lead, she giggled, then whispered back, "Off to our left. He's sitting next to the man from the treasury I told you about. Christian, he won't stop staring at me. I've seen him with Magnus Spelman, too."

Christian turned his attention to the person accepting an award then looked casually about the room. Since he had never seen the head of security at the treasury, it was impossible to distinguish one man in a black tie from another.

He turned back and whispered in Teira's ear. Then he kissed her cheek and went to stand next to a massive marble pillar in the back of the room where he could observe both their table and those around it.

The only person Christian didn't have a good view of was the man who had watched all this take place from a third table. He now stood behind Christian, silently observing it all.

25

"Well, whoever he was, he couldn't be the one who tried to drown me," Teira said. "He was too old. I mean, he looked like he was eighty or so."

She and Christian sat at their table talking while all around them couples rose to dance.

"Maybe," Christian said thoughtfully.

"He's gone now. He left right after you came back to the table." Teira took a steadying breath. "I wish you'd ask me to dance."

"Dance?"

"Why, I would love to! Thanks," she smiled coyly.

Christian grinned, stood, and took Teira by the hand. Then he led her to the dance floor. He held her close and she kept thinking how right it felt. She wished they could dance all night long. She smiled. Christian smiled back and held her a little closer. Just as he was leaning over for a kiss, there was a tap on Teira's shoulder. She turned in surprise.

"May I cut in?" a woman purred.

Teira refrained from groaning.

"We were talking over a serious matter," Christian said apologetically.

Teira remembered being introduced to the woman, Monique, earlier in the evening. She also remembered every one of the flirtatious looks she'd given Christian since.

"*Oh, mon cher!* You can do that anytime, no?" Monique pouted as she pulled Christian's arm.

It took all her self-control, but Teira refrained from grabbing the other arm for a game of tug of war in the middle of the dance floor. She relinquished her grasp and stepped aside. Teira all but waved good-bye as Christian sailed away in the powerful arms of the Frenchwoman. It would have been worse to watch Christian in the arms of the curvy woman with the pouty red lips and skin-tight gown except for the look of reluctance on his face. Monique was leading, and he was being pushed and pulled and dragged around the floor at such a speed that he had to concentrate to keep up. So, rather than feel sorry for herself, Teira laughed delightedly at Christian's plight. Meanwhile, she was careful not to make eye contact with the men who looked her way. She had no desire to dance with anyone but Christian.

After that one seemingly endless dance, Christian made his excuses and practically ran back to Teira. Grabbing her hand he said, "I need fresh air, fast!"

Fighting the urge to laugh, she followed him out to the terrace where he leaned against the balustrade. "I didn't know you were so light on your feet," she said, suppressing a giggle.

"It helps that half the time she was carrying me around like a mop. My feet hardly touched the floor."

His comment made the dam burst. Teira laughed uncontrollably. Finally she said, "I think she likes you. Play your cards right and she could be yours for keeps."

"I hate to disappoint her, but I've got a thing for somebody else." Christian placed Teira's hand in the crook of his arm so they could walk together.

"Oh?" She took a steadying breath.

"Yes," he said as he turned to face her. They stood in the shadows of the terrace, discovering the truth in each other's eyes. Their feelings were so strong they could go unspoken—they both could feel the air of vulnerability mixed with excitement. Inside, the music played and people laughed; outside, two people discovered love.

"We didn't finish our dance," he said.

"Are you sure the last one didn't do you in?" She smiled.

"I'll always have something left for you. Shall we?"

"Certainly." Teira draped her arms around his neck and Christian drew her close. They moved together flawlessly until the music faded and their steps slowed to a stop. Still they stood together, motionless, looking at one another. Christian studied every feature and thought for perhaps the millionth time how beautiful Teira was.

What seemed an eternity was actually a heartbeat. Then Christian bent toward Teira and kissed her tenderly.

* * *

Christian held Teira's hand as they drove down the motorway talking about superficial topics. The night had been perfect.

Teira stole a glance at him. His spicy clean cologne teased her senses. Her heart skipped a beat, then made up time by racing. She felt as giddy as a schoolgirl.

After they arrived at her grandmother's house, Christian turned to Teira before he opened his own car door.

"Should I go in and check out the house?" Christian asked.

"I don't think it's necessary," she said. "I made sure the place was locked securely before we left."

"Before I walk you to the door, I have something for you." He retrieved an envelope from the glove compartment and handed it to Teira.

"What's this?" she asked, surprised.

"Open it." Christian said. He turned on the car's interior light.

Teira slipped her forefinger along the seam and carefully tore it open. Inside was a slip of paper with the name "Jakob Meier" along with a Swedish phone number and address. Confused, she looked at Christian. "Gosh, this is a most unusual gift. Thank you so much."

"You won't believe who that is," Christian said, tapping on the paper. "I know a guy from Sweden named David Solomon. He runs one of the offices. I met him when I first came to Denmark, scouting out the acquisition. He's a good man. We used to talk religion a lot when I was investigating the Church."

"Oh, is he a member?"

"Actually, no. He's Jewish. Anyway, we started talking about the war, and David told me about the rescue of the Danish Jews in 1943. He's not old enough to have lived through it himself, but his father did. It was unbelievable. Anyway, I told him your grandfather's name and related some of the good deeds he had done during the war. Then I asked David to ask around to see if anybody recognized Soren's name. I thought it would be good for you to hear about some of the good things your grandfather did from the original sources." Christian shrugged off her thanks and continued. "Yesterday when I was in Sweden, David gave me this name."

"Who is it?"

"This is the best part. Mr. Meier was only twelve when the Danish Jews were helped into Sweden by many courageous people, including your grandfather." Christian leaned in a little. "Teira, he remembers that night. Jakob remembers your grandfather and wants to meet you."

"How did David locate him?"

"It wasn't difficult. He'd been asking around at the synagogue for me. When he mentioned your grandfather's name to Jakob, the older man recognized it immediately."

Teira was stunned.

"He said it would be an honor to meet you and Grethe. If you'd like, we can drive there Saturday. I hear he has an amazing story to tell."

Teira was overwhelmed that Christian had gone to so much effort in her behalf. "I don't know what to say," she murmured.

"Say you'll let me take you there," Christian replied.

"Yes, please!" Teira smiled. "But what I mean is, thank you hardly seems adequate to express my gratitude." She looked down at the paper. "This is so thoughtful. It will mean the world to my grandmother."

"You're welcome." Christian smiled with pleasure.

"Boy, will you ever score big points with this one," Teira said. "Not that you haven't already won Grandma's heart."

"It's not *her* heart I'm trying to win," he said with a sly smile.

Teira kissed him on the cheek. "You've already won mine," she whispered.

Christian gathered her in his arms and held her for a time before he walked her to the door.

Teira looked up at him. "Everyone at the office was talking today. They saw us leave together for lunch the day I was . . . um . . . on the news." She sighed.

"You mean the day you went swimming in the Strøget fountain?" He chuckled.

"Okay, yes. That day. Anyway, I'm afraid a few rumors are flying around about me having a bit of a *thing* for you. And perhaps vice versa." Teira looked down at her feet. She knew how he felt about that kind of thing, how much he valued privacy above all.

Christian lifted her chin with his thumb and forefinger so that their eyes could meet. "I think you know how I feel. Is it your part that's the rumor?"

Teira felt herself blush. "Um, well, I suppose you could say I have grown rather . . . well . . . I mean . . . I guess I could admit that I feel . . . but if you want me to I could get over . . . that is . . . if—"

"Don't do that," he interrupted.

"Do what?" she asked, afraid of the answer.

"Don't 'get over' anything about me. Unless it's my faults." He grinned. Then he kissed her with a kiss that left her breathless.

* * *

Despite Christian and Teira's happiness, neither could forget there were issues left unsettled. On that following day, Christian, Teira, and Grethe shared an air of excitement as they crossed the oresund Bridge connecting Denmark with Sweden. The two women couldn't wait to meet Jakob Meier, and, seeing their enthusiasm, Christian was beyond pleased that he had been able to set up the meeting.

Several minutes later Christian stopped the car in front of a small cottage and double-checked the address. "I believe this is it," he said.

As if to confirm his words, the door swung open and a man appeared on the porch, waving. He wore a cardigan sweater over a shirt and tie. Waves of curly white hair topped his head. On his crown he wore the traditional yarmulke. His smile was as warm as the noonday sun.

Christian reached for Grethe's hand and helped her from the car, then did the same for Teira.

Jakob came eagerly out to greet them. After introductions were exchanged, they walked into the house where he introduced everyone to his wife, Anna. She had prepared a lunch of breads, cheeses, and a mouthwatering homemade soup. It was all topped off with pastries and coffee, the latter graciously declined by Christian and Teira.

At last they retired to the family room, where Jakob turned to Grethe. "I am so glad you could honor us today by coming. I will be forever grateful to the people who helped my family escape the Nazis." His rheumy eyes clouded. "Many of my relatives died in the Holocaust with millions of others." He shook his head sadly and was silent for several seconds. Then he looked at each of his guests in turn and began the tale of triumph and tragedy that fused the heart of a nation. "One tries to block frightening, painful images," he said, "but there are things we can never forget. Should never forget."

Jakob Meier began. “My family was lucky enough to be numbered among those who were rescued from the horrific plight of the mass genocide. There were one hundred and twenty Danish Jews who were not so lucky.”

Teira cleared her throat and spoke quietly. “We studied the Holocaust in school, and I’ve seen movies and documentaries about it. Still, I can’t begin to imagine how horrible it was. You must have been terrified, especially as a youth.”

Jakob nodded. “It was certainly one of the darkest times in history. But amidst all the anguish, strangers reached out to help one another without prejudice, saving many lives. Such people as your grandfather.”

“You do remember my Soren then?” Grethe asked hopefully.

“I do, because of what he did for us. In those days my family often gave thanks for him and the many others who aided our cause. Later, my parents saw to it that we never forgot those brave souls.” Jakob leaned back in his chair. “Werner Best, Hitler’s chief in Denmark, received orders in September to proceed with the deportation of Jews to death camps. There were more than seven thousand of us. Praise God, the information was leaked to the head of the Jewish community.”

“Is that how the word spread?” Christian asked.

Jakob nodded. “On Rosh Hashanah, the Jewish New Year, Dr. Marcus Melchior, the acting rabbi of the Krystalgaade Synagogue, implored everyone to go into hiding.”

“What happened then?” Teira asked.

"The country came together as one. There were already two German ships docked in Copenhagen's port and buses ready to transport the rest." His eyes shone. "But the Danish people would not stand by and see our extermination. They stood up for us. They hid us anywhere they could—the Bispebjerg hospital, a crypt at the Trinity Church, their own homes—everywhere they could find that might be safe. They fed us, protected us, and in the end they freed us." He shook his head in awe. "So many were involved—teachers, store owners, clergymen, doctors and their staffs, fishermen—everyone who possibly could took part in the rescue. Fortunately, Sweden was willing to take us in and help us there. Of those thousands of Jews I mentioned, fewer than five hundred were captured. But the Danish acts of bravery did not end there."

"What do you mean?" Teira asked.

"Danish officials were able to convince Adolf Eichmann to keep the Danish Jews from the extermination camps. They were sent to Theresienstadt. Working with the Danish Red Cross, the Danes sent more than seven hundred packages of food, clothing, and vitamins to their prisoners monthly. This was made possible because Werner Best wanted to improve relations with the Danish authorities, and Eichmann was presumably trying to idealize the propaganda and hide the mass murder of millions of Jews."

"Jakob," his wife interrupted gently, "these things they can read in history books. I'm sure they want to hear your story about Soren."

The old man nodded. "Our family left home in the middle of the night after the sirens had signaled curfew. I was terrified of those sirens—terrified of the gestapo who wanted us dead. My father had pulled me aside that day and told me that if anything were to happen to him, as the oldest I would need to care for my mother, sisters, and baby brother. We were to meet a man near Tivoli who would take us to a fishing boat that would get us to Sweden, but we were running short on time because the baby was ill. Taking a crying baby through the streets would alert the gestapo and we would surely be killed. Finally, William cried himself to sleep and we set off into the night with too little time to make our destination.

"Sure enough, the small group we were to travel with left without us, but there was one man who had remained behind to see if we came. It was Soren. He said he felt he should wait a little longer to see what had kept us. He risked his life waiting for us. Had he been caught after curfew, he could have been shot with no questions asked. He led us down to the docks and told us to hide. We huddled together, but in the cold night, William started to fuss again. Despite my mother's best efforts, he could not be calmed. Then we heard the click of a gun and my father put his hands in the air. A German soldier had his rifle aimed at my father's back. The soldier was merely a boy."

Jakob rubbed his chin. "While Mother begged and pleaded for him to spare us, Soren returned in a small, metal fishing boat with a fisherman named Gerritt Rykersen. He had agreed to take our family to Sweden. When Soren saw the soldier with his gun to my father's back, he jumped from the boat and implored him to reconsider. He said, 'I speak to you as from one soldier to another. There is no honor in carrying out this order. Let these innocent people go.' The soldier finally turned his back and my family jumped into the rowboat with Mr. Rykersen. Soren patted the soldier on the back and ran off into the night. I sat in the boat and watched him disappear into the shadows. I never saw him again, but I will never forget what he did for us. I could never thank him or the soldier, but Mr. Rykersen and my father remained friends until my father passed away eighteen years later."

The group sat quietly as Jakob reached for his handkerchief, dabbed at his eyes, and wiped his nose.

"Did the soldier know Soren? Is that why he turned away?" Christian asked. He hated to ask, but had to know.

"I am sure he did not," Jakob replied. "They talked as strangers. I've heard of other cases where the soldiers turned away, moved by compassion, though some were bribed. The Danish police and coast guard also helped by refusing to aid in the manhunt. The good of my countrymen does not end there. Most Jews left everything they had behind and ran with the little they could carry, thinking only of their lives. Although most didn't expect to ever return to their homes, many did. And do you know what they found? While almost everywhere else in Europe, Jews returned to find their homes vandalized and everything of value stolen, in Denmark their pets, gardens, and personal belongings were protected by their neighbors. It is an extraordinary and inspiring story."

Teira was moved to tears and Grethe wept silently.

A few minutes later, Jakob produced a box of memorabilia. Looking through the papers and books, Teira exclaimed, "It's amazing you've kept this all these years!"

She then looked at a book of newsletters Jakob's father had produced.

"My father felt that one way to repay the Danes for what they'd done for us would be to communicate to them any information he could get past the Germans. You know, of course, about their strict censorship," Jakob explained. "That's why he started this underground newsletter. He printed copies and then gave them to a fisherman who smuggled them into occupied Denmark. The Resistance passed the newsletters secretly, keeping as many people as possible informed of what really went on in the world."

"Look at this." Teira pointed to one of the newsletters. "It has names and pictures of people to watch out for."

"There were brutal animals afoot," Jakob said sadly. "Spies. Double agents. My father wanted his friends to know who they could and could not trust."

"Do you have anything on King Christian X?" Teira asked.

"What do you mean?"

"Well, this seems silly, but I toured Rosenborg Castle, and they spoke of a ring of his that came up missing about the time my grandfather died. The guide said its disappearance might have had something to do with the war effort, but I know the king had no real political power."

"He may have had no political power, but do not underestimate his influence," Jakob replied. "Denmark and Germany worked out the terms of the occupation early on. King Christian remained in Denmark. He continued to rule and was a prominent figure in the eyes of his people—a positive contrast to German militarism. In fact, he rejected many aspects of the occupation and spoke publicly against it. He was also known as a protector of the Jews. Here is a picture of him." Jakob pointed to a newsletter. "He rode his horse down the streets of Copenhagen every morning, unarmed and without guards." Jakob smiled. "He was much loved by his people."

"You're saying he's the kind of man who would gladly give his ring if it could serve his country?" Teira asked.

"Certainly. He would give life and limb for his kingdom, why not a stone?"

Teira nodded. "But would he have had any way to become involved in the war effort aside from acting as a figurehead?"

"If you want my opinion," Jakob said, "I don't believe King Christian sat by his front window watching the war pass him by. He cared too deeply. I would venture to say that many of the actions we *saw* him take were indicative of things he did behind the scenes—whether he had a great deal of real political power or not."

Teira was hopeful. "Do you have any guesses as to how he might have used his ring to aid the country's cause?"

"Exchanged it for information?" Jakob shrugged. "It's anybody's guess, I suppose."

"I thought of that too," Teira said, deep in thought. "But money would have been less conspicuous. What could a person do with a king's ring? Perhaps the man at the treasury is right. Maybe the king gave it to someone he trusted for some reason and was deceived."

Before anyone could respond, Grethe gasped. When Teira turned to her, her grandmother was pointing to the book of old newsletters. "No, no, no!" she cried, aghast.

"What is it?" Teira asked, alarmed at her grandmother's pale, distraught face.

"It's him! *He's* the one I gave the letter to that day!" Grethe cried.

"Are you sure, Grandma?" Teira asked, moving to her side. "Look very carefully. It's been many years." The photo depicted a group of people, mostly men, crowded behind one man who stood in the forefront. Although the picture was a bit out of focus and the printing was far from professional, most of the people were still easily recognizable.

"He haunts my dreams," Grethe said. "This is the one. I'm sure of it."

Teira met Christian's eyes. His expression said it all. Teira's stomach dropped and a chill ran down her spine.

"Take a look at him, Teira," Christian said, "and try to add about sixty-five years. Are you thinking what I'm thinking?"

She heard herself whisper, "Is it him?"

Christian nodded. Then he turned to Jakob. "Will you make a copy of this newsletter? I need the picture to be as clear as possible."

"Certainly." Jakob took the newsletter out of the protective sheet and set it against his computer scanner. "May I ask why?"

Christian ignored the question. "What can you tell me about this man?"

"Just that I know my father strove to be sure his information was accurate. Whatever the article says is most likely true." He took a moment to read it. "Looks like this man, Gunder Larsen, belonged to the Danish Nazi party. The article says he's dangerous—known to have cost many people their lives. But the young man pictured in the crowd with him, him I don't know."

"That can't be right," Grethe said, emphatically shaking her head. "This man *must* have been part of the Resistance group. He's the one my husband sent a message to." She pointed to the younger man next to Gunder Larsen.

"But Grandma," Teira interrupted, "look at the date of this newsletter. This picture and article were published almost four years prior to Grandpa's death. We don't know how long he'd belonged to the Freedom Council when Grandpa worked with him."

Christian cleared his throat. "There's one more thing. Teira and I saw him, or someone who looks very much like him, at a banquet last night. He was seated with the man from the treasury and he didn't look happy to see her."

"It's not the first time I have seen him. I have also seen him with Magnus Spelman," Teira confessed.

"But don't you see?" Grethe cried. "This makes Soren look even more guilty. It doesn't clear his name. It darkens it."

"What if that man you recognize intercepted the letter, Grethe?" Christian asked. "Maybe he never took the message to the council, but to the enemy instead?"

"But there is no way to prove that, is there?" Grethe asked. "All this has done is made Soren look like he was part of the conspiracy!"

"If I may be so bold as to speak?" Jakob asked. The others turned to him. "I know the rumors and the tragedy behind Soren's death. I have never believed a word of it. And while I know nothing of the letter of which you speak, I can assure you that the man in this picture, Gunder Larsen, was in the early days of the war active in the Danish Nazi Party. He was dangerous. He was trouble. I don't know who this younger fellow is with him, but it is hard for me to believe that he could have changed his views enough to become a member of the Resistance movement."

Christian turned to Teira. "We need to find out who he is."

"We could ask Olaf who he was sitting next to," Teira suggested sarcastically.

"Jakob, do you have a list of other members of the Nazi Party?" Christian asked.

"There are so many newsletters, I don't remember what is in them all, but I am willing to look. Also, if you can give me a name, I can research that way very easily. I have scanned all these documents into the computer to protect them. We can run a search to see what comes up."

"That would be great. If we leave now, we could make it to Rosenborg Treasury in time for the tour and see if we can come up with a name there. Can we call you this evening?"

"I will be honored to help."

On the way out, Teira thanked Mr. Meier tenderly for all he had done and offered to do. Not only had he opened his home, but he had opened his heart. She was truly touched by the life story he had shared.

* * *

A kaleidoscopic picture of that night whirled in his head.

Savage hatred engulfed him as he remembered how the man had slipped out the broken window and escaped through the darkened streets. After the man was gone from sight, he hurried into the building to see what was amiss. In a second he knew.

It was gone. All of it was gone.

In fury he swung out, flinging at anything his fists could reach. Tables and chairs overturned; papers lay strewn across the floor.

He would be destroyed unless he could first get to his destroyer.

And he would.

27

After dropping off a tired and discouraged Grethe at the center with a promise to call later that evening, Christian and Teira set off toward Rosenborg Castle.

"I love this place," Teira said as they neared the palace. "Have you toured it yet?"

"Yes. It's pretty remarkable."

"But their head of security gives me the creeps," she muttered. "Even seeing him at the dinner put a damper on an otherwise perfect evening."

"I'll do the talking," Christian said. "You stand next to me and do what you do so well."

"And what's that?" Teira asked.

"Look beautiful, of course." Christian winked. "Ready?"

"No, but let's do it anyway."

They paid for admittance, then walked past the armed soldiers who marched back and forth in front of the treasury. As they entered the first of the darkened exhibition rooms, Christian asked, "Do you see our friend anywhere?"

Teira looked around. "No. Should we ask somebody if he's here today?"

"Hold that thought. I want to check out something first. Let's walk over and listen to the guide tell the story of the ring once more."

Teira shrugged. "Okay. It's over here." She led the way to the display where they examined the remaining pieces. Within minutes a group joined them and the guide repeated the story almost exactly the way Teira had heard it before.

Christian asked the guide the same question Teira had at the end and got the same response. The guide referred him to the head of security, Mr. Jorgensen. She excused herself to move on with the group. In a couple of minutes, Olaf Jorgensen approached.

"For some reason, they divert all questions about the ring to him," Christian whispered. "That's strange."

When the man recognized Teira, his face turned to ice. "We meet yet again, Miss Palmer. What can I do for you this time?"

Teira bristled, but Christian said, "I'm the one with a question. I hoped you could tell me the name of the man you sat next to at the awards dinner last night."

"Any particular reason you ask?"

Teira could read nothing from his austere features.

"It's personal," Christian answered politely.

"Then I'm afraid I won't help you."

Christian's eyes narrowed. "It's not a state secret. All I have to do is ask for a guest list."

Teira spoke up. "Let's just tell him the truth, Christian, and save a lot of time and trouble." She turned to Jorgensen. "I told you before that I'm a history buff. I think the man sitting next to you was part of the Freedom Council with my grandfather and Magnus Spelman. Surely if he was, there is no need to keep his name a secret."

The world seemed to slow before Olaf replied. "Let's be frank, Miss Palmer. Your grandfather was a menace to our society. I assure you, my friend would want nothing to do with you, nor would he care about your so-called interest in our history."

"But he was a hero like Magnus," Teira protested.

"Of course he was," Olaf said, "which is all the more reason he doesn't want vermin such as Soren Pedersen's family scurrying around him."

Teira's jaw dropped. Christian stepped forward. "What did you say?" he said through clenched teeth.

"I would be very careful if I were you," Mr. Jorgensen said, hostility radiating from his eyes. "There are armed guards all around, waiting for my distress signal."

"Let's go," Teira said, tugging on Christian's arm.

As they walked out of the treasury, Teira tried to break the tension. "Did he call me a rat?"

"Either that or a relative of one."

"He has no idea how insulting that is. It's lower than low."

"I would like to have let him know how I felt about it," Christian said. "Why did you want to leave so quickly?"

Teira looked at him through the corner of her eye, but kept walking. "He's up to something. I never gave him my name."

Christian stopped dead in his tracks. "Not only that, but if he associates you with your grandfather, why does he know you as Palmer instead of Pedersen?"

"Either he has connections, or I'm being followed. Which do you suppose it is?"

"I'm sure it's both. But why? What are we missing here?"

Sensing his tension, Teira slipped her arm through his. "I told you he's nasty."

"What's his problem?" Christian asked in frustration.

"He's no different than Ulrike Spelman. Judging by the looks that man gave me last night, I would venture to say some people never forget their feelings of anger or hatred. Should we go see if Magnus knows the mysterious man from the banquet?"

"Would his son, the human barrier, let us within ten feet of the front door?"

"I guess not." Teira sighed dejectedly. "I don't know why he's so upset. And why make *me* pay for it? It's not like I'm the threat."

Christian looked at Teira long and hard. "Yes, you are. That's it. That has to be it."

"What are you talking about?"

"Grethe never questioned anything—it was too painful. Your mother grew up and moved out of the country. Then you came back and started asking questions, stirring things up. You're a threat, especially if there is something to hide. Whoever is hiding it thinks that you can uncover the truth. If nothing else, you're a threat to their peace of mind."

"But I've never had more to go on than a hunch," Teira protested.

"Whoever is after you doesn't know that. They must think you're a lot closer to the truth than you know. We're missing something vital here. What is it?"

"It has to be the ring," Teira said. "It's the most obvious answer. If security is so paranoid that only the chief answers questions about it, it must be linked to that."

"Possibly. Missing jewels would definitely fall under the head of state security, so that isn't so far-fetched."

"I have an idea," Teira said. "What if we go to my place and I make us some dinner? Then we can figure out our next course of action."

"That sounds great. On the way, why don't you call to check on your grandmother? She was still pretty upset when we dropped her off."

Teira agreed. A few minutes later she hung up with a sigh. "Grandma's out in the garden taking a walk. I'll try back shortly."

"I feel awful," Christian said. "This is my fault. I thought meeting Jakob and hearing how much of a hero her husband was would be a blessing."

"It was!" Teira said. "Didn't you see the happy tears? Christian, you did her heart a lot of good today."

"Yeah, I also saw the tears she cried when she saw a picture of a Danish Nazi who just happened to be the one her husband had her pass something to the day he was accused of treason."

Teira didn't know what to say. She knew he blamed himself for Grethe's disappointment. But what he didn't realize was that Teira carried a good dose of guilt herself. "You know," she said, "I've learned something important lately."

"What's that?"

"I learned how insecure I was. I don't know if this makes any sense, but I was angry with my grandfather for disgracing our family name. I felt it reflected on me. And while it is part of who I am, I've finally learned that in the end who I become is up to me. I can learn from my ancestors, but hopefully be wise enough to take what is good from them and let whatever might not be so good go." She paused. "And I learned not to resent a person I didn't know. Maybe, just for being my grandfather, Soren deserves my love and respect."

Christian smiled warmly. "Okay, it's settled. We go over to the senior center and hug Grethe until we all feel better." He reached for Teira's hand and kissed it.

Minutes away from the senior center, Teira's cell phone rang. She looked at the caller ID. "Must be Grandma."

"Ask her to join us for dinner," Christian said before Teira answered the call.

"Hello, Grandma?" There was silence while Teira sat listening. Her smile disappeared. Christian looked over in concern.

"No, of course not," Teira said. "I called only a few minutes ago."

More silence.

A look of alarm crossed Teira's face. "We're on our way." She snapped the phone shut and turned to Christian. "That was the senior center. Grandma's missing. They said she went out for a walk, but when they called her for dinner she was gone. They've searched everywhere, but no one has seen her."

"What do you mean she's gone? How can she be missing?" Christian asked incredulously. "Aren't they supposed to keep an eye—"

His tirade was interrupted by the ringing of Teira's phone. This time the ID was unlisted. She opened it with an anxious "Hello?"

"By now you know we have something you want," a harsh voice said on the other end of the line.

"Who is this?" Teira demanded.

"Contact the police and she's dead. Do you understand?"

"No!" Teira screamed. "Don't hurt her, please. She's an elderly woman. Take me instead."

"We have our bargaining chip. You get us what we want and you get what you want. You have until six tomorrow morning."

"Wait! I don't know what you want!"

"The game is over. Give it to us. We'll call you with drop-off directions. Make one mistake and your grandmother's dead."

"How do I know she's alive now?" Teira sobbed. "If you do anything to her, I'll—"

"You're in no position to make threats," the man growled.

Teira took a shuddering breath. "Neither are you." Her voice shook with fear and anger, but she would not allow herself to be bullied. "You know I know the right people," she challenged. She was bluffing, but it was all she had with which to fight for her grandmother's life. "I want a call from you every two hours to assure me she's all right. If you slip up, I'll call the police. In America we call it insurance. Do we have a deal?"

"Fine. But one slip on your part and she's blown away. Understand?"

"Yes," Teira choked. "Now, let me know she's okay."

Teira heard some muffled sounds and then her grandmother crying. It was Teira's undoing. "Don't you hurt her!" she screamed. "Don't hurt my grandmother!"

"Six AM," the man growled.

"I don't know what you—" Teira yelled, but the phone was dead.

Christian had stopped the car by then and grabbed the cell. When he realized it was dead, he held a nearly hysterical Teira in his arms as she tried to relay the conversation. Above her head he squeezed his eyes shut as fear shot through him. He'd been sure Grethe would be safe at the center. How could he have underestimated them like this?

Emotion clogged his throat at the thought of the dear, sweet woman in the hands of monsters. He reached for his own phone to call the police, but Teira stopped him. "No!" she said. "They'll kill her!"

28

To their surprise, Magnus Spelman himself answered the door and stepped back to admit them without a word. He led the way to the front parlor and motioned for them to be seated. Before they could take a seat, Ulrike barged in like a wild bull, powerful and furious. Teira wouldn't have been surprised if steam had flared from his nostrils as he stampeded around the room.

"What will it take?" he demanded. "A restraining order? You will leave these premises or I will have the police escort you out once and for all!"

Christian fought back the fury that threatened to consume him. It was bad enough to see Teira mistreated by Jorgensen and now Ulrike, but with Grethe's abduction on top of it all, his tension was at an all-time high. His dark eyes glistening with anger, Christian turned on Ulrike and Magnus. "You do that! Call the police. Once they get here maybe we can get to the bottom of how you're connected with Grethe's disappearance."

"Stop this at once!" bellowed Magnus, catching everyone off guard, especially Ulrike.

"What are you talking about?" Ulrike demanded, ignoring his father's outburst.

"You heard me. She's gone and we think you're both connected to her disappearance."

"You're out of your mind!" Ulrike roared. He took a step toward Christian.

Christian wasn't about to back down.

"Let him speak!" demanded Magnus.

Christian reached into his pocket and pulled out the newsletter. It was folded so that the picture of the Nazi party leader didn't show. "Do you know this man?" he asked, showing Magnus the picture of the man they desperately needed to identify.

"Of course I do," Magnus said. "He is Haldor Andreasen. It's an old picture of him, but I would know him anywhere."

"How do you know him?" Christian asked brusquely.

"He was part of the Freedom Council with Soren and me. It's no secret."

"How long did you work together?" Christian asked. "Time enough to know him well?"

"We hardly knew him at all back then," Mangus said. "The war was near its end when he transferred to our group. He'd come from a sabotage ring. Of course, after the war we remained friends. What does this have to do with anything?"

Christian unfolded the picture and Magnus stared at it in disbelief. "I don't understand." His voice shook.

"Where I come from we'd call him a double agent," Christian said. "How is it that underground newsletters like these were circulated, yet no one saw this picture?"

"That is easy to explain," Magnus said. "It is not as though we sat back and read the papers at our leisure. If we were caught with one, it could have meant our death. They were meant to be read and destroyed. It was as simple as that. One would simply glance through and be rid of it. It is no wonder that no one noted Haldor in the crowd. We would not have looked for him, or noted him if we had seen his face, for he was not in our group then."

Christian continued his questions. "The day Soren was killed, Soren asked Grethe to send a message with Haldor, saying he would know what to do with it. Shortly afterward, you both made your way to the train station where you saw the enemy officials get off the train before the car exploded. The council never got word to send for help, but you saw Soren speak to the soldiers. After Soren's exemplary war record, what do you make of the accusations against him?"

"I never knew what to think of it all. It didn't make any sense to me," Magnus said mournfully. "I only told the council what I saw."

"Soren also sustained a bullet wound that day. What do you know of that?"

"I told Teira before, I knew nothing of any shots being fired. I saw only the explosion and debris fly everywhere. Soren was badly burned and bleeding. I carried him to a nearby home where the council met us. One of the two men was a doctor who tended him while I went for a truck. Then we took Soren home to Grethe. The doctor and the other man carried him in while I stood watch in the truck. I swear to you now, that is all I know!"

"How could you possibly miss a bullet wound?" Christian pressed.

Magnus shook with frustration. "I've told you all I know! There was shrapnel in the explosion, debris flew through the air, but I know of no bullet wound. All I saw were cuts and severe burns." His voice faded. "And they were everywhere."

"What of Grethe?" Ulrike interrupted. He was still cold, but not nearly as aggressive as when they'd first arrived.

"Grethe has been taken from the senior center where she lives," Christian said. "What do you know about that?"

"Now just one minute!" Ulrike said, his voice dangerously low. "What makes you think we have anything to do with it?"

Teira's cheeks were bright with anger. "How can you ask us that after the way you've treated me each time I've come to your home? Magnus has withheld information and I've seen him with Haldor myself! You don't think that's suspicious?"

"I'm a public figure," Ulrike admitted. "I was appointed to a high government position by the prime minister, I report to the Parliament, and I still have aspirations to further my political career. All of this requires a person of respect and decorum." He tried to explain. "I know it doesn't hold much weight with you, but my father was Soren's friend. It was bad for him after the war. You think he didn't have accusations thrown his way? I assure you that my father paid a price for being Soren's friend. He made himself look even more guilty when he tried to help Grethe, but he did it anyway. It may seem little in your eyes, but in those days it was much. Right or wrong, Soren was branded a traitor. He still is. I don't need the bad publicity by association. Every piece of negative gossip threatens my position. I may seem cruel to you, but those are the facts."

Magnus cleared his throat. "Soren and I were friends for years. I did love him like a brother. We may have distanced ourselves from Grethe eventually, but that doesn't mean we wish ill upon her. I have always thought very highly of her. If I have seemed to hold back, as you say, it is out of concern for my son—and because I didn't want to dredge up memories that are still painful. However, when someone's life is at stake, it is time to do what we can to help. What do you want of us? We will *both* be happy to assist."

"Teira was being watched by this man at the ball last night," Christian answered pointing to Haldor's picture.

Magnus nodded. "I noticed him watching her intently myself. I was watching you both at the banquet. I could see that you were troubled by something, so I stood behind you when you walked to the back of the room. I couldn't see what it was you were looking at."

"Do you know how Jorgensen is involved with Haldor Andreasen?" Christian asked.

"The Jorgensen who is head of security at Rosenborg Castle?" Ulrike interrupted.

"Yes," Teira said. "He was very unpleasant when we asked him for Haldor's name. He has to be involved somehow."

Ulrike said, "Olaf is closer to my age. I can't imagine what the two could have in common." He turned to his father.

"Please, Mr. Spelman," Teira added. "Is there anything you can think of that would help? What could we have that they want? Did it have anything to do with my grandmother meeting that man at Amaliehaven Royal Gardens the day my grandfather died? Or the letter she gave to Haldor? Or—"

Magnus's head jerked up. "What man did she meet at the gardens?"

"I have no idea. It was part of her report to the council though. Earlier that same day she met someone at the gardens. She was pushing a baby pram. The man bent over as though peering in to see the baby and something fell from his sleeve and went under the baby blanket. She rushed the buggy home. Later, my grandfather sent her on her way again with the note for Haldor."

"I knew nothing of this," Magnus said. "The interrogations were kept confidential. Grethe never discussed them. Nor did I. It was too painful." He leaned forward and asked, "What was in the man's sleeve?"

"She had no idea," Teira said. "Soldiers were everywhere. She hurried home to pick up my mother from the neighbors. When she returned, Soren was gone, but he later called to ask her to meet him behind a market for a second errand. This time she delivered the note to Haldor."

"Find what she received that morning and I believe you will know what these people want," Magnus said.

"Do you know who she might have met at the gardens?" Teira asked.

Magnus shook his head. "I don't. But Soren was good friends with many from the palace. The man could have been sent by King Christian himself."

Teira's eyes grew wide. "Magnus, have you heard the legend about the signet ring?"

"Of course."

"Is there any chance that it may have been given to my grandfather—for any reason?" Teira asked. He sat silently. "Magnus, did my grandfather have the ring?"

"We all suspected it at one time," he said at last.

"Why? What is so significant about that ring?"

"It had the power to condemn and destroy or to free and enlighten."

Teira pondered his words. "That's it then, isn't it? They think I have the ring. If I do, my grandfather is innocent because the king trusted him. If I don't, my grandfather still looks guilty and the ones who killed those people stay free. As long as there is no proof, my grandfather remains a traitor and Haldor remains a hero."

"Teira, I don't have any more answers today than I did back then," Magnus said. "I wish I did, but I don't know what happened. I'm sorry. It would appear, however, that given all you've said, your assumptions must be correct."

Teira began to tremble. "But I *don't* have the ring and they're going to kill my grandmother!"

"We're running out of time," Christian said. "Let's go back to the house and see if we can find it. Magnus, if you can think of anything at all, please call us."

"It won't do you any good to look in the barn," he advised. "It's new. The first was torn down and the new one erected. But if I know Soren, he would have put the ring somewhere with great significance.

Somewhere he would be sure it could be found if he could not retrieve it himself."

Ulrike stepped forward. "If you can accept my apology, the other side to being a public figure is that I'm in a position to help. I would like to. If there is anything I can do, you have only to call."

* * *

It was another twenty-five minutes before they pulled into the driveway of Teira's grandmother's home. They walked up to the front door and Teira reached for her keys. Christian stopped her. The door was slightly ajar. Christian held a finger to his lips. He moved Teira around until she was standing behind him. Then he cautiously pushed at the door. Ever so slowly it swung wide. Christian peered inside.

Teira looked around him. The place was in shambles. Christian motioned for her to go back to the car and wait for him, but she shook her head no and reminded him, "Together."

Quietly they walked through the broken glass and damaged furniture. "They must be gone," Christian said, the muscles in his jaw working out his tension. "But they've trashed the place. I'm sorry." He gently rubbed Teira's shoulders as they sagged in discouragement. When they began to shake, he pulled her against his chest and held her close.

She looked up at him. A tear rolled down her cheek. He wiped it away with his thumb. "We're losing time," he said gently. "Let's get to work."

"This is my fault, you know."

"No."

She nodded stubbornly.

"Don't worry, Teira. We'll get Grethe back safe and sound, you'll see. You just hang in there with me and stay strong, okay?" He released her. "Why don't we put things in the Lord's hands now? We'll exercise our faith and work like crazy to get our grandma back, hmm?"

"Sounds like a perfect plan," she said, trying to smile.

But inside she couldn't help but worry that perhaps this time the answer to her prayers was no.

* * *

Teira called Jakob Meier and got his promise to call back as soon as possible with anything else he could turn up on Haldor Andreasen. Within half an hour, Jakob kept his word. He confirmed that Haldor had indeed been an active member of the Danish Nazi Party. It was proof of what they had suspected. Jakob also said he had gone a step further to see if he could turn up anything else on the Danish Nazi Party. All he could find was a short paragraph on a few riots and protests and one that mentioned that their headquarters had been broken into near the end of the war. "That's not a big surprise," he said. "By then the country was quite bitter with anyone working for the enemy."

Jakob offered his help again if there was anything more he could do, then he and Teira ended the call.

Christian began his search in the attic while Teira went to the bedroom her grandparents had once shared—the one she was staying in. Like everywhere else, the vandals had been there as well. After searching through the drawers and cupboard contents that were now overturned and scattered, Teira walked to the closet to look through the top shelf. It too had been swiped clean of the boxes that had once been stored there. On top of a heap of rubble was her grandfather's uniform, slashed practically to threads.

She clutched it to her chest and fought back tears. "Oh, Grandpa, what have they done? You had so much respect for everything this uniform represented. I'm so sorry." Instinctively, she went looking for Christian. "Look what they've done!" she cried.

Christian turned from the trunk he'd been sorting through and rose to his feet. Brushing the dust from the knees of his jeans, he walked to meet her. Hurrying to meet him part way, Teira tripped on the same nail she had tripped on the last time she'd been up there.

"I need to fix that before someone gets hurt," she said with emotion in her voice. Holding out the garment, she showed him the ragged pieces of the once stately uniform. "It's ruined." Teira swallowed past the lump that had lodged in her throat and forced herself to blink away the tears that threatened to spill from her eyes. "Sorry," she apologized. "I get over-emotional when I'm tired."

"Yeah. Or when some animal comes in and destroys a family heirloom after kidnapping your grandmother." He sighed and looked around. "I don't even know what we're looking for. It's like searching for buried treasure without a map." In the next second he straightened his shoulders. "Come on, we're not giving up. We're not letting those creeps win. Later we'll figure out what we can do to preserve the uniform." He took it and set it on a nearby box.

Christian's words weren't very convincing. The uniform was obviously ruined, but Teira loved him for trying so hard to encourage her. With one last look at the shreds, she turned to walk away, but something caught her eye. Looking closer, she said, "Christian! What's that?"

He turned to look where she pointed. At the hem of the torn garment something white stuck out, barely noticeable. Whoever had slashed it had ripped just enough into the hem to reveal that something was inside.

Teira picked up the garment and looked at the hem. It had been restitched at least once by hand. Her heart raced. Whoever had slashed the uniform had done them a favor. He had brought to their attention something that he himself had missed. Teira ripped the hem the rest of the way and removed a folded piece of paper, tightly banded with the king's signet ring. She gasped.

"Bingo!" Christian said reverently.

They stared in wide-eyed astonishment at the ring Teira held in her trembling hand. Both were speechless.

Finally Christian let out a whoop and a holler. "You did it! You found it!" He picked her up and swung her around. "That's my girl!" he said excitedly. "Now we have a way to get Grethe back."

"What does the letter say?" Teira asked.

Christian grinned. "I don't know. Read it."

With trembling fingers, Teira unfolded the paper and scanned the few lines. Her jubilation died instantly. "Christian!" she said. "It's a ransom letter! My grandfather planned to abduct the king!"

Christian waited for Teira to return from the bathroom downstairs. She'd looked like he felt when they read the abduction letter—ill. He now feared this nightmare could end in the worst way possible.

Christian said another earnest prayer for Grethe's safety and added a plea for himself. He needed to keep a clear head if there was to be any hope of helping Teira through this disaster.

He heard Teira crawl up the ladder and watched her come toward him. He knew she was terrified *and* tired, both mentally and physically. It was three in the morning and they had been searching all night.

She forced a smile. "Well, that was the last thing I expected," she said just before she tripped on the protruding nail again. This time she came down on her knee with a crack. "Ouch!"

Christian winced and sprang up to help her. "Are you all right?"

"I'm fine. That makes three times that nail has tried to get me! Anyway, I've been thinking . . ." Her words trailed off as she stared at the nail.

Christian followed her line of vision—and her line of reasoning. "Why is that the only nail protruding?" he said. "It's the only loose board up here."

Teira looked around and located a hammer. Before she could hand it to Christian, her phone rang. "Let me talk to her," she said anxiously.

"Three more hours. You better have it," the man on the other end of the line snarled.

"Look, I have what you want," Teira said. "Just let me talk to my grandma. This time I want to hear more than crying."

There was a pause and then Grethe came on the line. "Teira? I love you. Tell Hanne—"

The phone went dead.

Teira's eyes glistened. Her hands shook as she snapped the phone shut.

Christian kissed her on the forehead. "She's all right. Focus on that."

Teira meant to hand Christian the hammer, but it slipped from her grasp and dropped to the floor. It landed on the loose board.

Christian looked down, his brow furrowed. "Did you hear that?" He knocked on the board. "Teira, it's hollow under there. Listen to the difference." He knocked on another area of the floor and then on the loose board again.

Teira dropped to her knees. "Can you pry it up?"

"Yeah. The nail's old and rusty, but it's coming."

In no time Teira and Christian lifted out a small section of floorboard. Tucked inside was a packet of folded papers.

"It looks like some sort of correspondence," Christian said. "We'll have to at least skim them to find out."

"I'm not so sure I want to know," Teira said. "Who knows what else my grandfather was hiding."

"I'll read them," Christian said. "Knowledge is power, as they say. Let's see what's in these letters." He divided the stack and they began to go through the papers.

Christian scanned an article and said, "Look at this, Teira. I think it's an overview of how the Resistance sabotaged the Germans. They were a lot bigger group than I imagined. It says here that by the end of the war there were almost fifty thousand of them. How do you like that?"

"It's easy to see how one bad apple like Haldor Andreasen could slip in unnoticed," Teira replied. "Does it say anything else?"

"Only that after the military had been freed from imprisonment they began to work alongside the Freedom Council. They gathered in special groups in Copenhagen and formed a brigade called Danforce. Officers were given leading positions around the country and the movement was secretly funded by the state. Of course the occupying forces retaliated. They had taken control of the government, newspapers, schools, and even the hospitals."

"My grandmother said they couldn't take my grandfather to the hospital after he had been burned or he might have been killed," Teira said. She stood and the papers fell from her lap. She crossed her arms over her chest and paced around the room. Then she stopped and looked at her watch. "Two and a half more hours," she informed Christian before beginning to pace again. "I wish they would call so they could take this ring and we could get my grandma back. I just want this nightmare to end. I'll bury the past and pretend this never happened."

"Teira, wait. Look at this."

Teira sat beside him. "What is it?"

"This stationary has a monogram and a crown. Look at the signature. It looks like this letter was written by King Christian X himself. Is that possible? I mean, look at the date. Isn't that the day your grandfather died?"

Teira took the letter from Christian.

"Read it," he said. "What does it say?"

Teira cleared her throat and began.

My Friend Soren,

I have received your correspondence in regards to my ring. It never occurred to me that you would take it upon yourself to recover it, let alone discover who the perpetrators were. I thank you most sincerely for your service, friendship, and integrity.

You can imagine my disappointment to learn that the betrayal was by our own countrymen, those affiliated with the Danish Nazi group. I am disheartened. Please keep the letter and ring as proof of their malicious acts. I will ask for their return when the time is right. Take care, my friend, for if they become aware that you have recovered such powerful evidence against them, we both know the fate that will befall you.

In your letter you mentioned that you feel there is a spy among you. Perhaps a test of trust would bring him out into the open?

It has come to my attention that a group of enemy officials will travel to Berlin today on the afternoon train. It is imperative that the train does not leave the station with those men aboard. We must impede their communication at once. The German Empire is starting to disintegrate.

As we gradually see the collapse of enemy fronts, it brings hope for the time we will see a liberated Denmark. It is my sincerest wish that that day draws nigh.

Once again, I am counting on you, my friend, to see this through. You have never failed me. Send for help, but only if you must. Otherwise, take your most trusted allies. I will await your successful report.

God speed,
CX

"Do you think this is authentic?" Teira asked. "Did Christian X write this to my grandfather?" She ran her fingers over the initials scrawled at the bottom.

"Sure looks like it to me," Christian said. "It could easily fit into the sleeve of a man's jacket and slip out under a blanket into the baby pram like your grandmother said."

"She and Magnus both said my grandfather had contacts at the palace. Maybe it was an informant that delivered the letter."

"It makes sense. From what I understand from this letter, the council might not have known Soren was going on the mission unless he somehow got word to them."

"Maybe that information was in the letter my grandma gave to Haldor to deliver."

"I think you're right. Soren had to know it was a mission he could pull off with Magnus, but he sent Haldor to ask for help to see if he would follow through. That's the test of trust the king told Soren to put him through. That still doesn't explain why Haldor would have you killed, though. Maybe he wants the ring. People have killed for less, but none of this links him personally to the crime."

"Something else is missing," Teira said. "Is there anything in those stacks of papers?"

"Not that I saw. What was in your pile?"

"Just a bunch of letters and reports on missions. I'll go through them again." After a time of reading through the documents, Christian heard her gasp and then squeal. "I found it! This is what Haldor wants! I'm sure of it."

Christian peered at the typed document.

"It's a report to Commandant Gunder Larsen, dated the day before my grandfather died," Teira explained. "It says that the attempt to abduct the king was unsuccessful but that they managed to obtain one of his most prized possessions and plans were being formulated for another attempt. It ends by saying that the ransom note and ring would be included with the report." She drew a breath. "And it's signed by none other than Haldor Andreasen."

"I'll bet anything that Haldor knows Soren had all this proof against him," Christian said, taking the report from Teira and placing it with the letter from the king. Suddenly, Christian shot a look at Teira. "Wait a minute—that's it!" he exclaimed anxiously.

Christian quickly scanned the letter from the king once more. "It says here that your grandfather recovered the evidence against the Danish Nazi Party. Didn't you say Jakob mentioned that someone had broken into the Nazi headquarters?"

Teira nodded. "It had to have been my grandfather. That's how he recovered the evidence to incriminate Haldor."

"And Haldor knows that Soren would have hidden the documents and evidence away somewhere," Christian concluded.

"We have everything we need," Teira said incredulously. "Do you know what this means?"

"I sure do. When they call, we'll be ready."

After gathering up all the evidence they needed, Teira and Christian formulated a plan of their own and headed back to Copenhagen.

"Don't you see what a big risk this is?" Christian said, staring at Teira as they sat at his house waiting for the call to come in.

"Yes, but she's my grandma. I have to do this," Teira answered. "I can't believe it's come down to this. For someone to hold so much greed and fear inside, to keep it alive for so many years!" Teira exclaimed.

"This man is obviously deranged," Christian said. "No sane person would be obsessed enough with the events of six decades ago to stalk you and kidnap your grandmother." Christian frowned. "He's dangerous, Teira. I don't know if we can pull this off by ourselves. I think we should call the police."

"If they were willing to kill me, they wouldn't think twice about killing her."

"Point taken. But the police are experienced in this kind of thing. Don't you—"

"I couldn't live with myself if Grandma was killed because I didn't follow their directions," Teira interrupted. "Christian, I . . . I'm too frightened they'll find out and kill her before the police have a chance to act. We don't know who all is involved, after all."

He nodded grimly. "Should we go over our plan again?"

Teira stood and started to pace. "I have it down pat. I just need to double-check the battery on the cell phone."

"You already have and so have I—twice," Christian reminded her.

Teira kept pacing. Finally, Christian stood in her path and put his arms around her waist to stop her.

"Sorry," she muttered. "I guess I'm a little more scared than I want to admit." Tears filled her eyes as Christian held her. "You don't think they've done anything to hurt her, do you?"

"No," he reassured her. "They have too much riding on the ring. She's their insurance. Getting what they want from you depends on her well-being."

"I should have taken better care of her," Teira sobbed. "How could I have let this happen?"

"I've asked myself that over and over," Christian admitted. "But Teira, we thought she was safe where she was. And we'll get her back."

* * *

It was just before six when the phone rang. Christian nodded. Teira answered and pushed the "record" feature. Then, with trembling hands, she waited for further instructions. She recognized the voice at once. It was Olaf Jorgensen.

"Are you ready for your instructions?" he asked.

"I'm ready, but first I want to hear from my grandmother." It was half demand, half plea.

A muffled groan came through the line.

"What have you done to her?" Teira asked, near panic. "Let me talk to her!"

"You'll do as I say or, believe me, she'll be in a lot worse shape."

"That's not the deal we made!" Teira felt hysterical. "You said you wouldn't hurt her!"

"What I said, if you remember correctly, was that I'd trade the old lady for the ring. Now I suggest we get on with the business at hand."

"Tell me what you want me to do. I'll do whatever you ask. Just please, don't hurt her." Teira broke down in sobs.

Christian gripped her hand tightly.

Teira gathered strength from him as she listened intently to the instructions. "I can be there in ten minutes," she promised.

After the call was disconnected, Teira looked at Christian. He took the phone from her fingers and snapped it shut.

"Where's the meeting place?" he asked.

"Christiansborg Palace." She shook her head. "That's a public place! How could they have taken her there without anybody knowing it?"

"Olaf Jorgansen's office is probably there," Christian said. "He must know the place like the back of his hand. And with today being Sunday, the government offices will be closed." Suddenly another thought occurred to him. "I know exactly where they could take her without anyone knowing! The ruins beneath the palace." Christian gathered Teira close while he described the vast caverns under the existing palace.

When he was done, Teira's eyes were filled with fear, but she stood and gathered her purse. Accepting the cell phone Christian handed her, she put it in the front pocket of her shirt, concealing it beneath a lightweight sweater. Then she turned and headed toward the door, looking over her shoulder at Christian.

"Wait! I'm going with you," he said.

"You can't." Teira's voice wavered. "They'll kill her and me both if I don't go alone."

"You're not going alone," he said matter-of-factly. "I won't let you."

"It has to look like I'm complying," she said. "I'll do what we discussed. You won't leave me, will you?"

"Not a chance. We're in this together. I'll give you a few minutes. Then you can bet I'll be right behind you."

Teira's eyes filled with tears as she looked back at Christian. Suddenly, she ran toward him and kissed him soundly. "Thank you," she whispered. "We're going to be all right, aren't we?"

"Of course," he said. "Just stick to the plan."

Teira nodded, turned, and walked out the door.

* * *

As he watched Teira walk away, Christian wished he felt as confident as he'd sounded. He was used to being in charge, calling the shots, and controlling the outcome. To accept a role where all he could do was wait and hope that Teira and Grethe would finally be safe was the worst kind of torture. An overwhelming feeling of helplessness swept over him. It was similar to what he'd felt when Sidney was in the hospital, but this time he wasn't as ill-equipped to handle the fear and desperation. He knew where to turn. He knelt and said an earnest prayer as Teira pulled from the driveway.

Christian understood Teira's fear of involving the police, but he didn't share it. Besides which, he knew that he couldn't live with himself if he didn't do all that he could to ensure both women's safety. He reached for his phone as he sprinted for his car.

"There's been a kidnapping!" he told the dispatcher. "I know where the hostage is."

Unbelievably, the dispatcher told him to stay where he was; they would send the police to him. It wasn't the answer he wanted.

Striving to control his temper, Christian tried to explain the situation. "There has been an abduction and, as we speak, the ransom is being paid. I need help immediately. I'm not about to sit around waiting for someone to come to me. Lives are in danger and I need the police at the meeting place. Now!"

To his astonishment, the dispatcher had more questions. Exasperated, he cut him off midsentence and raised the decibel level of his voice. "Look, this isn't a prank call. I'm telling you, I need help. By the time someone gets here to fill out a blasted report it will be too late. Show some intelligence and send help quickly to Christiansborg Palace. I'll meet the police there." He slammed his phone shut and maneuvered his car through the city center.

* * *

Teira found the side door of Christiansborg Palace that the kidnappers had directed her to and glanced around. No security guard was in sight. Surely there should have been someone on duty at this early-morning hour. Then again, after what these monsters had attempted to do to Kort Madsen and herself, it didn't take an overactive imagination to guess what they wouldn't think twice about doing to someone who impeded their plans.

When Teira entered the building as directed, the room was still in early dawn's light and filled with shadows.

Olaf Jorgensen appeared at the door. Teira's voice trembled. "I want to see my grandmother!"

Jorgensen grasped Teira roughly by the arm and dragged her farther inside.

Caught unaware, Teira stumbled and nearly lost her balance. She righted herself only to find a gun pressed deeply against the middle of her back. She knew which way to go by the pressure from the gun as Jorgensen pushed her along.

After passing several long hallways, Jorgensen pulled open a door that led to the old ruins below ground. Weaving their way around the walls and pillars of the huge, chilly underground domain, they walked deeper into the bowels of the old castle with every turn and passage. They traveled down long flights of stairs where the walls on each side were only partially standing. There were landings between the flights where the walls had disappeared so one could look out over a stone banister and see the hard dirt floor far below.

Goose bumps rose on Teira's arms and fear caused her to tremble. No one would hear her scream this deep below the surface of the earth. No one would find her here until it was too late. Her only hope of getting herself and her grandmother out alive was if the men wanted only the ring, and not the deaths of the two women they held captive.

31

With the gun now pressing between her shoulder blades, Teira stumbled along. "How much farther?" she asked, her voice quivering.

"Until I tell you to stop."

A pungent, musty odor filled her nostrils the deeper they went. Teira started to shake violently.

"You should never have come to Denmark," Olaf sneered. "Now it's time for you to pay the price for your insolence."

"We made a deal—the ring for my grandma."

"Ah, but you and your boyfriend know too much, I fear. Fortunately, we can take care of that. Accidents happen all the time, especially in decrepit places like this. No safety restraints, you see, and arrogant American tourists." His laugh terrified Teira more than his words.

Teira tried to calm herself as her mind raced. If she didn't have a clear mind, she wouldn't be able to use her head when she most needed to think straight.

At the last turn they came face to face with Haldor Andreasen. He sat on a low, crumbled wall. A gun lay on his lap and one of his hands lay on top of it.

Two more men stood nearby. Teira had never seen either henchman before, but guessed by the grin on the younger man's face that he had been the one who'd tried to drown her. To her surprise, Rolf wasn't there.

With the gun still at her back, she clutched her purse to her chest and felt the phone beneath her sweater. She'd been wrong about not calling the police. If only she could call them now.

Teira's eyes darted toward a figure slumped in the corner on the cold dirt floor. It was her grandmother, huddled against the wall with her head resting on crumbling stone. Duct tape covered her mouth and was wrapped tightly around her wrists, knees, and ankles. Her glasses lay a few feet away, smashed on the ground. A purple bruise darkened her cheek, and a cut on her brow still oozed blood. She looked up at Teira with soulful, frightened eyes.

Forgetting the gun at her back, Teira ran to her grandmother and enfolded her in her arms. "I'll get you out of here!" she whispered fiercely.

"Stop!" Haldor commanded. "Or we will kill her now!"

Teira released her grandmother, but the tears flowed freely down her cheeks. She wiped them away with the back of her hand as rage overcame fear. "You hateful man! How could you treat her like this?"

Haldor rose slowly to his feet. "I don't think we've had the pleasure of being introduced. Allow me to handle the niceties. You've met my nephew, Olaf?"

Nephew?

Haldor pointed to Jorgensen who now aimed the gun at Teira's temple. "He angers easily, so may I warn you to not upset him? Hmm?" Turning to the young man with the smirk on his face, Haldor cocked the gun and said, "This is Viggo." He fired and the youth crumpled to the ground. Blood trickled from his forehead where the bullet had entered. Teira screamed and Grethe turned her face toward the wall. Her shoulders sagged even further.

"Now, Miss Palmer," Haldor continued, "something that Viggo never understood is that I don't like people who make mistakes. He made one too many. Kort Madsen should never have lived to tell about his car troubles. That was Viggo's first mistake. His second was in not finishing you off that day in the sea. If he had, we wouldn't be having this inconvenient little meeting today. Believe me, I don't like to be inconvenienced any more than Olaf likes to be angered."

Teira looked away from the body with the blood pooling around the head. She covered her mouth with a trembling hand, desperately trying to swallow the bile that rose in her throat.

"Finally," Haldor continued, "allow me to introduce Valdemar, my apprentice. He holds much promise. And I am Haldor."

"What about Rolf Tycksen?" Teira asked. "Isn't he involved? You tried to kill Kort so you could put Rolf there to watch me."

"Not only beautiful, but bright," Haldor sneered. "However, you are only partially correct. You see, Rolf is a stupid oaf. He believes he is spying for the city. His only job was to report your comings and goings. He knows nothing."

Teira looked at Grethe tied up and huddled on the ground.

"And my grandfather?" Teira asked.

The grin on Haldor's face became something dark and menacing. "What of him? He's dead."

"You leaked the information that my grandfather was going to blow up the railroad."

"I did better than that," Haldor said. "When your grandfather found me out and took the evidence he needed against me, I decided to get him first. It was a brilliant plan that worked for over sixty years, until his progeny came along. But I will not let you bring me down. I won't!"

"I read the letter," Teira said. "He never intended to kill anyone. He planned to stop the train by dismantling the railroad. There was never meant to be a single soul on that train."

Haldor snickered. "Don't be naïve. Your grandfather blew up enough railroads that he could do it in his sleep. He didn't need any help. He tried to set me up, but I wasn't about to let him bring me down, so I got him first instead. What he didn't know was that I had already been informed of that train and what its purpose was that day. It may have been Soren's intent to blow it up before anyone loaded, but I filled it with our countrymen ahead of schedule. You can well imagine his look of horror when he realized how the mission would play out."

Teira shuddered as she thought of the grisly scene Haldor described.

"If Grethe had kept her mouth shut about seeing me that day she wouldn't be in the mess she is in today," Haldor said. "But it doesn't matter now. That information won't leave this room, and neither will you. Alive that is. Now that I have appeased your curiosity, you can join that pathetic grandfather of yours in the cold, hard ground." Haldor cocked the gun. "So, about the ring—"

Teira had never known such fear. Haldor stepped forward and grabbed her purse. He overturned it and dumped the contents onto the ground. A loud metal clank sounded as her grandfather's gun hit the floor.

Haldor's eyes flared and met Teira's. "What have we here?" he asked in a low voice. "It was stupidity on your part to bring a weapon. I believe you have pushed me far enough. Where is it? Where is the ring?" He picked up the gun and slipped it into the waistband of his pants, still holding his own gun in his other hand.

"How foolish do you think I am?" Teira said softly. "You thought I'd hand it over before I knew if my grandmother was safe? You let her go and I'll take you to it. Otherwise, the police and the monarchy will soon receive a message telling them where to find the ring and the rest of the evidence against you. It won't matter then if my grandmother and I are dead or alive. You'll be caught either way."

Haldor's roar echoed in the ruins as he held his gun above his head and fired. Rocks, dust, and dirt tumbled down on their heads.

Teira screamed and ran to cover her grandmother with her body. Thick dust obstructed her vision as she dodged too close to the wall, slamming her head against it and grazing her forehead. Still, she managed to protect her grandmother from the worst of the falling debris.

Olaf grabbed Teira by the hair and yanked her roughly back. Terrified, but thinking clearly, she stomped on the insole of Olaf's foot and elbowed him in the stomach. When he doubled over, she kicked the gun from his hand and out of his reach. Then she ran back the way they had come with Olaf close on her heels. She didn't get far.

As the dust settled, Teira had a clearer view of the scene before her. Someone was wrestling Valdemar to the ground. It was Christian. Close behind was a security guard.

"Christian!" she screamed, then barreled into Haldor with her shoulder as she passed him, knocking the gun from his grasp. She kicked it near Christian, who scrambled far enough away from Valdemar to grab the gun. He immediately turned and backhanded Valdemar. The thug tumbled down unconscious and bleeding from his nose.

The security guard ran for Haldor. Despite his age, the man wouldn't be taken easily. He fought with all his might though it was a losing battle against the much younger, stronger guard. He soon had Haldor in cuffs.

With Valdemar down, Christian grabbed for Haldor's gun. Olaf jumped him from behind. The two men wrestled for the gun. Christian was able to gain enough momentum to roll Olaf onto his back and pry the gun from his grasp by slamming the pistol-clutching fist against the hard floor. The gun went off before it flew out of both men's grasp. Christian rolled over with a groan. Blood seeped from his shoulder.

Christian had been shot. Unarmed now, he lay motionless.

32

Teira screamed in terror. "No!"

Christian rolled over. "Grab the gun!" he gasped.

Teira swallowed a sob and dived for the gun just as Olaf did. They collided, and the impact sent Teira to the ground. In an instant she was up, aiming the gun with trembling hands. "Don't move!"

Christian staggered to his feet; the front of his T-shirt bright red.

From the corner of her eye, Teira saw Valdemar sit up. It was enough of a distraction that Olaf stepped forward to wrestle the gun from her grasp. "No!" she cried and fought with all her strength to keep hold of it. Her strength was no match for his. Thinking that she could divert attention from Christian and her grandmother, Teira ran from the area.

She dodged back and forth haphazardly as Olaf chased her. Bullets ricocheted off ancient walls and embedded themselves in others as Teira continued to run as fast as she could. She darted behind a crumbling pillar, caught her breath, and ran for the stairs. If she could make it to the upper levels, maybe someone in the occupied part of the castle would hear her screams and send for help.

Olaf caught up with her and cocked the gun. He would shoot her at close range.

Panicked, Teira swung her arms and legs, hitting and kicking with all her might. She managed to knock the gun from him and kicked it over the edge of the landing. A shot rang out as the gun hit the ground several feet below.

Olaf grabbed Teira's wrists and wrenched them behind her back.

Teira screamed, her shoulders burning with searing pain. Olaf pushed her head and upper body backward over the deteriorating balustrade. Teira stared out at the ruins until the blood rushed to her head and made her so dizzy she had to close her eyes.

She screamed one last time as gravity and Olaf's pressure forced her downward. Her feet began to slip. A few more inches and she would lose her balance. One more push and she would plunge to her death.

* * *

Valdemar held Soren's gun to Grethe's head while the security guard held Valdemar at gunpoint, calling for backup.

"I wouldn't do that if I were you," Christian warned Valdemar. "Put it down now!"

Christian pulled out the gun that Teira had kicked from Olaf's grasp and held it up. When his hand trembled, he tightened his grip. "I mean it. I don't want to use this, but I will."

Valdemar smirked and cocked Soren's gun.

Christian stepped forward. "Give me the gun."

"Shoot her!" Haldor demanded from where he sat on the floor.

Christian took another step closer.

"I said shoot her!" Haldor yelled in fury.

Valdemar pulled the trigger. The only sound was a small, metallic click.

"Didn't Teira tell you?" Christian smiled coldly. "She hates violence and refused to carry a loaded gun."

While the security guard dealt with Valdemar, Christian took off after Teira. He heard her bloodcurdling scream and the single shot. Then nothing but silence. His heart plummeted. In that instant, he thought Teira was dead. He was gripped with a fear like none he had ever known.

* * *

"Why did you do it?" Olaf breathed into Teira's ear. "Why did you have to come and mess up our lives?"

"I didn't mean to!" she managed with what little breath she had left. "You'll never get away with this," Teira said, gasping for air.

The sound of a gun cocking made Olaf turn around.

"Take your hands off her and step away or you're a dead man," Christian said through gritted teeth.

He was there! Christian had come!

"Sorry, Tanner, but I'm not backing away," Olaf said. He grabbed Teira and placed her in front of himself as a shield. "You shoot me, you kill her. Either way, you lose."

"I won't miss," Christian warned, stepping closer.

This wasn't the end Teira had had in mind. Olaf dead, possibly Christian as well, and her body slamming into the ground below. She had to get out of the way. Somehow she had to loosen Olaf's grasp on her.

The floor swayed as Teira's head dropped and the blood rushed back. Gaining momentum, and with all the strength she could muster, she swung her head forward then backward. She slammed it as hard as she could into Olaf's face.

The impact knocked her senseless and into the darkness of oblivion.

* * *

Teira opened her eyes in a daze. Blinking rapidly to focus, she saw a couple of security men standing directly in front of her. They had Olaf in handcuffs.

She sat on the stair landing with her head on Christian's good shoulder. He leaned against the balustrade.

Teira lifted her head quickly. Then, with a groan, she realized that the sudden movement had sent a piercing pain shooting through her head.

"Welcome back," Christian said quietly.

"You're alive!" Tears sprang to her eyes.

"You didn't think I'd let them best me in a duel, did you?" he said weakly.

Teira looked at the pallor of his skin and at the bloodstained shirt. She swallowed a sob. "Is help on the way?" she asked hopefully. A single tear slipped from her eye and then another.

Christian nodded and leaned his head back against the wall before rolling it to the side to look at Teira. With his thumb he wiped away her tears. "I didn't realize you were quite so hard-headed," he said. "Not that I'm complaining." Christian's lips twitched in a weak grin. Then he closed his eyes.

Teira looked at the man who had come to mean so much to her in such a short time. She knew he was in terrible pain, though he didn't say it. Sweat dripped down the side of his face. His breathing was labored and his lashes looked dark against his pale cheeks. He'd never looked more handsome than he did at that moment.

She reached out and brushed a dirt smudge from his brow and wiped the sweat away. She thought back to the grease that had lined his face the day he tried to get that ancient lawn mower started. Could it have been almost three months ago?

It seemed a lifetime ago.

She didn't know how long it was before he opened his eyes. "You've saved me in more ways than one, you know," she whispered. "You've slain all my dragons."

"All in a day's work, fair maiden. But if the truth were told, we did it together all the way."

"How did you get in here?"

"Ulrike Spelman. He was right—he does have connections. When he couldn't get through to the night security guard to warn him I was coming, it was obvious something was amiss. So he called one of the other security officers at home. He's the one who met me here and let me in. He also helped us out with those guys."

Minutes later a policeman brought Grethe to them. Although weakened, she was in remarkably good shape for the ordeal she'd been through.

At the sight of the officer, Teira looked questioningly at Christian.

He smiled weakly. "I know it's not what we agreed on, but if anything had happened to either of you—"

"You did the right thing," Teira said. "I'm glad you called them. I just wish they would have gotten here faster.

Christian grinned sheepishly. "You and me both."

When Grethe saw Christian, she stumbled toward him and sat on his other side. Then she took his hand, kissed the top of it, and held it lovingly. At last the old woman sobbed and told him he would be okay.

Christian squeezed her hand comfortingly. "Of course I will be. We all will be."

Teira crawled over to her grandmother and the two embraced as Teira wiped her grandmother's tears. Grethe handed her the cell phone.

She took the phone and pushed a couple of buttons and listened briefly. A look of pleasure crossed her face.

"It worked! Grandma, you are brilliant! Christian said you'd know what to do if I could find a way to get this to you. We have Haldor's confession recorded."

"You took a big risk running over to hug me when you first came in," Grethe said. "I was surprised to feel the phone placed in my hands and couldn't believe none of them noticed you handing it to me. It took me a minute to understand. I knew I couldn't call for help because I couldn't speak. Then I realized what you wanted me to do. I didn't know if I remembered how to do it or if it would even work."

"It's not very loud, but the voices are clear," Teira said. "Remind me to write the manufacturers of the phone and thank them for all the amazing features!" Teira hugged her grandmother tightly.

Although Christian's eyes were drooping, he made a valiant effort to smile. "That's my girl. I knew you'd come through."

Within minutes, Teira told Christian that his chariot finally awaited him. The ambulance had arrived with the police and other officials.

Two men walked up and helped Grethe onto a gurney. Teira assured them that though her head was throbbing, she was capable of walking. At Grethe's insistence, Teira rode with Christian to the hospital while Grethe rode in another ambulance.

On the way, Christian asked Teira to call his parents and Mr. Blackman to tell them what had happened. The numbers were programmed into his phone. He was immediately taken in for surgery. As the time ticked slowly by, Teira waited for word from the doctor and answered question after question for the authorities. They wanted to know everything she had done since arriving in Denmark—every detail that led up to the chilling events in Christiansborg Palace.

It was during the questioning that Teira was able to put the last piece of the puzzle in place.

"Grandma, I understand everything that happened now except for one thing. I still don't know how Grandpa sustained a bullet wound in his side."

Grethe's eyes filled with sadness. "When Haldor held me prisoner, he found great pleasure in recounting his triumph over my Soren that horrible day. When your grandfather set the explosives to dismantle the railway, Haldor had filled the car with his own countrymen. Soren immediately attempted to remove the women and children, but he was shot for his actions. Haldor said he could not allow there to be any witnesses of what had occurred." She sighed. "While the soldiers made it clear to Soren what they thought of his interference inside the train, Haldor lit the fuse. The soldier who aimed for Soren's heart was a poor marksman. In his haste to get away, he missed. It was Haldor who drove the getaway car."

Teira wiped the tear that slipped from Grethe's eye, then took her grandmother in her arms.

"The man is truly evil, Teira," Grethe whispered.

* * *

State officials had already been called in, and a royal administrator came to the hospital to question Teira and Grethe.

"I'm sure you have some way to make sure the ring and letter are authentic," Teira said to the kindly gentleman from the royal administration.

"Of course," the administrator assured her. "Although, if the letter to your grandfather is real, it belongs to you. Perhaps you could put some thought into how you would like to preserve it. The Royal Archives, perhaps?"

"Am I required to release it to you?" Grethe asked.

"All we ask is that you let us verify its authenticity. After that it is yours to do with as you wish. However, we must ask that the ring be returned immediately, for obvious reasons. It is priceless and cannot be replaced."

Teira nodded at once. "I don't want to be responsible for its safekeeping. The sooner you have it, the better."

"Perhaps you would allow us to escort you to it now?"

She hesitated, thinking of Christian. At last, knowing the surgery would take another hour or more, she consented. "May I ask you a question, though?" When the man nodded, she said, "I know the crown jewels were bequeathed to the country by Queen Sophie Amalie. So, I was wondering what will happen to the ring now. I mean since this ring was owned by the king and not Denmark, shouldn't it be given to Queen Margrethe? After all, it did belong to her grandfather. It's a family heirloom."

The official smiled. "Her Royal Highness has already been made aware of this and anxiously awaits proof that it is the genuine article. The royal family has been most generous with their collections. I assume it will be put on display at the Rosenborg Treasury, but it is up to the queen. Now I have one more question for you." The man smiled again. "What can we do to show our appreciation for the return of King Christian X's ring?"

Teira thought of her grandfather and smiled. "I think we already have everything we want, don't we, Grandma?"

Grethe smiled and nodded as grateful tears filled her eyes.

"And what is that?" asked the man.

"Honor has been restored to our family's name," Teira said. "There is no greater reward than that."

33

After she was examined at the hospital and treated, Grethe was released. She and Teira were together almost continuously. They cleaned up the house together, and Teira brought down the treasures from the attic at Grethe's request for her to go through once again. Grethe read each letter from Soren and lovingly handled each precious item, reminiscing about the past.

On Tuesday night Grethe asked Teira to take her to the hospital to see Christian again.

The doctors had him so deeply medicated that he was able to visit only for brief periods before drifting into a drug-induced slumber. Because his parents and Mr. Blackman were due to arrive the next day, Grethe wanted private time with him before they arrived.

To their surprise, Christian was awake and sitting up in bed when they entered. "I wondered where my favorite girls were," he said with a sleepy grin.

"You look better every time I see you," Grethe said.

"I feel better every time I see you," Christian replied.

"Always the charmer." Grethe smiled as her eyes filled with tears.

Christian looked at her in alarm. "Hey! What's this?"

"I have so many things to be grateful to you for that it will take the rest of my lifetime to thank you."

"I'm the one who's in your debt," Christian said sincerely, looking at Teira.

"I am so sorry you were hurt helping my Soren's cause," Grethe said, "but I thank you for restoring his honor. I believe the time will come when he will want to thank you himself. Even more than that, thank you . . ." Grethe choked on the words as she began to sob, "for bringing my granddaughter home to me. She is *min skat.* The two of you have brought a smile to my heart and laughter to my life once more. I love you as one of my own."

Overcome with emotion, Grethe leaned over the bed and kissed Christian on the forehead. Then she placed the gold pocket watch that Teira had found in the attic into Christian's hand, wrapped his fingers around it, and slipped quietly from the room.

Christian wiped a tear from the corner of his eye. "Wow. She's a wonderful woman, isn't she?" He stared down at the precious family heirloom.

"She sure is!" Teira smiled through her own tears.

At long last Christian said, "I can't accept this. It was your grandfather's."

Teira looked at the watch. "It means a lot to her. She wants you to have it."

"I didn't even get to say thank you," he said.

"I think that's what she was trying to do." Teira smiled warmly.

Christian looked down at the watch. "It means more than I can say. Will you thank her for me until I can do it myself?"

"Certainly."

"Will you do one more thing for me?"

"Of course."

"Come here and kiss me. I've missed you."

* * *

Teira drove her grandmother back to the center and parked in the long drive. She turned to the older woman. "Do you have any idea how much I love you?"

Grethe looked pleased and nodded. "Half as much as I love you, I think," she said as she smiled. "Come in and visit with me for awhile, will you?"

"You look awfully tired and pale tonight," Teira answered in concern. "Are you sure you want me to stay?"

"It has been a long and busy day, but I would love to visit until I fall asleep."

"Do you need to see a doctor?"

"Good heavens no, dear! Stop fussing!"

Once Grethe was ready for bed, Teira covered her with the goose-down comforter. Grethe scooted over and patted the bedside. Teira sat beside her.

"What are your plans for the future, my dear Teira?"

Teira smiled. "How far into the future are we talking?"

"Tell me as far as you can hope for."

"Well, for now my job here is not quite finished, but when it is I hope to take you home with me to America."

Grethe looked at Teira in genuine surprise.

"Before you say no, I only ask that you consider it. Grandma, you have no idea how much we want you in our lives. I hate the idea of leaving you here alone. All my life I have wanted to be close to you, and now that I am, I can never be away from you."

Grethe sat in silence for some time before she finally spoke. "Our loved ones may have to go away for a time, but they are always close when we hold them in our hearts. I had to let your mother go because I knew it was the way to her happiness. Soren had to go because it was the only way for him to find comfort and peace. You will move on to fulfill all your dreams and ambitions and find your own happiness. The time will come when you will need to let me go so I can be happy as well."

"I do want your happiness, Grandma! My mother longs for it as well. She made a vow to see the day that you would truly smile again—from your heart. I thought maybe I could help her with that by taking you home with me. I don't want you to be alone anymore."

"Your heart is in the right place, dear child, and I love you for trying," Grethe said gently. "But all I want is to be with my Soren again. I miss him more than words can say. I am an old woman who has lived many long years. I see now that my beautiful family is grown—happy, loving, and living life to its fullest. What more could I want but to be with the man I love? I'm lonely for him. Changing the world around me is only geography. It does not change what is in here." Grethe patted her heart. "This is the only land I have ever known. I will wait for my Soren here. As for the promise your mother has made, you can rest assured that you have both fulfilled it many, many times over."

Teira sat silently and considered her grandmother's words. Grethe had people around her daily; she wasn't a loner as Teira had once believed when she first came to Denmark. She just felt lonely in a world without her husband.

"Tell me something, Teira," Grethe said. "Do you believe there is a hereafter?"

"I know there is, Grandma," she said with conviction. "I am sure of it."

"I believe there is too. I plan to meet my Soren there." Grethe yawned.

"It will be a wonderful reunion," Teira said with a smile.

"Jeg elsker dig, min skat," Grethe whispered as her eyes drifted closed. *I love you, my treasure.*

"Jeg elsker dig, Mor mor." Teira leaned over and hugged her grandmother tightly and kissed her. "You have come to mean the world to me."

* * *

After Teira left for the night, Grethe's eyes drifted closed and Soren came to greet her. She opened her eyes in the twilight and her heart gave flight. At long last he wrapped her lovingly in his arms and she knew joy as she had never known before.

* * *

Christian cried.

Teira didn't know if it was more difficult to tell him or her mother, but the glowing, angelic smile she'd seen on Grethe's face that next morning sustained her through the most difficult days ahead.

A week after the funeral, Christian sat with Teira on the couch in his apartment. He slid his arm around her shoulders and said, "I've been thinking—"

Teira looked up at him. "What about?"

"It's time for you to start believing in fairy tales again," he said mischievously.

Teira grinned. "It is, huh?"

"Well, I heard this wonderful story. Want to hear it?"

"I'm always up for a good story."

Christian settled back on the couch. "Once upon a time there lived a beautiful little girl who grew up to be a tremendously fair maiden. One day her Prince Charming came riding by to offer the damsel a future with him. Of course, she had to take time to think about it. After all, there were other dragon slayers and brave knights in the kingdom who pined for her. But this prince had one thing to offer her that none of the others did."

"And what was that?" Teira asked.

"His heart. He had never given it to another because it was meant to beat only for her. Now he would give it to the rightful owner—if she would have it." Christian noticed the moisture in Teira's eyes, hugged her closer, and kissed her on her temple. "This heart, he told her, was a magical treasure. With it he would cherish her forever. It held within it the power of more love than she had ever known. It seemed too good to be true, so the fair maiden asked Prince Charming at what price she could receive such a gift. He said that the chance to be with her was gift enough."

Teira wiped a tear from the corner of her eye and kissed Christian on the cheek as he continued.

"But his wise leaders warned him to be careful lest the wicked witch of reality did all she could to destroy the fairy tale by forcing harsh tests upon them. In order for their dreams to come true he must receive something in return. So he said simply, 'Your heart for mine.' He had the wisdom to see the goodness that lay within her heart and knew that if the two were joined together, no evil force could separate them. Their union would be one of eternal happiness."

"I think that is probably the best story I have ever heard in my life," Teira said with a smile. She blinked to clear the moisture from her eyes. "Do you believe in fairy tales, Christian?"

"Well, not exactly. But I think they're based on dreams, and I definitely believe in those."

"What are your dreams?"

"I want to settle down and build my own castle with my princess, have our own little royalty running around, fulfill our dreams *together.*"

They smiled at each other and Christian leaned over to kiss her.

"Mmm," she said, "that sounds wonderful. Maybe you're right. Maybe I should start believing again. So who was the author of your story?"

"Me. It may have been a fairy tale when it began, but with you it can be a reality forever."

ABOUT THE AUTHOR

Jeri Gilchrist resides in West Jordan, Utah, with her own real-life Prince Charming, Brad, a.k.a. Elvis. She is the proud mother of two sons, Tyler and Bryan, and a new daughter (-in-law), Felicia.

A big fan of love stories, Jeri likes romantic comedies, spending time with friends, and of course, reading and writing.

In her spare time she likes to scrapbook, make crafts, and play games with anyone up for a challenge, which is usually her son, Bryan. The time she values the most is spent with family and driving her dad half crazy.

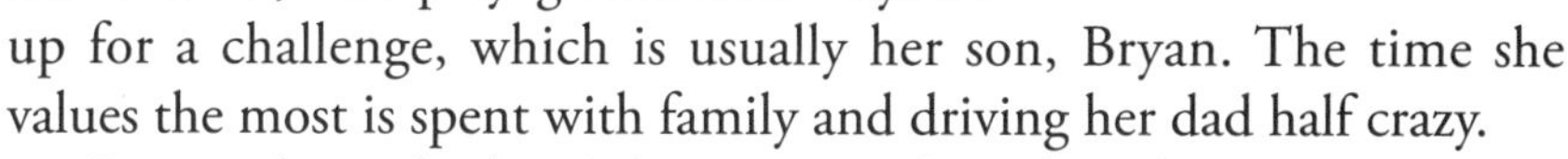

Jeri works with the Cub Scouts and teaches the 10\11-year-old boys in Primary with her husband. She also enjoys working with her "Temple Family" at the Jordan River Temple.